Sunshine Noir

Sunshine Noir

Edited by Annamaria Alfieri and Michael Stanley

Michael Stanley

Annamaria Alfieri

White Sun Books

Collective work copyright on the *Sunshine Noir* Anthology, © 2016 by Patricia King (Annamaria Alfieri) and Stanley Trollip (Michael Stanley)

Preface © 2016 Timothy Hallinan
Introduction: Clime Fiction © 2016 Peter Rozovsky
The Assassination © 2016 Leye Adenle
The Sultan Rules Mombasa © 2016 Patricia King (writing as Annamaria Alfieri)
When You Wish upon a Star © 2016 Colin Cotterill
The Logistics of Revenge © 2016 Susan Froetschel
Kronos and Chairos © 2016 Jason Goodwin
Blue Nile © 2016 Paul Hardisty
Housecleaning © 2016 Greg Herren
Corpus Crispy © 2016 Tamar Myers
The Cigarette Dandy © 2016 Barbara Nadel
Pale Yellow Sun © 2016 Richie Narvaez
The Man in Prampram © 2016 Kwei Quartey
Someone's Moved the Sun © 2016 Jeffrey Siger
Spirits © 2016 Michael Sears and Stanley Trollip (writing as Michael Stanley)
The Woman of his Heart © 2016 Nick Sweet
The Freemason Friends © 2016 Timothy Williams
Extreme Heat © 2016 Robert Wilson
Snake Skin © 2016 Ovidia Yu

ISBN-13: 978-0-9979689-0-3

To all those writers who set their stories in hot places

Table of Contents

Editors' note

Why Sunshine Noir?

"Nordic Noir stories," we hear their proponents say, "are a cut above ordinary crime fiction because the landscape and weather of the northern countries intensify the darkness of the crime and deepen the psychological complexity of the characters."

We writers of crime in hot countries beg to differ. Knowing full well that shadows are darkest where the sun is brightest and understanding, as we do, how heat can be more psychologically debilitating than cold, we decided to throw down the gauntlet to the Nordic noirists. We are here to challenge the dominance of dark-climate fiction; to show that stories set in sunny climes can be just as grim, more varied in plot and characters, and richer in entertainment value than those of the dark, grey, bone-chilling north.

To make our case, we've recruited crime-fiction writers from around the world. The authors in this volume will convince you with complex, beautifully written stories that span the hot places of the planet. Read these stories. You will agree.

The writers bring a variety of writing styles, which we have maintained to highlight their wonderful diversity.

Finally, we thank all the authors in the anthology for their enthusiasm and support.

You can follow us at www.facebook.com/sunshinenoir.

Annamaria Alfieri and Michael Stanley

Preface

In a sense, Sunshine Noir was my inspiration from the get-go.

The book that prompted me to create was *The Big Sleep*. It conjured in my mind a vivid picture of a cold glint of sunlight on the bumper of a car (probably a chromium-festooned coupe from the fifties). I was, I think, eleven, and it thrilled me to my shoelaces.

Dark doings in bright light. Until then, the books I'd read and the movies I'd seen had put evil firmly in the cliché-ridden dark. Horror stories weren't set in bright old houses. Vampires didn't stalk the world at noon. They didn't wear white capes.

Cold sunlight was new to me, and since I was living in Los Angeles at the time, I had lots of opportunity to explore the possibility. If Los Angeles has anything, it has a clement climate.

The train of thought that began with Raymond Chandler jogged my imagination's elbow with the notion of *inclemency*—in the sense of an utter lack of mercy—thriving like a toxic flower in a clement environment. Over the years, nothing I've learned has weakened the power of that notion. It still seems to me that evil is most striking in bright light. Cold hearts can thrive in hot weather.

Move over, mysteries set in Nordic places.

The bright, warm, lush world is a greenhouse for evil. That, to me, is a powerful image because it's a truthful one. These stories explore that greenhouse. Enter at your own risk.

Timothy Hallinan

Introduction: Clime Fiction

Peter Rozovsky

Jo Nesbø knows sweltering climates are seductive: he set *The Devil's Star* during a sweltering Oslo summer. And *The Cockroach*, Nesbø's second Harry Hole novel, takes place in "a steaming hot Bangkok", one website notes. Even the most successful Nordic crime writer knows hot weather is cool.

What makes it that way? Why a whole book of crime stories set in hot places? One story in *Sunshine Noir* tackles the matter directly:

> *"She could understand people watching Scandinavian noir in the heat, in Arizona or in Guadeloupe, where you longed for zero temperatures and biting air in your lungs. Here on Lake Ontario the low, grey skies of northern Europe were no more appealing than the encroaching darkness of a Canadian winter."*

Another story, this one by Kwei Quartey, opens with the backstory of a character who leaves Sweden for Ghana—a delightful joke whether the author intended it or not.

Readers (and reviewers!) could use a reminder that fictional crime is not exclusive to the Nordic countries, of course. But that's not the only reason. Consider drugs.

Don Winslow aside, the drugs of choice in North American crime fiction in recent years have been homegrown, cooked in rural meth labs or cultivated in cunningly disguised suburban grow houses. Not so long ago, though, drugs in popular culture were more an international thing: cocaine from Colombia, marijuana from Jamaica, opium from the Golden Triangle. The connection between drugs and hot weather, in other words, was stronger than it is today, now that Afghanistan has become the world's opium leader. Heat, dust, sweat, and drugs figure in Susan Froetschel's and Richie Narvaez's stories in *Sunshine Noir.*

If that has a whiff of old-fashioned exoticism, hold the thought. For now, ask yourself why should there be a renewed interest in tropical and subtropical locations? It's the geopolitics, stupid. Since the collapse of the Iron Curtain, the world's prevailing divide has shifted from East-West to North-South, and from ideological to economic. There's money to be made in the southern climes, and with money, even legal money that arrives with the best intentions, comes crime. Michael Stanley, who helped assemble this collection, has written a novel about China's problematic investments in Southern Africa. This is also where Paul Hardisty comes in, with his novels and with his story here about the hardships attendant on development work in poor countries that lack the finely developed ethical, financial, and physical infrastructures of the developed world.

Not all is geopolitics, though. Jeffrey Siger's and Colin Cotterill's stories are delightful mysteries with delightful twists and delightful characters in delightful locations. If you want gothic-tinged domestic mystery, you'll find it in *Sunshine Noir.* (Family secrets flourish in steamy air. Try Ovidia Yu's *Snake Skin.*) If you like bits of story that do triple duty as character marker, historical detail, and key to the mystery, you'll enjoy Jason Goodwin's *Chronos and Kairos.* If you like getting into a killer's head without wrapping yourself in a parka, or seeing the tables turned on petty tyrants, you can do so here. (No spoilers, though. Read the book to find out which stories I mean.)

Some of the stories take the *noir* part of the collection's title especially seriously, with characters making their way to their own doom and unable to do a damned thing about it. Once again, no spoilers. Heat—and what it does to people—can kill in Robert Wilson's *Extreme Heat*. Leye Adenle's *The Assassination* is a taut tale of death and political corruption that harks back to honorable precedents in crime and espionage writing but is redolent of its setting, which I take to be the author's country, Nigeria. And Nick Sweet's entry, so help me, with its straight-to-the-point storytelling and its wit, reminds me of nothing so much as Dashiell Hammett's Continental Op stories.

Sunshine Noir will take readers from Seville to Mombasa, from Algeria to Puerto Rico, from the Sonoran Desert to the Greek islands. Istanbul is on the itinerary, and so are Thailand, Ethiopia, Singapore, and the Dominican Republic. These stories will also take readers from blackmail and corruption through desperation, murder, and the brink of death, with a touch of perplexity and bits of humor along the way. So, why *Sunshine Noir*? Because these exotic locations are like the rest of the world, only hotter.

Extreme Heat

Robert Wilson

Jonny Sparks had dug a shallow hole in the sand, hoping for some cool against the desert heat. He cowered under a piece of tarpaulin he'd tied around a rock. It had taken everything out of him. The hot wind snapped at its fraying edges. It was late afternoon, and the temperature was coming off its high. He had no idea what that was now. He only knew that when he'd been in the car thieves' convoy at this time of day, the temperature gauge would have shown 47º C.

The gash in his side throbbed. He hadn't the strength to look at the state of it. He knew it was bad. An untreated stab wound from a hunting knife was never good news. At least the blade hadn't penetrated some vital organ. He took a sip from his water canteen, an old-fashioned type made of metal and covered with cloth. He had no idea how much liquid was left, but it couldn't have been more than an inch.

He'd been walking for three days—or rather three nights—no compass, no map. He hoped he was heading east, back to the main truck route through the northern Sahara that ran from Algiers down to Tamanrasset. He still hadn't crossed any tyre tracks, and his nerve, which had been rock solid with anger at what the car thieves had done to him, was starting to crack. He told himself there must have been sand storms. That the tracks had been obliterated, that the drivers wouldn't have been on the move anyway. As he lay panting through the long hot afternoons, his head pounding from dehydration, he listened for an engine. It was tricky, what with the wind and the crinkling heat, which turned stationary rocks into moving vehicles.

From under the tarp, he peeked out at the flat, hard, lunar landscape covered with broken rock and sand. He was in a valley between two escarpments. He'd been hoping to find the telltale ruts that trucks left behind. There was nothing, and by mid-morning he'd walked up the other side into the soft sand at the foot of the escarpment and dug his pathetic hole.

A fringe-toed lizard squirmed out of the sand and hot-footed across to some rocks. It looked left and right and disappeared into the shadows. Jonny passed a dry tongue over his cracked lips and suppressed an urge to pray. His mind drifted.

One moment he was back in London standing in front of his boss's desk on the 4th of April 1986 telling him why, at the age of twenty-five, he was turning down the chance to go to New York City to work on the Mars account. He was looking for a different challenge. He was going to hitch from London to Cape Town.

The next moment, he was sitting with his father in a pub in a Cotswold village, listening to him tell the story—for the first time—of his part in the bombing campaign that had reduced Dresden to ash. Then he was with his sister in Oxford, who was working all God's hours in the hope of becoming a surgeon, confessing to him that she hadn't had sex for three years. And finally he was with his mother, alone in her desperate flat in Hemel Hempstead, who, when he'd told her his plans, let out a little cry like a child lost in the woods.

And then came the middle-aged Frenchwoman on the ferry across to Algiers who told him: 'Africa is different. Nobody leaves Africa untouched. It gets into your blood. You can't help it. You lie on the ground, and the pulse drums into your head, your heart, your everything.'

'What's "it"?' he asked. '*It* gets into you. *What* gets into you?'

'You'll see,' she said. 'That'll be your adventure.'

The only time his mind didn't flit was when it converged on the immediate past and the car thieves. That moment when the convoy of stolen vehicles in which he was travelling arrived at a low, mud-brick building surrounded by worn tracks. Some tourists: a young couple in a VW Kombi, a couple of lads in a Land Rover, and two blonds in a Citroën 2CV, were going round and round, again and again. When they finished, they explained that it was a custom.

'You have to go round seven times for luck.'

Gilles, the Frenchman and gang leader of the car thieves, said it was bullshit, and the convoy set off without doing the seven tours of the building. In the next valley they came across some army trucks. Gilles decided against driving past. He didn't want to be stopped. The army knew that these convoys were taking stolen vehicles from Paris down to Togo, in West Africa, to be sold at a huge profit. There'd be a bribe, and Gilles wasn't prepared to pay. So they headed off-piste, and that had been the start of their trouble.

The first problem was steam pouring out of the Peugeot 504. The convoy pulled over. They opened the bonnet and staggered back. Head gasket blown. No spares, no sealant. These guys travelled light. They spent the afternoon stripping down the Peugeot and loading what they could into the back of the Land Cruiser. The two guys from the Peugeot were split up, one in the Land Cruiser, the other in the Citroën. They carried on, and by evening found themselves in a soft-sand field. At first it wasn't too bad. If you tuned your eyes to the different surfaces and you had a watchful co-driver, you could sprint from hard patch to hard patch. But desperation was growing in the convoy, and it wasn't long before the driver of the Citroën got stuck up to the axles.

The rest of the convoy found a place to park and came back to dig it out. The only problem: no sand ladders—the lightweight, holed-aluminium planks that desert travellers used to provide a hard surface for driving their vehicles out of soft sand. Night fell as everybody dug and pushed, pushed and dug themselves to exhaustion. After four hours, the Citroen had advanced thirty metres, with another fifty to go to get to the hard sand. Gilles told everybody to eat, get some sleep, and try again first thing in the morning when the sand was at its coolest.

Jonny Sparks had never been to the desert before, but on the way down he'd learnt a few things from locals and tourists who'd given him lifts. The first thing: he'd left it too late. The main tourist season was all over by the end of May, a few stragglers through June, but by the beginning of July it was done. And here he was, crossing the Sahara at the end of July during the hottest time of the year. The only people coming through now were the idiots, the car thieves, or both.

He'd got talking to these French and Belgian thieves when they were camping outside Ain Salah, about 700 kilometres northwest of Tamanrasset. Tam was the last major town before the greater emptiness of the southern Sahara. Jonny had already been in Ain Salah for a week, waiting for a lift. He was glad of their company, excited by their lawlessness. They asked him if he was headed for Tam. He was wary because the second thing he'd heard about was the ruthlessness of car thieves. But he'd run out of options. He should have listened to his instincts when they asked him for money for fuel.

He also realized what a barebones operation they were running. They had one rudimentary toolbox between the six different cars, no spare parts other than fan belts and spark plugs, and no sand ladders. They did have tinned fruit, plenty of water and, in his car, three bottles of whisky. He decided he'd go as far as Tam with them and then wait for a better-equipped convoy to come through heading south.

So here they were on their first night out of Ain Salah, maybe thirty kilometres off-piste, one car down and another on the brink of being abandoned. And it was then that Jonny found out how ignorant and nervous they were. Panic was making them hate each other. The whisky started fights.

In the morning, the sun rose relentlessly. The sand absorbed its brutal heat, and the dust created by the Citroën's wheels churning did something cataclysmic to the alternator. The battery died. They abandoned the Citroën. They set off again. With the spares rescued from the Citroën, there was very little room in the four roadworthy cars. They were all hung over. Whisky, tension, and dehydrated bodies; not a healthy combination.

They were driving fast, desperate to get back onto the main route to Tam. The driver of the Mercedes Estate didn't see the rock in front of him until he was on it. He swerved wildly—the left-front wheel hit the rock and sent the car into a rolling flic-flac. The Mercedes ended up on its roof. The front-left wheel sheared off and the axle buckled. It was a miracle to see driver and passenger crawling out of the wreckage with cuts and bruises and limbs still attached.

Gilles called them together, told Jonny to stay where he was. They had a discussion. Glanced over their shoulders to Jonny, sitting in the car. He began to feel like a tethered goat whose owners were thinking the time had come for roast kid. When they came for him, two of them had hunting knives drawn.

'Get out the car,' said Gilles.

Jonny did as he was told, stood with his back to the vehicle.

'There's no room for you. You're on your own from here.'

He looked from man to man. Sweat coursed down their desperate faces.

'I'll just get my things,' said Jonny, moving to the back of the car.

'Leave it,' said Gilles. 'Walk away.'

'It's my stuff.'

'You don't want to carry it in this heat.'

The two men with knives moved closer. Jonny held up his hands, backed away from the vehicle. They kept coming at him. Nobody said a word. Then they were on him, tore up his shirt, grabbed his money belt. In the scuffle, as they cut away the strap, they stabbed him in the side. He stiffened as the knife went in and the two men pulled away.

'*Connards*,' said Gilles, seeing the blood oozing out from behind Jonny's fingers.

They went through the money belt, took the cash—four hundred and fifty pounds—threw the passport back.

'*Allons-y*,' said Gilles. 'He won't last long out here. They'll think he had an accident … if they find him.'

They got into the cars. Jonny shouted at them to leave him some water. Nobody even turned. He tried to get to his feet but couldn't make it. He knelt on the ground, hand on his bleeding side. The cars pulled away in a cloud of dust. It settled slowly on the silent, bleached-out landscape.

The quiet was immense. The sun beat down like a hammer pummeling sheet metal. He crawled to the upturned Mercedes and eased himself through the shattered passenger window, glad to get some shade. Apart from pulling out the jerry cans for fuel, the Frenchmen hadn't stripped this car down. They had no room in the other vehicles. Jonny scratched around, looking for anything to eat or drink. He came across the old-fashioned canteen and a split, plastic jerry can of water, which still had three or four litres inside. There were three 500-gram cans of peaches in syrup. He went through everything, inspecting each item for usefulness before throwing it out. Scrambling back to the front of the car, he found the most valuable item: in the glove compartment was a Swiss Army knife.

***

Jonny came to with a grunt. Something had happened to him while he'd been asleep. He couldn't lift his arm. He was too weak to reach for the water canteen. His heart was racing. He focused his mind, and it came to him.

I'm dying.

'Am I dying?' he said, but no words came out of his cracked lips.

The fringe-toed lizard returned, scampering across the sand like a spirit. It stopped, did a *volte-face*, zipped across to some rocks, waited. An insect toiled over the sand. Total stillness. Then a lunge. A tongue flicked out, and the insect was in the lizard's jaws. It must be getting cooler for the insects to come out and risk death.

He had a sudden desire to cry. He was sad to be leaving this life. He had a vision of his funeral. His family in the front rows. His mates from school and university behind. Who would speak for him? Who could say that they knew Jonny Sparks? Fucking no one. Because you're not here. You haven't seen me now. I'm new. Even to me, I'm new. He sobbed. There were no tears. His eyes were crusty, and the lids scratched.

'I'm too dry to even cry,' he thought. 'In a few days I'll be completely desiccated. The husk of Jonny Sparks will be blown about in the wind, dashed against the rocks. A little more sand in the desert.'

And that was when he heard it.

The engine.

He tipped his head back and looked down the valley.

Another fucking rock shimmering in the heat.

A crunching gear change.

'Where are you?' he whispered. 'Where the fuck are you?'

He blinked.

'Don't lie to me. Don't you fucking lie to me this time.'

There it was.

A moving rock.

Not this time.

It's a truck.

It *is* a truck.

With a monumental effort, he raised a shaking hand.

'Over here,' he said, but no sound came out. 'Under the tarp.'

The truck. He could see it now. It was real. A Hanomag.

He kicked his leg against the tarp to make it shimmer. Anything to catch an eye. Why did he have nothing left? Why, at this crucial moment, did he have fuck all in the tank?

The truck sailed by.

Out of sight.

Gone now ... if it was ever there.

The rock sailed by.

Bye-bye little rock.

Little Rock Arkansas.

Home of the Clintons.

Or the Simpsons.

I'm home, Homer.

The Odyssey.

My odyssey.

The tarp was torn back. Jonny looked up. Two heads wrapped in *sheshes* with sunglasses looked down on him. Touaregs? They spoke in German.

'English,' he mouthed.

One of them reached for the water canteen. The top had gone and it was empty. He didn't remember taking the last slug of water. The figure in the *shesh* was wearing a dress. Is this a dream? Am I dead?

The one in the dress left, came back with water. The other took his head and rested it in her lap. They gave him small sips of water.

The one in the dress disappeared again, came back with a sachet. They emptied it into the water bottle, shook the bottle, dribbled the contents into his searching lips.

They talked to each other in German. He didn't understand them. They looked down on him blankly through black sunglasses, their heads massive in the wraps of their *sheshes*, which covered their mouths.

They were both women. He could hear them now. Life was swimming back up to him as if the tide was coming in. The liquid was making him feel himself again, his innards, the blood whizzing in his ears, his skin, the inside of his mouth was smooth once more.

The women spoke as they assessed him. Opened his bloody shirt, saw the wound in his side. Made a decision. Moved off as one. Came back with a sand ladder, rolled him onto it and pulled him to the truck. They were organized. They had pulleys and ropes. They hauled him into the back of the truck. Laid him on a mattress on the floor between the two seats that ran the length of the vehicle. Their first-aid kit was the size of the car thieves' toolbox.

The sunglasses were off now. Blue eyes looking down on him, telling him she was Petra. The other, in the dress, with soft amber eyes, was Ursula. Ursula was a nurse. They had a fridge on the truck. Jonny was delirious with happiness.

Ursula was a nursula with a cannula and saline.

She put him on a drip. Petra cleaned his wound, dressed it. They told him they were going to find help, climbed into the cab. The truck lurched forward.

The motion of the truck rocked him backwards and forwards between the two seats. Jonny fell asleep.

He woke with a start. It was dark. The truck was still. The saline bag hanging above him was empty. He jerked as he heard a noise outside. Men's voices. A woman shouting. Another screaming. Jonny's eyes widened as he heard someone he recognised: Gilles.

Two lights attached to the Hanomag truck illuminated the outside world. Jonny looked out of the corner of the window. An awning was fixed to the truck, supported by two poles stuck in the sand pulled tight by guy ropes. There was a gas bottle connected to a stove. A saucepan bubbled away. Between two folding chairs, some tools, including a hammer, were laid out on a piece of tarpaulin. Petra and Ursula must have been surprised by Gilles and what sounded like one of the other thieves as they cooked their evening meal. There was no one under the awning, but they couldn't be far away because he could hear their shouts.

Then Ursula came running under the awning. She was in her bra and pants, nothing else. Blood on her face. A guy Jonny knew as Jean-Michel was close behind, shorts hanging below his belly. He was holding onto them as if he'd undone them. Ursula was trying to get into the cab. Jean-Michel grabbed her by the hair, pulled her down, forced her face into the ground. He knelt behind her, tugged down her pants. Her arms flailed. Jean-Michel leaned his weight forward onto the back of her head and reached into his shorts.

Jonny pulled the cannula from his arm, opened the back of the truck, and let himself down onto the ground. He took the Swiss Army knife from his pocket, looked under the truck, ran around the other side, and came up on Jean-Michel from behind. He pulled the Frenchman's head back and ran the blade across his throat. Blood flooded over Jonny's fingers, and he pushed him away. Jean-Michel's arms twitched as he lay next to Ursula. His blood blossomed massively in the sand. Ursula rolled away from him, pulling up her pants.

Jonny picked up the hammer from the array of tools and stared into the night. He felt an immense strength running through him. Ursula was shaking. He listened, like an animal. Heard Petra's screams out in the dark.

He ran out from under the awning and homed in on Petra. She was no longer screaming. She was begging. A torch had been set in the sand. It cast a weak light on the two figures. Gilles was kneeling with his trousers down around his thighs. Petra was on her back, naked, legs splayed, the fight suddenly gone from her. Jonny's bare feet pounded through the dark. Without thinking, he slammed the hammer into the side of Gilles' face. The Frenchman fell sideways, and Jonny was on him, straddling his chest. He raised the hammer above his head. Gilles' cheek had been staved in. Blood and bruising bloomed black around his eye.

'Where are the others?' Jonny demanded.

'The army,' said Gilles, confused. 'They were stopped by the army. We were behind, digging out of the sand.'

'Where's the Land Cruiser?'

'About 500 metres back that way,' said Gilles, turning his head to the east.

Jonny raised his arm.

'Don't,' said Gilles. 'Please, don't.'

Jonny brought the hammer down, again and again into Gilles's face and head.

He stood up, dropped the hammer.

He reached down to help Petra. She didn't want to take his hand. Jonny called out to Ursula, who came running. The women looked at him, his hand blackened by blood. They staggered back to the truck.

Jonny stood under the dark canopy of the night. He looked up. He'd never seen a sky so full of stars and, as they breathed down their billion-year-old light, he felt the pulse of the ancient earth beneath his feet.

Blue Nile

Paul Hardisty

'Mengistu is a dog.' Teferi swayed in the wavering lamplight, turned his empty glass over, and placed it rim down on the table between them.

'Your president's reputation is ...' The young engineer paused, aware of his position as a guest. 'Controversial. The project was almost cancelled because of it.'

'I would use a stronger word, but I do not know it in English,' said Teferi.

The young engineer found the table top with the base of his glass, grabbed the edge of the carved-wood and woven-frond stool, steadied himself. Sweat slurried down the gutter of his spine, pooled between his buttocks. 'Describe it to me,' he said, shifting on his stool. His words circled around the mud-brick walls of the hut, came back as a distortion.

'It is when you are ...' Teferi paused, moved the middle finger of his right hand in and out of his left fist. 'To someone already dead.' He raised his hand, signalled towards the darkened end of the hut.

A man emerged from the edge of the lamplight carrying a bottle, shuffled to their table, refilled the young engineer's glass with a trembling hand. Some of the caramel-coloured liquid spilled onto the tabletop.

'*Ameseginalehugn*,' said the young engineer, the Amharic brutal in his throat. Thank you. The first and most important words to learn in a new country.

The old man nodded, disappeared back into the darkness.

'He is hungry,' said the young engineer with a tip of his head.

'Everyone here is hungry.'

'Not everyone.' The young engineer recalled the place on the outskirts of Addis Ababa where they'd stopped weeks before, at the start of the journey to the dam. While Teferi had bargained for supplies with the shop owner, he'd wandered the store, found his way to the back aisles. There, on a shelf against the back wall, sacks of grain piled high, dozens of them, fifty-pound bags of flour, plastic gallon jugs of canola oil set out in ranks. All emblazoned with the handshake logo of USAID, and the words *Gift of the People of the United States of America* stamped in black beneath. All for sale.

The young engineer felt the first tremor, the now familiar destabilisation of the ground under his feet, the lurch of gravity, a reversal of Coriolis, ten times stronger. He walked his fingers to and around the glass, spilled more of the stuff they were calling whisky onto the table.

Teferi sipped his drink. 'When will you finish your work?'

'Soon.'

'And then the dam will be fixed?'

'The dam is not broken, Teferi. The penstock is the problem—the pipe that carries water to the turbines. It was built on swelling soils, and it's shifting.' The young engineer lifted his right forearm, tilted it to an angle, pushed it upwards with the fingertips of his left hand. 'If it shifts too much, the pipe will rupture.'

'And then?'

'The lights go out. For a long time.'

Teferi nodded, scratched the top of his head. 'What remains for you to do?'

'The drainage galleries we've been installing will keep the penstock's foundations stable. The last one is going in tomorrow.'

'How many more days do you need?'

'Two or three.'

Teferi nodded. 'You must finish quickly.'

The young engineer did not reply, took a slug of alcohol.

'And then you must go home.'

A distant concussion walked through the hut, found his chest cavity, thrummed there a moment like some winged beast, fled.

'The rebels are close,' said Teferi.

'Will they cross the river?'

'Soon, yes.'

'What will happen if they win?'

Teferi grinned a moment, as many teeth as not. Then his lips closed and pursed and his gaze flicked away to the right, towards the entrance. The young engineer had seen the movement, swivelled on his stool. A man stood in the doorway. Kerosene lamplight lit one side of his face, left the other in shadow. Sweat stained the front of his uniform, dark wedges in the centre of his chest and under his arms. A handgun hung from a belt around his waist. He was small, his clothes outsized, like a boy playing at being a man. The soldier nodded to the barman, said something in Amharic. There were only four small tables in the place, each with a pair of stools. The soldier walked to a table set against the opposite wall, sat down, looked at them.

Teferi looked at the glass on the table between them. 'Finish,' he said. A whisper. 'We must go.'

The young engineer shook his head. 'Always it is this way.'

'You do not like our country.'

'I like most of it very much.'

'But not this?'

'Not how it is run, or who runs it.'

Teferi frowned. 'And yet we are here.'

'Please understand,' said the young engineer. 'I hope there is more good than bad.' That is what he had told himself, had convinced himself he still believed.

'Finish your drink. We will go before there is a problem.'

The young engineer drank. He stood, the mud floor shifting beneath his soles, started toward the doorway.

'*Koom*,' said the soldier. Stop.

The young engineer stopped, turned, and looked at the soldier. He may have been young, but it was hard to tell. Lines gullied the skin around his eye sockets. Sweat beaded on his forehead, greased his temples. Like everyone here, his bones seemed very close to the surface.

'Necrophile,' the young engineer said.

Teferi glanced at him, a question in the flex of his left cheek.

'That's the word.' The young engineer stared at the solider, made the same motion with his finger and fist as Teferi had. Then he raised his voice. 'Fucks the dead.'

Teferi grabbed the young engineer's arm, started guiding him towards the doorway. 'Please, do not provoke.'

The soldier called out in Amharic.

They were almost at the doorway now. Outside, the living din of the African night, the dark earth radiating the day's heat, the desperate, transpired humidity of a thousand days without rain, all of it accelerating the vortex in his head.

'Keep going,' whispered Teferi.

The young engineer stumbled, gripped his friend's shoulder.

'*Koom*,' the soldier repeated, louder this time.

They stopped, turned to face him. He was on his feet now, moving towards them, speaking rapidly. Teferi held his palms out and open, responding. The young engineer could make out a few words amongst the tones of reconciliation—*aznalehu*. excuse me; *i'bakih*, please.

The soldier was close now, a fist's throw away. His voice was shrill, constricted, loud against the night. He waved his hands in the air, alternatively pointing out into the darkness and at Teferi's chest.

The young engineer planted his feet, stared back at the soldier, adrenaline cutting through the booze. He was a head taller than the soldier and almost half again as heavy. He leaned in, stared down at the man.

The soldier pointed at Teferi, said something the young engineer could not understand. Anger boiled in his words. Teferi took a step back. The young engineer did not. The soldier was yelling at him now, jabbing his finger at him as if this alone could somehow translate, explain, solve. Then the young engineer realised that it was no longer about the things he had seen since he'd arrived in the Horn of Africa, the war raging closer every day as the rebels moved south, or even the simmering anger inside himself that he had brought with him to this fevered continent. It was something altogether more basic, this exothermic proximity, the heat generated when fight overcame flight.

'Fuck you, asshole,' the young engineer shouted, forcing the syllables out from deep within himself. 'He has as much right to be here as you do.'

Teferi grabbed his arm, started pulling him towards the door.

The soldier, initially taken aback by this foreigner's outburst, renewed his attack.

'Please,' said Teferi, hauling on the young engineer's arm. 'There is no need. Come.'

The young engineer twisted away from Teferi's grip, bunched his fists at his sides, and took a hard step towards the soldier. Surprised, the soldier lurched back. His foot caught a table leg, and he toppled backward over a stool, hands clawing at dead air. He hovered there for a moment, and then came down hard, the back of his skull striking the edge of one of the rough plank tables. It sounded like a car door closing, that hollowness.

They stood looking down at the soldier, waiting for him to get up.

But he didn't.

'Jesus,' said the young engineer. 'I didn't mean to ...' He stepped forward to help the soldier, but Teferi grabbed him.

'He's not moving.'

Teferi shook his head. 'We must leave. Now.'

'We should help him.'

'Please. Before someone comes.'

They ran to the car. Theirs was the only vehicle in the small, dirt clearing under the dark shadow of a sprawling mango tree. Soon, Teferi had the car hurtling towards the main road, the dim myopia of the headlights jetting through the hacked bush that crowded both sides of the red-earth track.

They didn't speak for a long time. After a while they left the main road and moved through darkened fields and sleeping thatch villages, the country increasingly rocky and covered in stunted trees. By the stars—Dubhe and Merak pointing to Polaris—the young engineer knew that they were heading north, towards the river.

'Where are we going, Teferi?' he asked, still shaking from the encounter at the bar.

'Before you leave, I must show you.'

'Show me what?'

'Not far.' Teferi guided the car up a narrow track through the brush. The vehicle lurched over the rutted, uneven ground, the suspension groaning. Soon the track ended. Teferi stopped the car, turned off the engine. They sat a moment, eyes adjusting. Slowly, the world reappeared, lit by precarious stars. 'Walk now,' he said.

The night was very still. The silence broken by a billion screaming insects. The young engineer followed Teferi up the rocky slope. Sweat ran cold at his temples, across his chest. A chill shuddered through him.

'That soldier ...' he said.

Teferi stopped, turned back to face him. 'It was not your fault,' he whispered. 'You must be quiet now.'

'If the police find out ...'

Teferi shook his head. 'Come, we must hurry.'

They climbed. Ahead, the dark silhouette of a ridgeline, constellations behind, the dust of nebulae. A sudden flash erased the stars, offered a silvered landscape of crags and stunted trees, a hacked-out geometry of shadows. As quickly, it was gone. The young engineer stumbled, disoriented, the ground flexing like hot rubber beneath him. Seconds later, the distant shock of thunder, felt as much as heard.

He kept moving, Teferi there ahead of him, almost invisible in the darkness. The slope had died away now, and ahead he could see some sort of precipice, and beyond that, the edge of a cliff, a pale fluttering sheet of rock. Eventually Teferi stopped and dropped to the ground, and signalled him to do the same. Side by side, they snaked their way towards the precipice.

The young engineer gripped the rock, felt the world spin beneath him. He closed his eyes, but that only made it worse. He pulled himself forward and looked out over the edge, down into the canyon. Far below, the Blue Nile, dark and scattered with stars. And beyond, across the divide, a million cooking fires strewn like glowing coals across the darkened sweep of the Eritrean plain.

'Somewhere out there,' whispered Teferi, 'is my home.'

And a million and a half Eritrean troops waiting to cross the river and crush Mengistu. 'Family?' the young engineer asked.

'My wife and three children, God bless them.'

It was the first time in the eleven weeks they'd spent together that Teferi had spoken of such things. They lay still for a time and peered across the river.

Teferi touched his arm, said, 'Wait here. I will be back soon.'

'Where are you going?'

'Do not move from this place. Do you understand?'

In the distance, how far away he could not judge, a string of tracers arced red across the plain. And then the sound came, the raptor trill of automatic gunfire. He turned to answer, but Teferi was already up and moving away, towards the dark cleft of a draw in the valley. The young engineer watched him until he disappeared.

For a long time he lay among the rocks and gazed down into the canyon at the dark surface of the water. He could hear the river coursing through the rocks, feel it cutting its way down into the flesh of the highlands on its way to meet the White Nile at Khartoum and then on to Egypt and the great delta and the Mediterranean. In this, he felt insignificant and small, and then he thought about the soldier in the bar and if he was okay and if he would report what had happened and if the police would be waiting for him when he returned to the dam.

More than an hour passed before Teferi returned. When he did, a quarter-moon was rising in the east, and he was very quiet and would not answer any of the young engineer's questions. They walked back to the car and drove back to the dam in silence.

***

Three days later they arrived in Addis Ababa. Abandoned vehicles choked the roads. Smoke veiled the city, pillared hot into the sky from the hulks of burning tanks, smashed buildings. Dead animals littered the roadside, the bloated carcasses of horses, goats, dogs. Soldiers streamed into the capital, many without weapons or leaders. Children wandered naked and aimless, lost in the confusion, crying for their parents.

The young engineer sat in the front passenger seat, stared out of the open window at the world gone crazy. Before leaving the dam, he'd supervised the installation of the last drainage gallery, stayed another day testing its performance and evaluating the data. There had been no trouble, no sign of the police, no mention of the soldier in the bar. The next day, he'd reported his findings to the dam manager, proclaimed the penstock safe. The dam manager had thanked him and advised him to leave the country immediately. The rebels had crossed the Blue Nile that morning and were bearing down on Addis, Mengistu's troops in full retreat.

Teferi guided the car through the melee towards the airport. 'Not far now,' he said, easing past an abandoned fuel truck.

'That soldier, the one who hit his head.'

Teferi said nothing, kept driving.

'He died, didn't he?'

Teferi shook his head. 'Do you have your tickets, passport?'

The young engineer patted the breast pocket of his jacket.

'Thank you for helping my country,' said Teferi. 'It has been good to know you.'

'Likewise,' said the young engineer, meaning it, feeling something else too. It felt vaguely like cowardice.

Teferi reached into the back seat, produced a small package, handed it to him.

The young engineer opened the newspaper wrapping. It was a small, stringed musical instrument, like a crudely made ukulele.

'It's a *kra*,' said Teferi. 'The instrument of my people.'

The young engineer plucked one of the strings. 'Thanks, Teferi. It's not necessary. But thanks.' Yes. Cowardice.

Ahead, an army checkpoint, the airport terminal building a couple of hundred metres beyond. The sound of a jet powering up for take-off. Car horns blaring. Teferi slowed the car, stopped at the barrier. A harried-looking officer peered inside the car, checked their documents. He'd just handed the young engineer's passport back to Teferi when he looked up in the direction of the city and froze. The young engineer just had time to spin in his seat before the shock wave hit. The blast knocked him back, sucked the air from his lungs, blew out the windows in the building across the street. He caught his breath, looked back towards the city. A huge pillar of brown smoke mushroomed into the sky.

'Jesus,' he said, turning towards Teferi. 'You alright?'

Dust billowed in the air around them like fog, as if the ground were an old rug that someone had picked up and snapped.

Teferi nodded, jutted his chin towards the roadblock. 'Look.' The soldiers were picking themselves up from the glass-strewn tarmac and walking away. 'They are going home. It is over.'

A convoy of Mercedes Benz sedans flashed past towards the airport, four cars in all, police escort front and back. Teferi handed the young engineer his passport, slammed down on the accelerator, sent the car hurtling after the convoy. They pulled up in front of the terminal just behind the last Mercedes.

Teferi turned to him. 'Go quickly,' he said. 'The airport could close at any time.'

People were piling out of two Mercedes, big men in superbly tailored suits, gold flashing against dark fingers and wrists, equally big women swathed in multi-coloured cloth and elaborate headdresses, half a dozen overweight children. Porters loaded mountains of luggage onto waiting trolleys.

Teferi spat. 'Our government.'

The young engineer hoisted his pack and stepped onto the pavement. He looked back across the city, counted eleven, twelve, thirteen columns of smoke rising into the sky. A jet screamed by overhead. He wanted to remember it, all of it. He closed the car door, leaned back in through the open window. 'Where did you go, Teferi, that night at the river?'

His driver looked at him a moment, clenched his fist around the steering wheel. 'We are a poor country, my friend,' he said. 'The dam is very important. No one else could have fixed it.'

The young engineer nodded, understanding.

Teferi smiled. 'This,' he said, waving his hand towards the city, 'is the beginning, God willing.'

The Assassination

Leye Adenle

The bank manager shook hands with Otunba. The driver held the door open. Otunba's account officer waited by the manager, one step behind him. She unfolded her hands from her back, but Otunba did not shake her. He sank into the back of his Mercedes and let out the remainder of a fart he'd been letting out in sips.

"We are going to the club."

"Yes sir."

The driver took one hand off the steering wheel to wave back at the manager, who was still outside the bank with Otunba's account manager.

A black Camry with tinted windows started to pull out.

"Hurry. I need to use the toilet."

"Yes sir."

***

Prince returned the wine because the waiter had opened it before bringing it. He asked for new glasses too, because the ones set before him were for white wine, not red. He looked up at Otunba unravelling his *agbada*, only to throw it over his shoulders again; it was the way he announced his arrival. Otunba nodded and walked round the bar to the toilets.

"Sir, what about this one?"

The waiter had brought a bottle of wine that he presented like a fishmonger showing a prize catch.

"It's alright. Don't open it. Wait. Don't go away."

Otunba emerged from the door, grappling with his *agbada* over his head. He twirled it round his hand as he walked and handed it to the waiting waiter, who had to take it.

"I see you have ordered," he said. "Ah, Carlo Rossi. Good."

When the waiter had left, Prince began his rehearsed lines.

"Otunba, I spoke to the party members today—"

"And what are they saying? Do they still want me to run?"

"It's not that straightforward. I spoke to them today and—"

"They want me to step down for Alhaji Abiodun?"

"It's not that simple ... I spoke to them—"

"I have told them 'Refund my expenses to date and then we can talk.'"

"Otunba, let me try and explain it. I spoke—"

"There is nothing to explain. Nothing more to discuss, in fact. I have done my account. If they want to talk to me, I will talk to them, but only after they refund my expenses."

"Otunba."

"Prince, forget them. Let us eat first."

"Otunba, they won't let you run."

"How can they stop me? Ehn? How?"

***

The driver thought to run across the road to buy roasted corn. They had been out since seven; he had been up since five. They had been to Mushin, to visit Otunba's spiritual adviser, then to Apongban, to see his Imam, then Tantalizers in VI, then the bank. They got to the club at eleven; it was four now.

***

"Anyway," Otunba said, as he washed *egusi* soup off his hands into a bowl held before him by a waiter, "Kike's illness has assured me victory. When they sent cancer to my house, they thought it would kill me, they didn't know they were shooting themselves in their legs."

"Madam's illness started in London."

29

"Is that what you believe? Is that what they are saying?"

"Otunba, you asked me to talk to them and I have. They don't want you to run. My advice is for you to step down."

"Prince, what are you saying? I should step down? After all the money I have spent? After they have tried to kill me? See my Kike? That cancer she has was meant for me, you know? Step down? After all that money?"

"If they can do that to your wife, what will they do to you?"

"They can't do anything. They have done their worst and my head has rejected it. It is just sad that Kike is still following her born-again people. That's why the protection I did for her did not work. But she will survive this, and I will collect my money back."

"My father taught me something. He said, 'Whenever I want to leave to use the toilet, I must finish my drink before getting up.'"

"Meaning?"

"You cannot be too careful. Be vigilant. You don't know what these people can do."

"Don't worry, Prince. I know this game better than them."

***

The driver saw Otunba and his friend in the mirror. He hid the rest of his roasted corn in the glove compartment and licked his teeth clean.

"Suzy."

"Yes sir."

***

Suzy watched from the window. She hissed and made a phone call when the Mercedes drove into the compound.

"Uncle, he is here o."

"Ok. Thanks. Keep him there till tomorrow."

"Ah. Tomorrow *ke*? Me, I want to go out o. They said the man has AIDS, how can he stay till tomorrow and he will not touch me?"

"Use a condom."

"I should use condom? Ehn? I should use condom? If I am your sister, is that what you would say? I should use condom?"

"Suzy, we don't know that he has HIV or not. It is just a rumour started by his opponents."

"They say his wife has almost died finish."

"She has cancer."

"They say it is AIDS."

"It is not."

"How do you know? Are you a doctor?"

"Just keep him there. I will settle you tomorrow."

"Prince. Me, I am tired of all this o."

"Keep him till tomorrow."

***

Police officers climbed out of the station wagon before it had come to a stop. Their arrival frightened the workmen across the road. Behind them, a bullet-proof Range Rover also stopped. Another convoy speeded down the road from the other end. The windows of the adjacent SUVs slid down and the men in the backseats had a conversation.

***

Otunba told the driver to go and get himself something to eat and be back in twenty minutes. The driver watched him enter the house, then made a phone call.

"Sir, we are at Aunty Suzy's house."

"Good. Let me know when you leave."

It was too late to get *amala* at the Buka on the adjacent street. The other place he knew in the area was Mr Biggs, so he stayed in the car. He also needed to pee. He searched the car park in the rear view mirror. There was only one other car in the compound; a black Camry.

***

"Hello sir."

31

"Hello."

"Sir, it is me, Mutiu. Alhaji Abiodun's driver. You gave me your number, sir."

"Oh yes. How are you? I promised to add to the thing I gave you the other day."

"Yes sir. Sir, I am not calling to remind you, sir."

"Ok. But I have not forgotten you. Where is your boss?"

"We just left Magodo, sir. You said I should call you when we see the party chairman."

"Are they meeting now?"

"Sir, they have met."

"Really? Did they mention my friend?"

"Yes sir. Should I come to your house to tell you what they discussed?"

"That's not necessary. Do you have a bank account?"

"Yes sir."

"Send me the details and I will send you something."

"Thank you, sir."

***

Traffic back to the Island had subsided. The driver drove as quickly as he could without having to use the horn to move slower vehicles out of the way. By ten-thirty they were back in VGC.

"I will need you at five o'clock sharp," Otunba said.

The driver started his walk out of the estate. None of Otunba's friends had given him any cash. He would have to pay his bus fare to Maryland from the 200 Naira he had started the day with. He remembered the roasted corn. He checked his pockets, for he couldn't remember collecting his change. He cursed and stopped in the middle of the road. Hands on hips, he considered his options. He would have to return and sleep in the night guard's post.

***

The black Camry drove past the building and stopped down the road. The doors remained shut.

***

At 1 AM, a patrol van drove past the Camry, past Otunba's house, and continued round the bend. A man stepped out of the Camry and walked to the house. The night guard's snore stopped at its top. The man continued to the front door, four bullets left in his revolver.

***

Otunba woke. He listened to his wife's faint breathing and silently got out of bed. He went to the opposite room, turned the handle, and looked back at his door. He switched on the light to wake the nurse, in case she had fallen asleep.

***

In the dark foyer, the gunman put out his gun hand and his other hand to remember which side was left. He found the housemaid's door and tested the lock. He climbed the stairs, three bullets left. He stooped at the landing when he saw light under a door. He held out his hand and went to the other door. The room was dark, but he could make out a shape under the sheets. It was too small to be him. He backed up to the wall and waited next to the door.

***

The nurse clenched her fists on the duvet and pretended to sleep. He peeled it up from her legs and climbed onto the bed. He placed his hands on her thighs and tried to part them. She stiffened. He pinched her, and she kicked and turned, her eyes squinting against the light. He put a finger to his lips.

"I'm on," she said, trying to sound drowsy.

"I will use a condom." He pulled his night pants down and stroked himself.

"Where is it?"

"What?"

"The condom."

"I will go and get it."

"Go and get it."

He rubbed her legs, his hands moving up. She squeezed her thighs tighter. He kneaded her butt and rolled off the bed.

"Go and wash up. I'll be back now."

He opened his door and walked to his side of the bed. He listened to his wife then pushed his hand under the mattress. He took a condom out of his wallet and put the wallet back under the mattress. He turned and saw a man pointing a gun at him.

"No!"

He jumped onto the bed and dragged his wife's frail body onto him. She woke up groaning.

The gunman switched on the light and she saw him too. She gasped.

Otunba peeped and saw the gun was still aimed at him. "Please, don't shoot. I beg you, don't shoot."

The gunman tried to get a clear shot.

"Please, I beg you in the name of God, please, don't shoot."

The wife watched, stretched into a shield by her husband. The gunman backed to the open door, stepped out, his gun still trained on them. He knocked on the opposite door.

"Don't come out," Otunba shouted, but the nurse opened her door and the gunman got her too.

Otunba remained behind his wife, denying the assassin a clean shot. He begged for his life, and cried and begged some more, but the gun kept seeking his head. He took a deep breath, filling himself with his fate, and pushed his wife away.

"Wait. Not yet."

The man lowered his weapon.

"I know who sent you. I know I cannot pay you not to do what you have come to do. You see that picture there? There is a safe behind it. Take the money inside. I am hiring you to kill the person who sent you."

The gun rose and a bullet puffed through its silencer. Then it panned to the wife.

"You bastard," she said. "You were meant to kill him outside the house."

Chronos and Kairos

Jason Goodwin

'What I like about you Ottomans,' Palewski said, 'is your sense of time. It's so unhurried. So natural. You sleep when you are tired, eat when you are hungry. You pray by the heavens, by the appearance of a star, or the decline of the sun. In the West, everything is chopped up, measured, inspected, and divorced from nature. Time in the West is mechanised, and I despise its clockwork tyranny.'

'Mmmm,' Yashim murmured, guiltily fingering the pocket chronometer he had received only that morning. It was the first time he had ever carried a watch, or indeed looked at a clock with any regularity, and he was finding it curiously compulsive.

He decided not to mention it to Palewski, who was indulging in one of his Ottoman rhapsodies.

'Open-hearted, open-handed! That's your empire, Yash, and always will be! And that's the style of the old commonwealth, too,' he added. Yashim had been expecting this: Palewski was forever extolling the virtues of his Polish–Lithuanian commonwealth, of whose utter overthrow he was the sole diplomatic survivor. 'Generous to our friends, and magnanimous in victory! "Don't count the minutes", that's my motto.'

He flung up the sash window and stood there, grinning at the sun.

A finch trilled in the wisteria. From where he sat, Yashim could hear an iron-shod barrow bouncing along the road and the cry of a simit-seller in a distant street. And the quiet, rhythmic tic-toc, tic-toc of his beautiful watch.

Surreptitiously, for the fiftieth time that morning, he flipped the gold lid with his thumb and glanced at the face. And, for the fiftieth time, he felt that little glow of delight. It was like having a loving pet, he thought. Something tiny and quiet that followed you through the day, and was always ready for you.

Its tininess had affected him especially. Yashim was one of those people who are entranced by miniaturisation. He had once spent an hour (maybe it was more?) enjoying a sensation of silky fuzziness in his belly as he contemplated, through a magnifying glass, a grain of rice that had been polished, smoothed and minutely inscribed with several key suras of the Koran. He loved to press his nose to warm meadow grass and then, as his focus adjusted, enter the miniscule theatre of insects and fronds, where petty dramas were enacted before him in a six-inch patch of grass. He liked ships in bottles, which the Maltese sailors sold at the Karakoy quays, and fine embroidery, and the doll's house he had once seen at the Russian Embassy, equipped with tiny place settings and a miniature sleigh.

At the back of the watch was another lid, and inside ...

'What have you got there?'

It was Palewski, drawing his head in from the window.

'Oh, nothing. I was just thinking it's time to be getting along,' Yashim said. He snapped the watch shut and stood up, yawning. 'Must be nearly noon,' he remarked.

'Oh Yashim, Yashim. Don't you listen to a word I say?'

'I'm teasing you, my old friend. You are perfectly right. We must not become entrapped in time's tyranny. I'll see you later, no doubt. Thank you for the tea.'

***

Forty-seven minutes to drink tea! Pausing at the corner of the street, Yashim could hardly credit it, though whether it was the amount of time that had elapsed that surprised him, or the fact that he could measure it so neatly, he wasn't quite sure. He supposed it was the latter, because he had nothing to compare it with. Drinking tea with Palewski always took, what, the time it took! Now it appeared that was forty-seven minutes. He imagined it was sometimes more, and sometimes less. Maybe not much less. He had had the impression of making a short visit. A visit, it turned out, of three-quarters of an hour.

And it had taken him slightly longer to get there in the first place, hadn't it? Leaving Balat, where he lived, to take a caique along the Golden Horn, had taken forty-two minutes! Then seventeen to work his way uphill, in Galata, to the Polish Ambassador's residency. A total of fifty-nine minutes. Practically an hour!

Had he known he would spend an hour travelling to see his friend for forty-five minutes, he might not have gone at all. Thereby saving himself the hour … and the forty-five minutes, too.

It was rather an imposition, Yashim thought, as he made his way downhill to the Bosphorus shore. On the way, crossing the Grande Rue, he glanced up at the beetling Frankish edifice that housed the Levantine Insurance Co., behind whose blank windows worked over seventy men, young and old, toiling over ledgers, figures, and reports as the sun beat down on the glass and turned their offices into furnaces. Yashim knew: he had been there, summoned by the fat Greek director to look into the sudden death of his friend and long-time partner, Levi Kothman.

***

'Dead! I cannot bear it. What I tells his family, eh?' Koulotris had been red-eyed from worry, fatigue, and sudden squalls of weeping. The room was hot. He had mopped his bald head and dabbed at his eyes with a huge, spotted Manchester handkerchief. 'Yashim *efendi*, I need you. Wherever it takes you, go. Personally, I am afraid he took his own life, but ...'

'But?'

'In business, you can never be too careful. Kothman had a beautiful wife, three lovely children—oh, God!—and a stake in this business. A half-stake. We were like brothers, *efendi*. We built the insurance trade, in Istanbul at least. Before we come—pah! Nothing. Can you help me?'

'What do you want me to do?'

'Investigate.' Koulotris leaned forward, and his chair creaked. 'Find out what happened. If he killed himself—I don't know. Anything is possible. There was a brother, I think, not honest like Kothman. Talk to him, if you can find him. Give me something to tell the people. His wife, his children. In Istanbul everything is always gossip, rumour. Forgive me, you know that's true? I have seventy people here, all depending on me like a father. And now I'm alone. People talk, say crazy things. Ah, Levi, Levi.'

At the last moment Koulotris grabbed the handkerchief and rubbed it across his face.

'I think I understand, Koulotris *efendi*. You want a clear account of the events that led up to your partner's death.'

Koulotris held out a hand, palm upwards. 'This is friendship. It is also,' he added, holding out the other hand, 'business. And in business, it is good to make everything clear.'

He weighed his hands in the air, like a set of scales.

'Perhaps you should tell me about finding Kothman's body. It was you, you say?'

Koulotris dragged a hand down his face. 'Me. I came into work. No Kothman. Not a big problem. I opened all the letters, then I told the people what to do. Then I went out to buy a cigar. After that, I strolled along by Dolmabache. You know the caique-landing there, at the end? So, I had the idea to take one, go to Uskudar, buy some halva and baklava for my wife. Sounds crazy, but she likes the ones from Uskudar.'

'I've heard of them,' Yashim murmured. Nothing struck him as more reasonable than to cross the Bosphorus for a special treat. 'Where does—did—your partner live?'

'In Uskudar. Which is why, when I was in the halva shop, I thought I would buy some extra for his children. I'm sorry.' He clapped the handkerchief to his face and blew his nose. 'His children.' He heaved a sigh. 'I arrived, with my packets, and the butler let me in, through to the garden. He has a kiosk there. That's—that's where he was.'

'The butler was there when you found him?'

'The butler... I don't remember. No, he must have turned back. The family were having lunch, you see. I called for him, that's right, and together we—' Koulotris spread his hands. 'Tried to clean up.'

He grimaced at the memory.

'He had been shot?'

'No. His throat was cut. With a razor.'

'So there was a lot of blood?'

Koulotris winced and closed his eyes. 'A lot.'

'Had he, do you think, defended himself?'

'How could I tell?'

'I don't know. Signs of a struggle, something broken, his clothes torn. Did he have any marks on his face?'

Koulotris shook his head. 'I don't remember well, but no, everything was in order. Just the razor.'

'On the floor?'

'A long way off from his body. Like—he threw it.'

'Or someone dropped it?'

'Or someone dropped it.'

'And who, in your mind, would want to kill him?'

'Nobody. He was a good man.'

'You mentioned a brother?'

'Yes. Simon, or Simeon. I don't recall. Kothman didn't talk about him, but I had the impression he was involved in shady business. Kothman always told me to not let him in if he came to the office. They were not on friendly terms, that much I know.'

'Has there been any event, anything new, that might make Kothman want to take his own life?'

'I don't see it. Business good. Family happy. But who knows?'

Koulotris and Yashim had left the building with the uncomfortable sense that all seventy people whose livelihoods depended on the Greek magnate were holding their quills in mid-air, watching him go.

***

That had been yesterday. Since then he had spoken to the distraught widow, and the butler had shown him the garden in Uskudar. The butler, too, had been very upset. Neither thought it likely that Kothman had killed himself: to his widow, it was impossible: 'He cannot even bear the sight of blood.'

The butler was adamant that someone must have come through the garden door, although the door itself was locked and the key was in the house.

Yashim felt the watch bump against his midriff, and paused to pull it from his pocket. He put it to his ear and smiled, involuntarily. It was like having a rather solemn colleague, having a watch. Always ticking, always attending to the matter in hand.

Further along the road he paused to look into a shop window, one of those new Frankish shops with great slabs of glass on the street and all the goods neatly displayed behind them. This one was piled with boxes and jars, carefully labelled in three scripts—Greek, Ottoman and Latin—with exotic names from all over the Empire and beyond: Ladakieh,

Trebizond, Manila. Yashim read the labels with interest, then turned and continued down the street.

At the bottom, feeling hungry, he bought a mackerel sandwich from a man who had set up a brazier on the prow of his fishing boat and placed a row of stools on dry land for his customers to sit on; a boy went to and fro with a tray of tea glasses dangling from his finger. Yashim chose not to sit, but to eat as he walked. In the end, he licked his fingers, rubbed them on the hem of his jacket and, feeling the watch, drew it out.

According to his new friend, it was exactly twelve o'clock. What did that mean? Yashim wondered? Were the muezzins being slow to call the faithful to the noon prayer? He raised his head, listening, and a caiquejee caught his eye, gesturing across his oars to the slender workhorse of the Istanbul waterways, the gondola of the east.

'Uskudar? Kadikoy? Anywhere you want, *efendi*!'

A muezzin began to call from the minaret of a mosque.

'Uskudar,' Yashim said.

He settled slowly into the caique, feeling its balance against the slightly choppy waters of the Bosphorus, and the caiquejee swept them into the channel with one powerful stroke of his bulbous oars.

Yashim surreptitiously drew out his new toy. Here was a novelty: how many minutes would it take to cross the Bosphorus? It was a question that Yashim had never thought to ask. Perhaps as long as the muezzin's chant, he would once have said, or longer. But now he could pin it down exactly, like a European.

On the crossing, he looked about for new things to measure, eager as a boy with his first gun. He tried to measure the rhythm of the caiquejee's strokes, but the effort muddled him: it seemed to be twelve a minute, but he wasn't sure. The watch, fine as it was, told the hours and the minutes but not the seconds ... or so he thought ... until he noticed with delight that the little disc he had thought put an eye in the face of the machine was in fact a miniscule second-hand, tirelessly plotting its dull little circuit of the disc. He squinted at the watch in the bright sunlight. Twelve seconds. Perfect. A passing covey of shearwaters, four seconds a beat. His own breathing: eight seconds from breath to breath.

At the Uskudar stage, he thanked the rower, paid his coin, and stepped ashore. The air on the water had given him an appetite. Koulotris had praised the baklava nearby: Yashim knew the place he was referring to, run by two Armenian brothers whose fame had reached the farther shores of the Bosphorus, so he hurried down past the mosque and plunged into the warren of backstreets, following an instinct for baklava.

He found the place without getting lost and ordered two baklava, vermicelli and pistachio, with a coffee, not sweet. He ate the honeyed pastries at the counter in four minutes, the same time it took an elderly gentleman who had entered just ahead of him to have two boxes of pastries packed up and tied off with string. Yashim bowed and let him pass through the door first, in deference to his age and his burden.

As he found himself in Uskudar, he could think of one or two questions he might ask the unfortunate Jew's wife, and another for the butler. Remembering the way from his visit the day before, he walked briskly through the streets to the house.

The place lay in mourning. Levi Kothman had been laid to rest in the cemetery of the synagogue only that morning, and a number of guests had assembled in the sunshine of the garden to pay their respects. Yashim wondered how many of them knew why the kiosk had been so freshly scrubbed, as they wandered in and out to take advantage of the shade.

Koulotris knew, of course. He had found the body. He stood alone at the edge of the garden, scowling with grief, or fury. Yashim could not tell which. Kothman's wife, small and yellow and with eyes that missed nothing, sat ramrod stiff on a chair, her hands in her lap, nodding to her guests as they filed past.

43

Yashim caught the butler as he passed with a tray of little sweetmeats.

'A question,' he murmured, and asked it.

The butler pondered the question. 'The family. Me,' he replied.

'Koulotris?'

'Yes, of course.'

Yashim waited for a gap in the file of guests and bent close to Kothman Hanum's ear.

His question surprised her. 'At noon, every day! By the muezzin. There is no question.'

Yashim nodded. He brushed past Koulotris, who was still standing mournfully by the wall.

'May I call on you tomorrow?'

'Have you learned anything?'

'That the Kothman family eats at noon. What I can't decide is—the matter of the cigar.'

Koulotris shrugged and turned his jaundiced eyes towards Yashim.

'I asked for clarity, not riddles, *efendi*.'

Yashim bowed.

***

'I hadn't expected you back,' Palewski said, pulling the door open.

'It's after seven,' Yashim said.

'Ah, time for a spot,' Palewski suggested hopefully. 'How do you know?'

'I have a useful new friend.' Yashim fished out his watch and held it up to the light. 'The famous Hunter that belonged to Compston's father.'

'The boy at the British Embassy? Why have you got that?'

'Because today I too became a hunter. And with the help of this one, I tracked my quarry.'

'And slew it?'

'That must wait until tomorrow. Let's go up, and I will tell you what the Hunter told me.'

In the drawing room he sat in his favourite armchair and kicked a leg over its crooked arm.

'Koulotris gave me a precise itinerary for the day he discovered his partner's death. A cigar, a little walk, a trip on the Bosphorus. He went to Uskudar. He was in a playful mood, it seems, and stopped for some baklava. Then he went to find his partner, who was dead, while the family took lunch.'

'Isn't that odd? Why didn't they miss him at lunch?'

'They were about to—but Koulotris beat them to it.' Yashim dangled the Hunter and watched it swing. 'How long does it take a caique to cross the Bosphorus at Dolmabache? On a good day?'

Palewski shrugged. 'I don't know. Twenty minutes?'

'That's what everyone thinks. It takes thirty-nine minutes. Maybe longer, if the passenger is fat.'

'Meaning your friend Koulotris? What of it?'

'Meaning, quite simply, that he could not possibly have done in a morning what he told me he had done. He arrives at work at nine o'clock and does his correspondence. At the very least, according to a thoroughly modern clerk in his offices, that takes him at least three-quarters of an hour, but usually an hour or more. Let us assume he leaves at a quarter to ten, however. Nice and early. He goes to the only tobacconist nearby and buys a cigar. Seven minutes. From the tobacconist's he saunters—but let's say he waddles quickly, like me—to the waterfront. Another twenty-six minutes, by Mr Compston's watch. At the waterfront he strolls—but let's say he makes a beeline for the Dolmabache caique—and finds one. The time is now twenty-five minutes to eleven, because the Hunter told me so.

'The caique: thirty-nine minutes. Twelve minutes to reach the baklava shop, and another four minutes ordering and the boxes being made up. Twenty-three minutes to Kothman's home. What time is it?'

'No idea.'

'Seven minutes to twelve.'

'And so he arrives just as the family are getting ready to have lunch. All very interesting, Yashim, but I really can't see the Hunter has done very much except put Koulotris on the doorstep at the appointed time.'

'Well of course, the Hunter doesn't lie. You know it can even count the seconds? Amazing. A caiquejee rows ...but let's speak of that later. Right now, I know something that Mr Compston's Hunter cannot tell, for all its tiny cogs and whirring springs. Koulotris left the office at least forty-five minutes later than we assume.'

'You asked the clerk?'

'Not yet. I will. But he will point out that, in addition to his correspondence, Koulotris attended to his absent partner's letters. It is a fifty-fifty share. Doing all that he did, he arrived at Kothman's too late for the lunch.'

'Meaning?'

'Meaning that the cigar and the stroll and the baklava are not part of the real story. I think Koulotris left the office and made his way straight to Kothman's house. Twenty-six minutes to the caique, thirty-nine on the water, and eight to the house, making one hour and thirteen minutes. It is, by a conservative estimate, twenty minutes past eleven.'

'How does he get in?'

'At the back, using the key. Only he and the family know where it is: easy to borrow it one day and have it copied. Kothman is in the kiosk. Koulotris surprises him. Cutting his throat creates a lot of blood—he springs back and flings the razor aside. The Hunter doesn't tell me how long that all took, but it's about right. Koulotris slips out, dusts himself off, and turns up at the front door in time to find the Kothmans in the dining room and the paterfamilias bloodily dead. Possibly by his own hand, which would be advantageous.'

'One quibble.' Palewski opened the sideboard and brought out a misshapen green bottle. 'How did he know that Kothman wasn't coming in to the office—and would be waiting in the kiosk?'

'I imagine he arranged it easily. He got the ne'er-do-well brother to suggest a meeting—or maybe he wrote the letter himself. Kothman had forbidden him to visit the office and would be reluctant to receive him in the house inhabited by his wife and children. His garden office, the kiosk, was the obvious solution. Koulotris knew he would be there.'

Palewski poured two glasses. 'This, Yashim, is a liqueur from somewhere, not sure where, the label fell off. Why did he want him dead, then?'

'Oh, that's like the insides of Compston's watch. Beyond my understanding. I expect we'll find that Kothman wouldn't sell his stake, or wanted to sell out, or resisted Koulotris's plans in some way. That's business, my friend. I'll find out tomorrow.'

The Woman of his Heart

Nick Sweet

Things had been quiet in the city for a while, and then everything happened at once. First, a twenty-nine-year-old Russian by the name of Vladimir Vorosky was murdered in his own bed. Then the body of Fernando Llorente, a twenty-two-year-old local tough, turned up in the river.

Inspector Jefe Velázquez took less than two hours to discover that Fernando Llorente had worked for Raul Ramirez, the man who ran the biggest criminal gang in Seville. The biggest, that is, until the Russians appeared and started battling with Raul's crew to see who was going to have the run of the city.

Next, Inspector Jefe Velázquez received the call he would never forget till the day he died—the one where he learned the woman of his heart, lady bullfighter Pe Naranjo, had been kidnapped. The kidnapper, who spoke grammatically sound Spanish with a Russian accent, said he wanted a certain DVD as ransom. Velázquez was turned into a chili, as the locals say, and he dug his nails into his flesh in order to try to contain his feelings of rage. 'I don't know anything about any DVD,' he said.

'But Raul Ramirez does—he got a lad by the name of Fernando Llorente to steal it for him.'

'So it was you that killed Llorente ...'

'I heard he had a nasty accident, but you must refrain from jumping to rash conclusions, Inspector Jefe.'

The man hung up.

***

Velázquez climbed into his Alfa Romeo and headed over to Raul Ramirez's *puticlub* in the Poligono Sur. He drove with both his foot and the windows down, the hot night air messing with his wavy, jet-black hair, the blue T-shirt he was wearing under his black leather jacket wriggling up his back like a damp snake. He parked any old how, then jumped out. There was a queue of ten or twelve people outside the club, and the bouncers were patting people down for weapons before letting them in. The club stood at the end of a rank of warehouses, and a small posse of girls stood on the opposite corner advertising their wares.

Velázquez hurried to the front of the queue, flashed his ID at the bouncers, barked '*Policia!*', and went inside. The place was hot and sweaty as an old sock, and loud music was pumping out, some kind of electronic dubstep shite. A slim, young blonde was wrapping herself round a pole like she thought she was a sexy boa constrictor, and she was giving the old farts at the bar a very public viewing of her privates while she was at it. Velázquez made straight for Ramirez's office, which he knew from having been here before was up the spiral staircase.

'You can't go up there,' a man called after him. 'It's not open to the public.'

'I've come to see Raul,' Velázquez said over his shoulder. He couldn't be sure Ramirez would know anything about the kidnapping, but the man practically ran the city's criminal underworld single-handedly. Or had done until the Russians showed their faces and offered him a little unhealthy competition, and so he was in a better position than most to know what was going down. Ramirez's boast was that a dog couldn't take a poop in the street in Seville without him getting to hear about it. Well, now it was time to put that particular theory to the test.

'He's not come in yet. You'll have to wait.'

Velázquez stopped and turned as he heard the hired muscle coming up the stairs after him. Stocky guy with a brush of spiky blond hair, dressed in black trousers and a tight black T-shirt that showed off his muscles. The Inspector Jefe took out his gun and pointed it at the man's gut. 'I'm a police detective,' he said. 'Now give your tongue a rest and let me into Raul's office.'

The man took a bunch of keys from his pocket and opened the door. Velázquez prodded him in the back and said, 'Get inside.'

No sooner had the muscle shut the door than Velázquez clubbed him on the back of the head with the butt of his gun. The guy went down and stayed there.

Velázquez used his lock picks to open the drawers of Ramirez's desk. He found a DVD in the bottom one.

***

Twenty minutes later, Velázquez was trying to keep his temper under control as he sat at his desk back at the *Jefatura* watching the DVD, along with the rest of his team. There were those who said his usual manner was that of someone who'd taken the bad milk, to use the local lingo, but he was well beyond that now.

The film was a sick piece of work. It had no soundtrack and lasted just over twelve minutes. It was just over twelve minutes *too long*, so far as Velázquez was concerned. Or it would have been, if it weren't the only thing that could save the life of the woman he loved. In the short film, four sickos took it in turns to rape a boy who couldn't have been any older than eleven or twelve. You only got to see the boy from the back on the footage, which was going to make identifying him difficult to say the least. It broke your heart to have to watch the poor lad screaming his way throughout the entire ordeal. It was enough to make anyone want to throw up.

As for the four men, you only got to see the face of one of them.

Velázquez called in on the techie, Luz Cano, and told her he needed a favour. They were really going to have to throw the house out of the window on this one, he said. So whatever she'd been doing, he needed her to drop it. His girlfriend had been taken, he explained, and he needed Luz to make a blow-up of the man's face ASAP. When the enlargement was ready, the Inspector Jefe and his team set about checking it against the mug shots on the national computer database. But they didn't come up with a match, which meant that the man didn't have any form. The man's face apart, the only other distinguishing feature on the footage was a figurine that stood on a shelf in the background.

It was a highly distinctive model of a female nude, a 'Picasso-meets-Giacometti' sort of piece, as the Inspector Jefe coined it; stick-thin and complete with displaced eyes, ears, and breasts. Velázquez gave his number two, Sub-inspector Gajardo, and Agente Jorge Serrano the job of finding out what they could about the figurine's provenance, in the hope that it might provide a clue as to where the footage on the DVD had been shot.

The air conditioner in Velázquez's office was on the blink, as usual, and rivers of sweat coursed down his back as he watched the DVD for the third time, along with Agente Sara Perez and Oficial Merino, just in case they'd missed some vital piece of evidence that might serve as a further clue. By now Velázquez was so angry he was again turned into a chili. He was fantasizing about getting the men in the video on their own, somewhere quiet, and tearing them limb from limb.

He told himself getting angry wasn't the way to go about things. You had to keep cool so you were able to think things through. Easier said than done, of course, when it was the woman of your heart who had been kidnapped.

His mobile started to vibrate against his thigh. He fished it out of his pocket and saw that the call was from his number two. 'What's new, José?'

'My source tells me the figurine's the work of a Sevillano sculptor by the name of Alfredo Ferrer.'

'Spoken to him yet?'

'On my way to his place on Calle Gerona right now,' Sub-inspector Gajardo said.

'What's the number?'

***

Seeing Sub-inspector Gajardo standing by his Volvo up ahead, Velázquez parked with two wheels on the pavement, then climbed out. An elegant, narrow street in the Old Quarter, or *casco antiguo*, Calle Gerona was quiet at this hour. The low mumble of a television set could be heard—someone up watching the late film—but there was little else to disturb the slumber of the local residents, most of whom would be safely tucked up in bed for the night.

'This is the place, boss,' Gajardo said, pointing, and he and Velázquez hurried over to the door. The Sub-inspector—twenty-eight, tall, slim and smart as ever in his navy-blue suit—pushed the buzzer. A gruff, masculine voice said, '*Hola?*'

Gajardo told the man who they were. 'We need to talk to the sculptor Alfredo Ferrer.'

'That's me. What do you want?'

'If you come and open up, *señor*, then we can tell you.'

'I'd just got into bed,' the man said. 'Can't whatever it is wait until the morning?'

'No.'

'The mother that bore you,' the man cursed.

'It's an emergency.'

'Okay, hang on a minute.'

Velázquez heard the sound of somebody moving on the other side of the door. Then it opened and they found themselves looking at a big bear of a man with a bushy, black beard. He stood at around six-two and was wearing an old pair of jeans that were smudged with stains and a T-shirt that did nothing to hide his burgeoning beer belly. He shat in the milk, as they say, in a guttural tone of voice, so that he sounded less like Velázquez's idea of an artist than one of the *ultras* who swear obscenities from behind the goal at the Ramón Sánchez Pizjuán Stadium or the Estadio Benito Villamarín on a Saturday.

Sub-inspector Gajardo took out the enlargement of the figurine that Luz Cano had run off from the DVD. 'We need to know if this is your work.'

Alfredo Ferrer took the photo and looked at it. '*Que sí.*'

'You are quite sure?' Velázquez said. 'This is important.'

'Of course I'm fucking sure. I do know my own work.'

'How many copies of it did you make?'

Ferrer's dark eyes were big with outrage. 'I'm an artist, not a fucking factory. *Cojones!*'

'Who did you sell it to?'

'Man by the name of Jorge Villalba.' The sculptor lifted an ursine paw and scratched his beard. 'Some sort of big cheese in the Town Hall, by all accounts.'

Velázquez showed the sculptor the blow-up of the face of the man on the DVD. 'This him, by any chance?'

Alfredo Ferrer nodded.

'Ever been to the man's home?'

'*Sí.* He invited me over for a drink when he bought the figurine.'

'Where does the man live?'

Alfredo Ferrer told the Inspector Jefe. 'But what's all this about?'

Gajardo said, 'Just routine.'

The sculptor's dark eyes narrowed. 'Sure,' he said, 'and I'm really the Pope, only don't tell anybody.'

Velázquez turned to Gajardo. 'Let's go.'

***

They set off for Calle San Vicente and got there in next to no time. The place turned out to be a flat in one of the beautiful old palaces that were once the preserve of the local aristocracy. Velázquez rang the buzzer, but nobody came. 'We need to get in there,' he said, 'and take a look around.'

'Gonna need a warrant, boss.'

'No time for that.' Velázquez pushed the buzzer to the flat below Jorge Villalba's. No answer. He pushed it again, once, twice, and then a third time for luck. A woman's voice said, '*Hola?*' and Velázquez identified himself and said that he needed to enter the building. The woman complained that she'd been asleep, but she buzzed them in anyway. They took the elevator up to the third floor; then Velázquez took out his lock picks and set about getting the door open.

Once inside, they began looking through the spacious and elegantly furnished rooms. 'Some pad this guy has.' Velázquez's sweeping gesture took in the Steinway baby grand, the original oils on the walls, the chandelier, and the general atmosphere of luxury and wealth.

'How the other half live,' the Sub-inspector said. 'Imagine having a pad like this to bring the *chicas* back to.'

'You're going to do the business with a girl,' Velázquez replied, 'it's all the same where you do it, no?'

'Place like this'd be bound to impress them, though,' Gajardo begged to differ. 'Find yourself in bed making a powder with them before you know it. Wouldn't even have to work at it with the usual charm offensive first.'

'Maybe,' Velázquez allowed, having long suspected that the Sub-inspector would give up the bachelor life in a moment if his ex-wife, Almudena, should offer to take him back.

They were busy looking the place over as they talked.

Then Gajardo noticed the figurine sitting on the mantelpiece. 'Hello-hello. Look what we have here, boss.' He pointed. 'Seems like this is where they must've shot the film.'

Velázquez went over to take a closer look at the figurine. It was the one in the film, no doubt about it. The piece was so distinctive there was no way you'd ever come across another one like it. And the sculptor had assured them that he'd not made any copies. The Inspector Jefe shat in the milk under his breath.

'Now what, boss?'

'We wait, José.'

They made themselves at home in the living room, and felt anything but at home while they went about it. The second hand on the grandfather clock over in the corner dragged like a bastard in a bitch of a mood. Finally, they heard someone out at the front door, followed by the sound of the door opening, then footsteps in the hallway, and a man walked in. He was wearing a light linen summer suit, a navy-blue shirt open at the collar, black leather moccasins and had a droopy Frank Zappa moustache. Velázquez recognized him from the blow-up Luz had made. The man's eyes and mouth opened wide when he realized he wasn't alone.

'The fuck're you two doing here?' he said and took out his mobile. He'd just started to dial when Velázquez took out his ID. 'Inspector Jefe Velázquez,' he said. 'Homicide.'

'The fuck's this about?'

'You're under arrest.' Velázquez gestured to Gajardo, and the Sub-inspector set about cuffing the man.

'You two pricks don't have any idea who it is you're dealing with,' Villalba said. 'I'm an important man in this city.' He shook his head as if in disbelief and shat on the mother who bore the Inspector Jefe in a sneering tone of voice. 'Both gonna be on traffic duty for the rest of your careers as from tomorrow, you persist with this bullshit.'

'Don't think so, Señor Villalba. You see, we've seen the little film you and your friends made.'

'What fucking film's this?'

'Sure you can guess.'

The man's eyes flashed as the seriousness of the situation sank in. 'The fuck is it that you want from me?'

'Names.'

'I've got one name for you to start with. Emilio Rodriguez.'

'Who's he?'

'My fucking lawyer, who'd you think?'

Velázquez cracked a smile that was about as sincere as a banker with a portfolio full of subprime mortgage loans. 'Not gonna be able to help you with this one, though, I'm afraid.'

'In too deep.' Sub-inspector Gajardo held his nose. 'Can smell you from this distance, old chap. Got shit dripping from you.'

Just then, they heard someone out at the front door. Velázquez held his finger to his lips and they waited in silence as whoever was out there made their way along the hallway. Then, a stocky guy of forty or so, dressed in jeans, cowboy boots and a white T-shirt entered the room. The intruder's graying hair was tied back in an improbable pigtail, his barrel belly hung over his belt, and a nest of dodgy tats snaked up his arms. But the Inspector Jefe had more important things to worry about than the intruder's personal appearance—like the fact that the man was holding a gun. A Beretta M9, if Velázquez wasn't mistaken. Which he rarely was when it came to firearms—not at this distance, at any rate.

Gajardo aimed a sidekick at the intruder's arm, and the gun went sliding across the floor. The man went after it, but Velázquez tripped him. Then Gajardo was on him, and the two men began to wrestle on the floor. It looked like the intruder was about to get the better of the Sub-inspector, but it didn't matter because Velázquez had already picked up the weapon.

'That's enough of this fucking around, Raul,' the Inspector Jefe said. 'Unless you want me to use you for target practice, that is.'

The intruder sat up.

Finding himself free to move, Gajardo got to his feet. 'Look who it isn't,' he said. 'Raul fucking Ramirez, of all people ... *Joder!*'

'I can explain.'

Velázquez said, 'I think you'd bloody well better.'

'The Russians have got this bastard here by the balls.' The gangster got up and pointed at Jorge Villalba. 'He's some species of big cheese at the Town Hall—been busy giving our Russian friends permits to run bars, restaurants and *puticlubs* all over the city and beyond. It's a fuckin' outrage.'

'He's being blackmailed, I take it?'

Ramirez nodded. 'Man's an animal .... Can't keep his filthy paws off young boys. Likes to throw parties, if that's the right word for it—invites his friends round and they get hold of some poor kid and take it in turns to rape him.' The gangster shook his head and sneered as if to show his disgust. '"*Sick*" isn't the word for it,' he went on. 'Anybody else would be ashamed, but this bastard thinks it's funny. Backfired on him this time, though, 'cause someone made a film of what they got up to and it fell into the hands of our Russian friends.'

'And you got your mitts on a copy, too, Raul, so I hear.'

'Vladimir Vorosky, the Russian who was murdered, wanted to part company with his compatriots and come in with me, so he ran a copy off,' Ramirez said. 'That was what I asked for as the price of entry.'

'But the copy he made for you was stolen from his flat by Fernando Llorente.'

'Vorosky started to sound like he was having second thoughts and wanting to kiss and make up with the Russians, so I had Fernando break into his place and steal it—then Fernando was killed.'

'Did Fernando kill Vorosky?'

'No, he found Vorosky's body in the flat when he broke in. The Russkies must've got wind of what Vorosky was up to and snuffed him out. Came as quite a shock to Fernando—he wasn't expecting that, I can assure you.'

'The Russians must've failed to find the copy of the DVD,' Velázquez said under his breath, as if he were thinking aloud. 'Or maybe they didn't know about it. But none of that explains what you're doing here.'

'Not a lot of people know this, but Fernando was my son. I only found out last year after they tested our DNA and it matched. Anyway, I thought this son of the great whore 'ere might be able to tell me somethin' about the Russians that'd help me to find out who killed Fernando.'

'So you were planning on hunting down your son's killer and avenging his death?'

Raul Ramirez looked at Velázquez. 'When are you gonna learn that you've got to make a choice, Inspector—it's either my lot or the Russians in this city.' He shook his head. 'All this sittin' on the fence shit just ain't an option anymore. Things have got out of hand. All you're doing is throwing water into the sea.'

'You're starting to sound like Henry Kissinger, Raul.'

'Be serially fucked by a donkey, if I know what you mean by that.'

'He's the guy who said, "My enemy's enemy is my friend—"'

'Man knew what he was talking about, Luis.' The gangster relaxing a little now, as if he reckoned he was in a position to negotiate. 'Your problem is, you're an idealist.'

'You're just as bad as the Russians, Raul.'

'You're forgetting one thing.'

'What's that?'

'Wasn't *me* that kidnapped your girlfriend—and that's a truth as big as the cathedral of Burgos.'

'How do you know about that?'

'I've got eyes and ears all over this city, in case you didn't know.'

They both went quiet for a moment, then Ramirez said, 'You see, Luis, people like me have limits. That's where I'm different from the Russians, because they don't have no limits at all. And the only way to deal with people like that is to play them at their own game.'

'Meaning what, exactly?'

'If you was to set up a meeting with them, and tell me where to expect 'em, then—well, I could take the problem off your hands...'

Just then, Velázquez's mobile started to vibrate. He fished it from his pocket. '*Hola?*'

'Have you got the DVD, Inspector Jefe?'

'Yes.' Velázquez recognized the Russian's voice. The man's Castilian was fluent and correct enough but sounded about as Spanish as goulash and vodka. 'Why are you so interested in a DVD with a bunch of sickos abusing a young boy on it?'

'I have my reasons.'

'Which would be blackmailing a certain big cheese at the Town Hall whose face is clearly visible on the footage. Is that it?'

'You are thinking too far ahead, Inspector Jefe. That can be dangerous.'

'You obviously don't play chess.'

'You're wrong, Inspector. I am a Russian. In Russian we all play chess—but life isn't a board game.'

'I'd prefer to play chess than watch sick DVDs.'

'Please allow me to remind you, Inspector Jefe, that it is only the existence of the DVD that is keeping your precious girlfriend alive.'

'I'd say we have business to do,' Velázquez said. 'I want to meet with you face to face—you bring Pe to me and I give you the DVD.'

'I will need to check the DVD you say you have is the one I want.'

'So bring a laptop.'

'Okay, we'll do it tomorrow, but you must come alone.'

'So you can take the DVD from me without handing over Pe, is that it?'

'Why would I do that, Inspector Jefe?'

'Listen,' Velázquez said. 'I'll be bringing my partner with me, and you bring one of your guys—but just one man, okay? That'll even it up. Try anything cute and the deal's off.'

'Okay, but I decide the time and the place.'

***

Just after three the following afternoon, Velázquez was waiting outside of a nondescript little café on Juan de Mariano, as arranged. Hardly the sort of place you'd ever expect anything exciting to happen. He was nervous and fidgety, and kept looking at his watch.

Eventually, a top-of-the-range BMW pulled up. Velázquez exchanged glances with Gajardo, both men aware that the moment of truth was near.

Two men climbed out of the car. One was tall and of medium build, dressed in shades, a smart, plain-grey suit that looked like it was probably made by Adolfo Dominguez or someone, pale-blue shirt, and black shoes you could have used for a shaving mirror in an emergency, and he was carrying a laptop. The second man was a blond ape, dressed in jeans, Nikes and a white T-shirt that was a size or two too tight.

They came over to Velázquez and Gajardo, stopped just in front of them on the pavement.

'Nice day for it,' said the one in the suit.

'Usually is in Seville,' the Inspector Jefe said. 'But I thought it was only the English who like to talk about the weather.'

'Always been a big admirer of the English.'

'Not many of them here, except for the tourists and the odd language teacher.'

The Russian cracked a cobra smile. 'To business, then,' he said. 'Have you got the DVD, Inspector Jefe?'

'Where's Pe?'

'In the car.'

Velázquez looked over at the parked BMW, but it was impossible to see in through the tinted windows.

'Bring her over here.'

'First I need to see the DVD.'

'No, either you bring her out here now or the deal's off.'

The Russian looked at Velázquez and didn't say anything. Velázquez tried to look the guy in the eye, but just saw his own reflection in the man's Ray-Bans.

'You can leave your gorilla here, outside the café with Pe and Sub-inspector Gajardo,' Velázquez said. 'You and I go inside and you check out the DVD. Then once you've satisfied yourself it's the one you want, you leave with the DVD, and Pe stays with us. That way everyone's happy.'

The Russian and Velázquez stood eyeballing each other.

A long moment passed.

The Russian said, 'And what are you gonna do if I say no?'

'I'll do whatever I have to, to bring you down—whether it's inside or outside of the law.'

'I could have you shot, you want to play it like that ... Or we could make it look like an accident. Don't go thinking that wouldn't be easy.'

Velázquez shrugged. 'I'll take my chances.'

The Russian cracked a grin, then he nodded to his bodyguard, and the man went over to the car. Velázquez watched him open the door and help Pe out. She looked over at Velázquez. If she was scared, then she certainly didn't show it. *That girl hasn't half got some* cojones, Velázquez thought, his pulse pumping up the volume a notch as he watched the man take Pe by the arm and bring her over to the pavement.

Pe was looking pale and tired, but she was still beautiful for all that. She was wearing jeans that fit her long legs to perfection and a red T-shirt that was full of creases and stained in places—hardly surprising in the circumstances. Her long black hair was tied back in a ponytail, the way Velázquez liked her to wear it. Somehow it gave you a better view of her smooth skin and perfect bone structure.

'Are you all right, Pe?' He made a brave attempt at a smile.

She nodded.

'Okay, Inspector Jefe,' the Russian said, 'how about we go and see to our little business matter …'

***

Velázquez followed the Russian into the café. The place had a tiled floor, and there were pictures of bullfighters in action on the whitewashed walls. A number of men, all of them the wrong side of sixty, were sitting or standing at the long bar; others were sitting at tables. There must have been twelve or fifteen people in the place. The propeller fan that hung from the ceiling stirred up the hot air a little, but did nothing to cool the place down. Velázquez and the Russian sat at one of the vacant tables by the window.

The Russian booted up his laptop, and Velázquez handed over the DVD.

A young waitress came over and asked what she could get them. Velázquez said '*Dos cafés con leche, por favor*' just to get rid of her.

The waitress smiled and went away.

Meanwhile, the Russian had slipped the DVD into his laptop.

Velázquez looked through the window and saw Sub-inspector Gajardo and Pe standing out there, along with the Russian's bodyguard. Rivers of sweat were coursing down Velázquez's back.

The seconds dragged while the Russian concentrated on what was going on on the screen of his laptop. Then the man closed the lid of his Mac, clearly having seen enough. 'Please allow me to congratulate you on an excellent piece of work, Inspector Jefe. Now you are free to take the girl.'

Velázquez got up and left the café with the Russian close behind him. When they got outside, the Inspector Jefe reached into his jacket for his gun, just in case there was going to be any fun and games. The Russian's bodyguard drew his gun at the same time.

Velázquez stood in front of Pe and said, 'There's no need for anyone to get hurt here.'

The Russian didn't even turn to look back as he made his way over to the BMW. The blond ape followed him, keeping his gun pointed at Velázquez all the time. The Inspector Jefe watched the pair climb into the BMW and drive off. The next moment Pe was in his arms. 'Oh, Luis,' she sighed, 'I knew I could count on you.'

***

That evening, Velázquez took Pe to Dos De Mayo, the tapas bar on the Plaza de la Gavidia. They found a table near the window, then Velazquez went up to the counter and placed an order for a variety of tapas dishes and drinks. Pe had her nose stuck in the local newspaper, *El Sur*, when he rejoined her.

She looked at him across the table and said, 'Listen to this.' Then read: '"A frantic car chase through the centre of Seville ended in a deadly shoot-out this afternoon. Two men, both thought to be Russian nationals, lost their lives."' She frowned. 'I don't get it—who killed them ...?'

Velázquez shrugged. 'Must've been some rival gang, I guess.' He sipped his *cerveza*. 'But who ever really knows what the hell goes on in this crazy city?'

Snake Skin

Ovidia Yu

Straits Times 'Top of the News'

A fire raged through a house in Bougainvillea Estate in the early hours of Thursday morning.

In under two hours, the two-storey bungalow off Farquhar Road, where businessman Jerome Khong, 64, lived with his family, was completely destroyed. The conflagration claimed the lives of Khong's 28-year-old wife, Songsuda, and his business partner and house guest, Mr Emmanuel Okonjo, 32.

Mr Khong's daughter, Marie, 40, was asleep in her room upstairs when she woke coughing due to the smoke in her room. She rushed to the other rooms on the second floor to wake her father and domestic helper, Flordeliza Avelino. In a panic, the three escaped down the outside back staircase, climbing down through thick, black smoke billowing out of the kitchen. Only after they reached the road outside did they realise that Mr Khong's wife and guest were still in the house.

"My wife must have heard something downstairs and gone to look. She must have been trapped downstairs by the fire," a shaken Mr Khong said. "There was so much smoke nobody could have gone back in to find her and Emmanuel."

Mrs Khong was found in the toilet of the guest bedroom downstairs and Mr Okonjo in the guest bedroom. Both appear to have died from extensive burns.

Six pump ladders and five supporting vehicles were activated, and the fire was put out just after 5 AM.

***

Marie

I normally enjoy the taxi ride home from Changi Airport, but on this last trip I dreaded getting back to my father's house. Actually, it was not my father's house. It had been my late mother's house, the last of her investment properties that she had left to my brother Malcolm and me, on the condition that we would let our father live in it for the rest of his life.

The haze was all over Singapore. It looked like mist around the street lamps and dark trees, but it smelled like ash, the ash of burning rubbish rather than incense, even in the few steps from the air-conditioned arrival hall to the air-conditioned taxi. Like many born in the Year of the Snake, I don't like extremes of temperature, whether hot or cold. Usually on such homecoming rides, I would already be texting friends, arranging meet-ups to satisfy my cravings for fragrantly steaming Hokkien prawn noodles topped with crispy lard cubes and black char kway teow fried with bloody cockles.

But this time I had not told any of my friends I was coming back. This was family business.

Why hadn't my father told us he was getting married again? After all, my mother had been dead for almost three years. And in hospital, just before she died, my ever-practical mother had addressed the possibility of Dad remarrying: "It would be good for him to get somebody to look after him. But my jewelry goes to Marie."

The taxi stopped.

184 Bougainvillea Crescent was not the house we had grown up in. Malcolm had been doing National Service and I was away at Columbia when my parents moved. Still, we each had our own rooms in the Bougainvillea Estate house—all of us, including Mum and Dad, who had separate rooms. "Now we're getting old, we don't sleep so much," Mum said. "This way at night we can do our things without disturbing each other."

Bougainvillea was a 'good class' residential estate, and the house was one of the smaller ones beyond the expensive bungalows. Given its distance from the main road and the temperature in Singapore, it was inconvenient without a private car. But though Dad's eyesight made it dangerous for him to drive, he refused to consider living in a Housing Development Board flat, or even a condo. Mum had considered these options (citing their price and proximity to public transport and hawker centers), but Dad valued appearances over convenience. Since Mum's tenants were moving out of the Bougainvillea property, moving there had been the obvious solution. She had always been the practical one. "Choose your battles," she'd always told me. "Remember it's not worth fighting unless you can win."

I hadn't returned to do battle with my father and his new wife, but I did want to hear the news my father said he had for us, news he wanted to deliver in person. Though what could trump his 'just married' letter? I also wanted to take a look at his new Thai wife, Songsuda. I would be calm and friendly, I reminded myself, no shock or surprise. This was not a battle worth fighting.

But once inside the house I was taken aback to find it full of packing boxes. My father was sitting alone on a folding chair next to a barcalounger wrapped in plastic.

"What are you doing? Did you pack all these?"

"Of course not, *lah*! We had a removal company come and pack. They're not finished yet."

"Why? Is it termites? Are you renovating? And what is the big news you couldn't write in your letter?"

"I am selling the house," Dad said. "Songsuda and I are planning to move to Australia. Even at my age, it is easy for me to get in with enough money and a Singapore passport."

"What money?"

"You know I have a life interest in this house. So if I sell the house and move to Australia and buy a house with the money, I get a life interest in that house. It's the same thing. And for the same money I can get a much bigger house there. All I need is for you and your brother to sign the consent to sell. Thanks to your mother, I cannot even sell my own house."

I managed not to remind him that Mum was the one who had paid for the house. All Dad's money had disappeared into various get-rich-quick schemes.

"You worked all this out yourself?"

"With my wife. She has the forms for you to sign. And you must go and get your brother to sign also." My father looked towards the kitchen. It was clearly a signal, but no one appeared. Dad looked much older than I remembered, his speech seemed to come with more effort. I had wondered whether his sudden marriage would rejuvenate him. I was not sorry to see it hadn't.

"Dad, why didn't you tell us you were getting married?" It was such a cliché, but I said it anyway. Hadn't I flown back from New York just to say it?

"Look, we didn't want to make a fuss. We just wanted something simple, that's why I didn't tell you two. Anyway, you know now, so what difference does it make, right? And Malcolm isn't even coming back."

"Where am I going to stay if you're selling the house?"

"You will stay here of course! Your bedroom things are still upstairs. We'll get the disposal people to come after you leave, so you better take everything you want. You better tell your brother to come back and take what he wants also."

"You can sleep here, but I don't know whether you can eat here." Dad's new wife came out of the kitchen at last. I had expected some statuesque Thai beauty, but Songsuda was small all over. She had small hands, ears, eyes and mouth and a protruding lower jaw that made her look as though she was perpetually bracing for a fight. "Your father's servant is so spoilt. She won't cook for anybody except him!"

I had to get something to eat before I sorted out the servant situation, I decided. "If you haven't had dinner, I'll take you both out to eat." It was one of the things I liked best about being back in Singapore, how easy it is to eat out. At least that could not have changed. "Let me just go and wash up first."

I went upstairs with my bag. At the top of the stairs I stopped and opened the door to my brother's room, feeling an echo of the old guilt for going into his room without permission. The air inside was heavy and stagnant. The books and guitar Malcolm had left behind were on a shelf, thick with dust. The last time we were both in Singapore at the same time was when our mother died. What I found most sad were the stuffed toys, forgotten on the window seat. I picked up Mr Zonks, the striped zebra with a dashing blue necktie that our Aunt Kitty had knitted for him.

In my equally dusty room, I found the one she made for me, with its bright pink flower bandanna—Lady Mathilda. I put both of them on my cabin bag and went back downstairs.

"I'll drive. You still have the old car, right? Is it still working?"

"Of course! I have somebody give it a run every now and then."

The car keys were still on the hook by the front door.

"It's late, but Chomp Chomp will still be open." The nearby Serangoon Garden Food Centre, known to locals as Chomp Chomp, catered to late eaters. I would be able to get my Hokkien prawn noodles there, and some spicy, grilled stingray.

"The air is too bad to eat outside. Your father is old, okay? Do you want him to get sick?" Songsuda said.

I looked at Dad. Songsuda ran a small hand over his balding head. "You should take your old father to a nice place to eat. Somewhere not so cheapskate. Somewhere with air-conditioning." She clearly thought going to a hawker centre was beneath her.

"Okay. Wherever you suggest."

Songsuda and my Dad sat together in the back of his old Mercedes while I drove. Songsuda chatted happily about Burger King, especially the Double Cheese Burger with Bacon. I was not getting the hawker food I had been looking forward to.

"Dad, what about your cholesterol?"

"Your Dad ate dinner already. His fat servant made for him rice porridge. Every day rice porridge. Even if she makes for me, I would not eat!"

"I thought you hadn't eaten yet, Dad!"

"Your daughter doesn't like me!" my father's new wife said in a singsong voice. I could not tell whether it was an effect of her Thai accent or if she was flirting with my father, or deliberately trying to provoke me.

"Of course Marie likes you," my Dad said from the backseat. "Marie, tell Songsuda that of course you like her."

"Wait ... let me concentrate on driving." I turned into the Burger King car park.

"My daughter Marie was born in the Year of the Snake," I heard my Dad say, "like my late wife. Both so cold and suspicious!" He laughed, which made him cough. It was one of his favorite jokes.

I didn't like his old jokes, and I didn't like his new wife.

I didn't like the way she twined her young body around my old father and flicked her tongue on his ear in between eating her fries.

I didn't like her multi-color snakeskin shoes with impossibly high heels. I have always been averse to snakeskin, and I've never understood the attraction of high heels.

"Those look dangerous."

"Hey Marie, you don't care my shoes. You are my stepdaughter, not my stepmother!" Songsuda shrieked with laughter. "Maybe if you tried wearing shoes like that, you can find yourself a husband."

"Or you can work in a massage parlour," Dad said. "I told the woman at the massage parlour, 'get me a beautiful girl', and she told me this one's name 'Songsuda' means 'beautiful girl'!" Dad laughed. It was a feeble old man's laugh, with pauses to catch his breath.

Songsuda did not find this funny. She stopped licking Dad's ear and ate her fries.

"Dad, should we take home something for your breakfast?"

"That's all right. His fat servant will make his breakfast," Songsuda said. "She cooks for him, but she will not cook for me."

"Fat servant?"

"Flordeliza," Dad said. "You don't remember Mum's fat Flor?"

"I didn't know she was still with you! Why didn't you tell me? I should have said hello to her!"

"Your daughter shows more respect to your servant than to your wife," Songsuda observed. "She never even say to me, 'Would you care for some dessert, Miss?'"

I could have pointed out she was a 'Mrs' not a 'Miss', but I went to get her cinnamon melts and a chocolate cone, and thought about Flor.

***

Flordeliza Avelino was the live-in domestic who had come to look after my mother when Mum's cancer took over her pancreas. I had welcomed Flor's presence. She was a dark, plump, lazy woman with some basic nursing knowledge. Her main function had been to keep my mother company and act as a buffer between her and Dad.

My parents had not got along after my father's retirement. Until then, they had never spent enough time together to realize they didn't like each other very much. After Mum died, having someone in the house to clean and cook for Dad assuaged my conscience when I returned to America. Aunty Kitty had warned me to watch out for 'foreign maids' trying to seduce my father, but I laughed off the suggestion. I couldn't see why any woman would be interested in my father when there were so many younger and richer men available.

***

When we got back to the house, there was still no sign of Flor. I went out to the tiny porch off the living room and looked at the dark, neglected garden. There was a snuffling sound and I looked down to see Coco, my mum's Pekinese.

"Coco remembers you!" Flor came round the side of the house. "Now she is old she doesn't like to go in the garden, but she wanted to go outside to find you."

"Flor! It's good to see you again!"

"Oh Miss Marie. You should have come back earlier and stop that woman. That woman put a spell on your father!"

Flor was older and fatter but otherwise the same. She was holding on to Coco's leash. The dog's fur was patchy. From the way she walked and sniffed, I could tell she had trouble seeing and hearing, and from the way she smelled, I guessed she was unwashed and incontinent. She bumped her nose against my leg, and I patted her dutifully, feeling the stickiness of old dirt.

"Your Papa's wife don't like her in the house. So now whole day she is tied up behind the kitchen."

I almost asked Flor whether she had been tied up behind the kitchen too.

"I didn't see you just now. I didn't even know you were still here looking after my Dad,"

"It's not my fault," Flor said quickly. She had picked up my implication that she had failed. "I look after your Dad here. But he goes out for his massage, what can I do? Next thing I know he is telling me he is married, he brings that woman here. I ask you, what can I do?"

Nothing draws people closer as fast as a common enemy.

"That woman is taking advantage of your father. Do you know she has a boyfriend? A black boyfriend who comes and stays here? Some people no shame!"

"You mean an Indian boyfriend?" Flor dealt with the Singaporean prejudice against Pinoys by being even more aggressively prejudiced against local Malays and Indians.

"Not Indian—worse than that!"

"Worse?"

"I no need to say. You will see for yourself."

***

Emmanuel Okonjo turned up two days later. He was a tall, slim, dark man with very short hair and a goatee. Apparently he was a regular visitor and the bed in the downstairs guest room (once my mum's) had been left unpacked for him.

Dad introduced Emmanuel as his friend, his business partner. "He is helping me to look for investment opportunities in Australia, for when I move there. Things are much cheaper there than here."

"What kind of business are you in?"

"Actually in Singapore I am a student," Emmanuel said.

"What are you studying?"

"Why, don't you believe me? You think I am too stupid to be a student? You want to see my visa? Hah?"

I had not thought of disbelieving him till then. I shrugged to show I had only been making conversation, that he was overreacting.

"I'm studying business," he said.

I could have asked him where he was studying, but he might have taken that as another challenge.

***

Emmanuel appeared in the kitchen the next morning when I was sitting down to breakfast. I kept my eyes on the *Straits Times* and read reports on the aftermath of another major drug-syndicate bust in Malaysia. Emmanuel fixed his own instant coffee and put a cold curry puff into the microwave, seeming to know where everything was. Flor had made me toast with a couple of soft-cooked eggs with pepper and soy sauce, but she disappeared as soon as he appeared. Apparently she did not cook for Emmanuel either. He pulled out the chair beside mine instead of sitting across from me. I moved my chair slightly away.

"Do I make you uncomfortable, Marie? Because I am so black?"

Actually, I was uncomfortable because his clothes smelled bad. The sweat-stink odor of too much waxy antiperspirant trapping bacteria in the material. Another example of a problem exacerbated by attempts to get rid of it.

"I need space," I observed neutrally. I had Coco on my lap, and I could feel the growls trembling inside her.

"Maybe, Marie ... you need a black man." His eyes, fixed on me, were very serious. "Have you ever had a real man, Marie? Women like you, you don't even know what a real man is."

"What are you doing?" Songsuda appeared and stood across from us, arms akimbo and hips tilted. She looked like a jealous wife, though her husband was in bed upstairs. I looked back at her calmly. She tossed her head as though shaking off the sight of me and turned to Emmanuel. "Don't waste your time on her. She has no money. She tells her father she is a big shot with computers in America, but does she send money back to her father? Does she? No! In fact, her father has to go on sending his money to her! You call that working?"

My father did not send me his money. Malcolm and I got a monthly allowance from the account our mother had left. It was far from enough to live on in New York, but it was the same amount as our father got. It must have come as a shock to Songsuda to find out that despite the big house my father lived in, he could not touch the capital in the bank. Even the house— bought by my late mother in my name and Malcolm's—was his only to live in. After his death the house, like whatever was left of my mother's investments, would be divided between Malcolm and me. It was not that my parents had been on bad terms. They had been on very good terms as long as my father disappeared to the office and left my mother to take care of everything.

Emmanuel kept his eyes on me. "There's all kinds of working. I was a street boy. I put myself through school by selling bottled water by the roadside and selling men's underwear door to door. That was how I learned how to do business. That is why I'm such a good businessman now."

"What's your business?"

Emmanuel glanced at Songsuda, who had grabbed a pastry out of the fridge and was eating it cold. Given the way that woman ate, I didn't know how she stayed so small. Maybe she was bulimic and puke-destroying her insides. The thought cheered me up.

"Shoes," Emmanuel said with a loud laugh. He sounded as though he was joking, but I didn't see the joke. "Come and see. Your pretty stepmother here loves my shoes. All women love my shoes!"

Why not? Especially as I could see his invitation annoyed Songsuda. I put my bowl on the floor for Coco to lick up the egg yolk I had left for her and followed him into the guest room.

Emmanuel's room was a lot less dusty than mine and Malcolm's. At the foot of the bed, there was something that looked like a cross between a fridge and a steamer trunk. It was plugged into an extension cord, and there were dials showing temperature and moisture levels. It looked as though it had been designed for wine. But when Emmanuel opened it with a flourish, I saw it contained shoes.

"Snakeskin shoes," Emmanuel said, "The best. Are you scared of snakes? Women are all scared of snakes, but they all like snakeskin shoes. Crazy, no?"

I wasn't scared of snakes, and I didn't like snakeskin shoes. I didn't like snakeskin on anything, other than snakes. Snakeskin is either molted by a living snake or taken from a killed snake. These shoes had come from live snakes, killed to become human footwear. I picked up a snakeskin shoe and examined it. Cold like a snake, it was fascinating.

"Don't let her touch!" Songsuda protested.

"You like them, yes?" Emmanuel asked. "Have you ever seen such shoes? Do you know where snakeskin comes from?"

"Most snakes shed skin regularly. It's called ecdysis. A shed skin is almost double the length of a snake because each of its scales is wrapped on the top and bottom." I had done a school project on reptiles. It's strange what stays with you from school.

"Whatever," Emmanuel said.

Songsuda rolled her eyes and pulled him out of the room, slamming the door. Without thinking, I pressed my ear to the familiar gap in the door frame and heard her hiss, "I'm sick of this! I am sick of the old man. He keeps touching me. What are we waiting for?"

"You only just got back! You cannot go away again so soon without attracting attention!"

Songsuda had returned from a visit 'home' to north Thailand a day before I arrived.

"And your Jerome has to sell the house first."

"Don't call him my Jerome. You don't know how long that will take! Anyway, you said we will have more than enough money!"

I did not hear Emmanuel answer. When I opened the door they were gone.

Hearing the way Songsuda said 'we', clearly excluding my Dad, made me worry. Now she had her Singapore passport, she did not need him anymore.

"Are you sure about going to Australia?" I asked my Dad, when we had a moment alone. "You don't know anybody there. You don't know what life is like there. Why not go there for a holiday first and see if you like it before selling the house?"

"If I go for a holiday, I got to spend money to stay in a hotel. Where am I going to get that money? Are you going to give it to me? If not, you don't come and talk so much. I'm going to be an investor and let my money work for me. You must sign the consent to sell the house and make your brother sign also. You tell your brother if he doesn't sign I will report him to the police as a homo and get him arrested!"

"If you go to Australia, what is going to happen to Coco?"

I watched Dad's rheumy eyes squint with the effort of recalling Coco.

"Coco was your mum's dog. Your mum went and died and left me to look after everything without leaving me any money!"

"Yes, Dad," I cut off the familiar rant. "But Coco is still here. Flor is looking after her. What's going to happen to Coco if you sell the house and go to Australia?"

"Flor can take Coco. Flor always looked after Coco for your mum."

"Dad! If you go to Australia, Flor will have to go back to the Philippines or find another family to work for here. How do you expect her to take Coco?"

Dad shook his head dismissively. "You worry more about that dog than about your own father."

I added Coco to my list of things to do something about. Part of me wanted to fly back to New York (without signing the consent to sell), leaving Songsuda and Emmanuel to do whatever they wanted with Dad. But there was more at stake here than Dad's comfort. And to be honest, I didn't have enough in New York to sign away half of a property valued at 5.2 million Singapore dollars. The house was decrepit, but in space-starved Singapore, people would pay that and more for freehold land in an approved residential zone.

***

The next morning Coco was dead.

Flordeliza banged on my bedroom door, and I managed to understand through her tears of rage that she had found Coco's body outside the kitchen door, surrounded by bloody vomit.

"I am going to tell your Dad! Tell him that woman he brought here poisoned your poor Mum's dog!" Flor marched on towards the master bedroom. I grabbed a shirt to pull over my nightie and hurried after her, unsure whether to attack or defend my father's new wife.

But Dad was alone in bed, sitting up with his breakfast bowl of oatmeal and soft-boiled egg whites on the bed tray. Flor must have fixed his breakfast before opening the back door to feed Coco.

He squinted at us. "What are you talking about? Where is Song?"

"Coco is dead!" Flor wept. "That woman was talking about getting rid of the dog, and now the poor dog is dead! Sir! I tell you that woman poisoned your wife's dog!"

"Come on *lah*, why would Song do something like that?" My father smiled the genial smile that had exasperated my late mum so much. His 'do-nothing smile' she used to call it. No matter what she said, he would smile that stupid smile and make some inane joke. Dad looked towards the doorway, and I saw Songsuda had appeared with Emmanuel. "Song, come and tell these silly people that you did not poison the dog."

Songsuda rolled her eyes and said nothing.

"The dog was old. That is how old dogs die, same as old people. Their insides break down," Emmanuel said confidently. I saw his glance pass over Dad and Flor then settle on me, waiting for me to challenge him. He was probably getting ready to tell me he was qualified in the treatment of old dogs and old humans.

"I'm taking Coco to the vet," I said.

"*Hiyah*, the dog is dead already, what for make such a big fuss?" Dad shook his head. "If you're so upset, I'll get you a new dog."

I suppose he meant well. Hadn't he got over Mum's death by getting himself a new wife?

"No more dogs! I hate dogs. Anyway, she doesn't even live here!" Songsuda raised her plucked eyebrows at me. "If you liked that smelly old dog so much, why you never take it to New York with you? Hah? Why you leave it here to burden your old father?"

I went back to my room to dress without answering.

When I went downstairs, Flor was waiting for me. She had wrapped the dead dog in an old towel and put it in a plastic bag that she was carrying flat across her arms like an offering.

"Can I come with you, Miss Marie?"

"Of course, Flor. Just let me put on my shoes."

***

The vet phoned two days later and told me what I already knew. Coco had been poisoned.

"People put out rat poison and dogs ... you know how dogs eat anything."

I did know. I had already found rat poison in the storeroom.

It was clear Flor suspected Songsuda of killing Coco from the way she glared at her and ignored her orders, despite my Dad's attempts to joke her out of it. Dad needed Flor because Songsuda didn't cook. I didn't know how she was going to feed him in Australia. Song seemed to find it highly amusing. She reminded me of rich, powerful kids in school making life hell for the poor old teacher hanging on for her pension.

Later, when Emmanuel went out to see to his 'business', Songsuda came to watch me packing up my and Malcolm's things.

"I know who killed the smelly dog."

I continued shaking out and folding Malcolm's shirts. Songsuda did not need encouragement to talk. She could not stay silent for long, and since she did not like talking to Dad and could not talk to Flor, that left only me.

"Your Papa loves me. He knows that I don't like the dog because it is smelly and tries to bite me. He likes me to be happy, and I am not happy when the dog is around. That's why your Papa poisoned the smelly dog."

She stopped and waited for me to defend my Dad, but I did not.

It was the kind of thing my father would do. It was also the kind of thing he would never admit to. Years ago, the night before we left to spend a week in the Cameron Highlands during the school holidays, I got upset because my guppies could not come with us.

"I don't want to go!"

"They can survive one week without food," my mother said.

"Don't worry about the guppies," my father said.

The next morning all my guppies were dead, floating upside down in the tank, with tiny swollen bellies. My mother promised me new fish when we got back. My father said nothing except "better flush them down the toilet". He did not look at me, like he was not looking at me now. My practical, pragmatic mother did look at me, probably assessing whether I was going to be difficult. I never found out which of my parents killed my fish.

"Did you hear what I said?"

I nodded. "Do you think Malcolm will want his Matchbox cars?"

Songsuda didn't bother to answer. She had already made clear what she thought of my *kathoey* brother. I didn't have to understand the term to know it was something derogatory.

"I know you don't like me. But when you go back to America, you need somebody here to look after your father. But in exchange you also got to help me."

"Flor will look after Dad." I said. I turned back to my packing.

Flor would always be there to look after my father. Or so I thought.

Two hours later, Flor was upstairs looking for me, in tears and wailing in anger. For an instant, before I made out what she was saying, I thought my father was dead. I was wrong. Unfortunately.

"Dad, did you fire Flordeliza?"

"Women can never get along," Dad said in his feeble genial voice. "If only you all can get along then no problem. But if cannot, I got to side with my wife, right? Anyway, we are leaving Singapore soon. Do you expect me to take that Fatty with me? Haha. You want me to take the servant, take the dog …. If you sign for me to sell the house, I take everything with me!"

I wondered whether I could blame it on dementia.

***

Flor stopped cooking altogether after that. She locked herself in her room and said through the door that she would stay in there until her flight back to the Philippines. I had no idea who was supposed to book that flight—certainly not my Dad. He didn't even know how to make himself a cup of tea. Well, that was Song's problem now, I thought.

But when I heard a loud discussion going on in the kitchen, I decided to use my Dad's needs as an excuse to make my way down the stairs very slowly.

"They would look at you!" I heard Song saying, "They would question you and arrest you! They don't look at me, because I am Mrs Khong. I have a Singapore passport. You need me!"

"The Americans would look at you. American Immigration doesn't trust you Pinoys. But Marie can get into New York, no problem. She has an apartment there. She would just be going back to her apartment. Nobody will look at her twice. Right, Marie?" Emmanuel raised his voice. I had not been as quiet as I thought.

I went down the last two steps and into the kitchen.

"Well, what do you say?" Emmanuel looked at me.

"There's a death penalty for carrying drugs."

"Only if you get caught." I saw a glint of appreciation for how quickly I had caught on. I distrusted the man, but could not help feeling pleased.

"It's probably easier getting drugs in from Singapore than anywhere else in the world," Emmanuel said. "The reputation of this country is so good, once they hear you are coming from Singapore, nobody looks too hard at you."

"What do you want?" Songsuda glared at me.

"I want to fix something for my dad."

She didn't move out of my way.

"I thought I would make lasagna," I said. "Dad used to like it. Maybe he'll try to eat some."

"Don't bother. He can eat instant noodles. But don't expect me to fix it. I am his wife, not his servant."

I had to decide what to do. No, that's not true. I already knew what I had to do, I just had to figure out how to do it.

"I bought some ginger beer when I went to get the beef and tomatoes," I said. "And there's some pineapple juice and vodka. Want some punch while I cook?"

Their greed combined with their laziness made them move out of the kitchen, leaving me alone to work.

***

The beef lasagna smelled good. Emmanuel inhaled greedily. He clearly thought I had been won over. I made a point of preparing a beautiful portion for Flor as well as for Dad and pouring a mini jug of punch that I took upstairs to her.

When I got back to the kitchen, no one was there. Emmanuel called to me from the guest bedroom, and once there I heard Songsuda vomiting in the attached bathroom.

"Go and call the fat servant to come down and clean up this mess." He sounded disgusted. Songsuda clearly had not made it to the toilet in time.

"Flor won't come. Dad fired her, remember?"

"Then kick the stupid *buwisit* out and call the agency to send another servant!" Songsuda shrieked. With her make-up smeared with sweat and worse, she was a plain, flat-faced woman with blotchy skin. She retched, and Emmanuel heaved her roughly back into the toilet before she made too much of a mess. I worried how much was coming out of her.

"What's wrong with Songsuda? Why is she throwing up like that?"

"She took something. She thinks she is having a baby. A black baby, so she is scared. Your father is an old man with a car he can't drive, and a wife he can't fuck!" Emmanuel threw back his head and laughed, overcome with his own wit. But his laugh was feeble, and he didn't look too good himself. He stood his suitcase on end and pushed it under the toilet door handle so that it could not turn to open. "I don't want her stinking up my room with her vomit. Bitch tried to get rid of it without even telling me. I got so mad I slapped her—just a couple of times, but she deserved it. My baby. My son. She tried to kill it."

"How are you feeling?" I saw discomfort in the tense hunch of his shoulders and the protective hand he kept rubbed over his eyes trying to stay awake as he slumped back on the bed.

"Crazy tired. That fat bitch servant is using her black magic on us because you all think Song poisoned that goddam dog."

"Let me out!" Songsuda was banging on the bathroom door, but not too loudly. She didn't want my father to hear and come downstairs.

"I know Songsuda didn't poison Coco," I said. "I did."

***

"Miss? Miss, can you hear me?"

It felt like years later when I opened my eyes to find someone holding my hand—my wrist actually, fingers firm on my pulse—and a broad, concerned face looking into mine.

"I am Section Commander Damian Loh. Are you Miss Marie Khong?"

"Yes, I'm Marie—my father is inside the house—he's old ..."

"Miss Khong, take it easy. Your father is safe."

"And Flor—his helper—her room is next to his ..."

"Miss Flordeliza Avelino is also safe. Can you tell me how many other people were inside?"

I looked across the road at the house. It was still burning, flames fluttering and dancing out of windows (Mum's curtains, I thought) as sections of roof collapsed in ashy surrender.

"My stepmother. She would have been with my father ..."

Damian Loh nodded; a nod of acknowledgement, not agreement.

"Any idea what time the fire started? Do you have a family altar in the house by the way? With joss sticks? Or a prayer bin indoors?"

"I was awake until about 2 AM—jet lag—but there was nothing wrong then. And no. We make offerings at the temple."

"It looks like the fire started around 3 AM, in the downstairs guest room. The room Mr Okonjo was occupying?"

"Yes. He's a business contact of my Dad's."

"And you made dinner last night?"

Did he suspect me of putting something in the lasagna?

"What?" I stared at him blearily. I had just been rescued from a burning building. No one could blame me for not remembering whether I had cooked dinner.

"Your domestic helper says that she did not cook dinner. She said you did?"

"I'm sorry, I can't remember ..."

Again he made a note. I felt myself tense, watching him.

"Do you remember using a grill, barbecue, candles?"

"No." I breathed easier. "I think—I made lasagna."

Another note.

"What do you do, Miss Khong?"

"I'm in IT."

"You have a lot of shoes, in a funny kind of leather, no?"

"Oh, the shoes in the car are snakeskin. I'm trying to design shoes with removable heels that can be worn flat for work and fitted with heels for after hours."

"Must get my wife a pair," Damian Loh laughed and shut his notebook. "You're all right, but take it easy, okay? I sent your father in for observation. The fire was likely caused by lithium-ion batteries overheating in a fast charger in Mr Okonjo's room."

I realized he hadn't been suspicious of me. He had just been making sure I was not in shock and coherent. He had not been paying attention. Like most people, he did not know the cost of snakeskin removed from live snakes, how their heads are nailed to trees and their skins slowly peeled off. This is after they are pumped full of water to make their skins easier to remove. Many snakes are skinned alive, suffering for days.

But not knowing things is what keeps people happy. That's why Rohypnol—roofie—is so popular. It's not just a date-rape drug, though that's probably why Emmanuel had the pills I found in his room. Mixed into alcohol, roofies work magic, turning the worst thug into a sleeping beauty. It is probably detectable if you know what you are looking for, but I doubted anyone would test the roasted remains of Songsuda and Emmanuel. I did the formal identification of their bodies in the morgue, and I will never forget the sight of blackened scales of skin crisping off them, or the smell so like *char siew* pork that filled the room.

Luckily, the house was insured against fire. Since Dad no longer had anyone or any reason to move him to Australia, I used half the insurance money—my half—to set him and Flor up in a comfortable condo. The other half I sent to Malcolm, telling him to invest in an apartment for himself and Amel. There were tears of gratitude from both of them for my 'sacrifice', and I now have a standing invitation to their new apartment on the Rue de Courcelles, close to the Parc Monceau.

But while I did use my share of the insurance money to settle Dad, the street value of what is in the heels of those snakeskin shoes will more than make up for it.

Corpus Crispy

Tamar Myers

Assistant Professor Delbert Finkter had written the best American novel of the twenty-first century. It was so good, in fact, that future generations would rank him up there with Henry James, Ernest Hemingway, and William Faulkner, among others. Unfortunately, this masterpiece had never been published. Given that every rejection letter Delbert had ever received over the past thirty years had been a form letter, all virtually identical, he couldn't even be sure that his nine-hundred-page manuscript had ever been read.

This maddening situation was what Delbert Finkter referred to as the Catch-22 of the publishing world. Publishers would not read unrepresented material, and literary agents would not represent unpublished authors. Great American literature of the sort Assistant Professor Delbert Finkter had created had to be plucked from a slush pile by some college-aged intern who couldn't write the instructions for boiling water.

For a serious writer, especially a great American novelist like Delbert Finkter, self-publishing was completely out of the question. That route was for narcissists, who merely wanted to see their words on a printed piece of paper. Self-publishing was for bored and unfulfilled housewives, who needed the validation that they weren't finding at home. As Delbert, now in his late forties, waited for the twits in New York to select his great creation from one or more of the slush piles (Delbert believed that rules against multiple submissions did not apply to him), he supported himself by teaching English and American Literature and Creative Writing courses at Desert Gulch Community College in the Sonoran Desert of Arizona.

Desert Gulch lies at the foot of the Superstition Mountains, just forty miles east of Phoenix, which is the hottest metropolis in North America. Delbert was born in Desert Gulch, on a day when the mercury reached a record high of 118° F in the shade. Except for the years that he had spent earning his degree at Arizona State University in nearby Tempe, Delbert had never been away from home. He lived in the two-bedroom bungalow that he'd inherited from his parents when he was only twenty-three.

In the winter, he spent his free daylight hours hiking in the Superstition Mountains, looking for the fabled Lost Dutchman's Gold Mine. In the summer, when only mad dogs and Englishmen would have been foolish enough to venture out into the Sonoran heat, Delbert enjoyed writing constructive letters to several dozen newspapers and magazines whose editors (and subscribers) needed to be enlightened. Although Delbert was a loner, he was at heart a generous man.

In Delbert's forty-ninth year, the month of August was the hottest on record. Temperatures soared over 100° F every day but one, when it reached a more *comfortable* 95° F, as the weather girl said with unnecessary sarcasm. On the second day of Creative Writing 101, even Delbert, who normally didn't mind things a bit warm, found himself feeling irritable. And who could blame him? Although almost September, it was 120° F, and despite the thermostat being set at 70° F, the presence of twenty human bodies raised the room temperature to just over 80 degrees. It's one thing to be hot outside, but quite another to be hot and trapped indoors with a room full of billions of mutating, heaving, roiling bacteria and viruses.

Although most of the students in Creative Writing 101 were college age, the class did include three senior citizens who'd been permitted to audit the course. Delbert did not approve of the college's policy of permitting wannabe writers in his class who were not paying for that privilege. He viewed them as dilettantes, who should be at home scrap-booking or working on their memory boxes. He despised their agreeable smiles and incessant head-nodding, as if they approved of every word that fell from his lightly rouged lips.

On that hot August afternoon, Delbert was especially irked just by the sight of Thelma Dustrey. Delbert had known the wizened septuagenarian his entire life. Mrs. Dustrey owned and operated what she had the nerve to call "riding stables" and a gift shop for tourists who wanted to explore the Superstition Mountains in search of the "Dutchman's" lost gold mine. What she really sold was kiddy rides on burros, short, guided trips on ancient mules, and Chinese-manufactured junk. Mrs. Dustrey also sold treasure maps that were worth less than a used taco wrapper.

Delbert had been extraordinarily generous in the initial class session and had given his students an easy assignment: write *anything*, just keep it under five hundred words. Simple, yes? Most senior citizens wrote about their grandchildren, or their pets, or some boring bus trip with other retirees. However, this woman had written a story about a gold prospector whose greed led him to die of thirst in the desert. It was a retelling of the legend of the Lost Dutchman's Gold Mine in the Superstition Mountains.

The 'mine' was supposedly composed of a vein of gold worth hundreds of millions of dollars in today's money that had been discovered by a German named Jacob Waltz in 1892 ... *or not*. There were more versions of the story than there were fools serving in the United States Congress. To accommodate the public's fascination with the tale, Arizona maintained the Lost Dutchman's State Park on the west side of the mountains, complete with a museum and a gift shop, where one could purchase supposed replicas of the Dutchman's map.

Thelma Dustrey's short piece about this legend was written as a murder mystery. Two things in the piece immediately stood out to Delbert. One, the woman possessed a fair knowledge of the mountains, and two, she was a surprisingly good writer ... for an old biddy. She might even be publishable at some point. However, the egotistical woman had typed a note at the bottom of the second page, stating that she hoped to get the story into print if it was any good. Delbert, who spent his winter days searching for the lost treasure, and whose nine-hundred-page Great American Novel still languished at clueless New York publishers, was not amused.

"I hold in my hand," he said, "some of the best first submissions that I've had the pleasure of reading during my quarter-century of teaching here, and also some of the worst." Delbert slapped a single sheet of paper on the desk of a handsome, blond man with a square jaw and eyes the color of the finest Ceylon sapphires. "Matt, way to go. Yours was the best."

Delbert walked halfway across the room to stand directly in front of Mrs. Dustrey. "But your paper, I'm afraid, is what the folks in New York call—and let me be really clear about this— they call it 'garbage'. Your writing is nothing but clichés. Students, would you like to hear me read some of Mrs. Dustrey's submission?"

"Please don't," Thelma Dustrey said.

"But I must," Delbert said. "The written word is meant to be read, to be shared." He cleared his throat so that he might force his high tenor voice up a full octave. "'The heat of a Sonoran summer is enough to drive even Satan underground. When the mercury climbs above 120 degrees, the earth moans for mercy. Boulders and rocks appear to pant, and mirages melt without as much as a shimmer.'"

He paused dramatically, just long enough for the inevitable laughs. When none were forthcoming, Delbert Finkter peered over his black, heavy-framed glasses in what one might construe to be mock annoyance.

"Oh come on, people. Granted, the rest of you are like ninth-grade dropouts, not university material, but even you must recognize the overuse of alliteration, and the ridiculous, over-the-top imagery here. Rocks that pant, indeed!"

Then Mrs. Dustrey, who possessed a weather-blasted face, and who was dressed in thrift-shop rejects for goodness' sakes, had the temerity to wave her hand. And practically in his face too!

"Sir," she said, "I didn't write 'rocks that pant.' I wrote 'Boulders and rocks *appear* to pant.'"

Delbert sighed dramatically. "Well, *excuse* me. Even if I were to gloss over all the other things that are wrong with your story, there remains the fact that you completely ignored the cardinal rule of fiction-writing that I so arduously endeavored to drill into your empty heads last week. Class, what is that rule?"

Much to Delbert Finkter's surprise no one stirred. Clearly, a few of the students had remembered it because not all of the assignments had been terrible. The handsome blond with the jewel-colored eyes certainly had.

"No wonder you did so poorly on this assignment," Delbert hissed. It was a proper hiss, replete with s'es. "The cardinal rule of fiction-writing—of any writing, really—is know your subject. Write what you know. Miss ..."

He glanced down at the papers in his hand, even though he remembered the offender's name. "Miss Dustrey has tried her hand at a sad little tale of revenge set in our noble and mighty Superstitions. Wouldn't you know, it's another tired version of that damned lost mine. It's what I call derivative fiction-writing. Her attempt at humor also falls flat in her title selection: *Corpus Crispy*."

The class, to a student, roared with laughter at the title. The handsome, blond male seemed to laugh the loudest. Not only that, but he leaned over and whispered something to Miss Dustrey behind one of his strong, manly hands. Why didn't these numbskulls understand that they should be laughing *at* her? The sound of this laughter, and the sight of this man's betrayal—well, of a sort—caused Delbert's cheeks to burn hotter than the pavement outside the classroom. And this on a day when the air temperature was 120° F. Delbert pressed his the thick, black glasses down on his restrained, even dainty, Caucasian nose so hard that they slipped, and he had to grab them.

In desperation, he gestured to the window, where the great massif of the Superstition Mountains loomed, the many caves and crannies along their vertical surfaces in deep-purple relief, thanks to the late afternoon sun.

"There is where Miss Dustrey has set her story, but I doubt that she has ever stepped off the trails of the Visitors' Center in the State Park. No, I take that back, I don't think she's even gone inside the Visitors' Center. If she had, then she would have read some of the articles and seen the displays, and at least picked up some of the literature on the Lost Dutchman's Gold Mine. If she had done her research, then she might have read that Weaver's Needle—which is a one-thousand-foot-high monolith—appears on the supposedly *authentic* map that dear, dead Jacob left behind. It, however, is not even mentioned in her story."

Finally, a malicious chuckle or two, maybe even three, from some of the male students. Thrill-seeking fools were forever scaling the towering needle. People even slept up there—in more ways than one. Delbert had once considered climbing the monolith when he was younger, but what held him back was the fear that he might be tempted to jump.

But Delbert's hard-earned chuckles were cut short by the aggravating Mrs. Dustrey. "But I did write about what I know best," she said. She ended her sentence with a rising note, like a

Canadian, or a Brit, or a whiner. Delbert especially hated whiners.

"No, you did not," he said. "I have hiked the Superstition Mountains every spring for the past twenty-five years, and I have never come across a potable source of water as far into the massif as the one you've written about."

The gnarled old woman didn't even have the guts to meet his penetrating gaze. "The reason for that is," she said quietly, but without hurrying, "is because the map that everyone thinks Jacob left behind is really a phony. At my riding-stables, the Busted Bridle, we sell authentic maps to the lost gold mine. Our maps that are based on the one that the Apaches used when they were mining the vein, back in the day."

A number of people sniggered at this, a reaction that Delbert encouraged by waving *his* arms wildly. "Is that so? Let me get this straight; you sell authentic treasure maps to loot worth hundreds of millions of dollars, yet no one has ever found it, including yourself?"

He could tell that he was hitting his stride now, because the class roared with laughter, and it was not directed at him.

Mrs. Dustrey looked up, but just barely. "Yes. But you see, sir, the map is in a sort of hieroglyph—"

"*What?* You mean the Ancient Egyptians wrote it?" That line should have been a winner, but it fell flat. It had to be that the students were associating this thorn in Delbert's side with their own sweet little grandmothers. The only solution that he could see was to shame Mrs. Dustrey into dropping his class.

"Miss Dusty—"

"That's *Dustrey*, sir."

"Whatever, it's all the same to me. Miss Dustrey, you should be grateful that you are only auditing this course, and that you will not be receiving a letter grade on a permanent transcript."

This time Mrs. Dustrey dared glance at him, but Delbert hadn't finished.

"Because, my dear, you couldn't write your way out of a paper bag. On that account I think you should do yourself a favor and avoid ridicule by withdrawing from the class. As this is only second time that we've met, I believe that you can get almost a full refund."

A ripple of gasps played around the classroom, but the old bag seemed totally unfazed by his ugly words. She merely shrugged and then offered the smallest suggestion of a smile in return. Or was it a loser's smirk? Delbert hated it when smiles bordered on smirks; that's when he wanted to haul off and slap the offending expression off the person's face, regardless of their age or gender.

At any rate, the bitch had brought it on herself, first by interrupting him, and then by not giving him the courtesy of being offended by his insult. If she really was a writer, she would have been crushed by his comment. Those who said that Assistant Professor Finkter was a cruel man were nothing but ignoramuses who'd had it easy in life. Even the Bible stated that the chaff had to be separated from the wheat and discarded. Delbert Finkter was merely doing his part to winnow out talentless dilettantes before they had a chance to add their drivel atop the legendary slush piles of New York publishers. For that, the entire industry, other serious writers included, owed him a debt of gratitude.

The rest of the class period did not go as Delbert had planned either. Traditionally, the second class meeting of the semester was the one that he enjoyed the most. This was the day that he got to pop the silly dreams of his bubble-headed students like they were a bouquet of party balloons landing in a cactus patch. And no, it wasn't because Delbert Finkter was a mean-spirited jerk, like someone had called him years ago— and since then as well—it was because he already knew what it was like out there in the world of commercial publishing. Delbert Finkter knew what it felt like to be rejected and have his dream destroyed. Delbert Finkter knew what it was like to live a ho-hum existence in the armpit of Arizona, in a town built over Hell itself. No, Delbert Finkter was a good man, a kind man, a man who wanted nothing more than to spare young, vulnerable souls the anguished existence that was his.

When the period was over, Delbert asked Mrs. Dustrey to stay behind so that he might apologize. However, a genuine apology was the last thing on his mind. When some other students—girls, undoubtedly sycophants, hung back as well, Delbert made a great show of gallantly escorting them from the room.

"Now," he said to Miss Dustrey, when they were alone, "tell me more about this map of yours."

"Well, sir, my granddaddy's granddaddy won it in a bar fight from a settler who was given it by one of the original Apache who used to live on this land. The Apache used the watering hole when they were high up in the Superstitions on long hunting trips. The mine is marked because the Apache used gold for personal ornamentation before the white men came."

"Why?" Delbert barked. "If the gold is marked on your maps, why hasn't anyone found it?"

"Because, sir, like I said earlier, the maps are kinda hard to read. They're all symbols and such."

"I have a PhD in Old English, for Pete's sake," Delbert said. "So I'll be the judge of what's hard to read. Are your hiking trails clearly marked?"

"Yes, sir. We have three trails that could all be a possible solution to solving the gold riddle."

"And you've already followed all three of these trails?"

"No sir. I'm afraid of snakes, and I'm afraid of heights. However, I did manage to get pretty far back on one of them, the one with the fresh-water spring, but then I had to be rescued because of my vertigo issue."

"Is that so?" Delbert said. "Well, tomorrow is Saturday, so I have no classes. What time do you open?" Delbert said.

"Six. Do you want me to save you a mule?"

Delbert shuddered. "Mules stink. Especially in this weather. I can hike on my own two legs, thank you. I'm not over the hill yet."

***

It was a good thing that Thelma Dustrey's old Chevy knew the way back to the Busted Bridle. She was blinded by tears, which fell with the rapidity of coins from a slot machine when a winning combo has been pulled. Thelma never cried from physical pain, mind you. As a girl, Thelma had never known her father, but she had never given her mother as much as a squeal's worth of satisfaction, not once during all the whippings that woman had given her. As an adult, Thelma hadn't as much as gasped when her first husband, Bobby the Bastard Rodrigues, chopped off two of her toes with a meat cleaver because she had complained that shoes that bought on sale were too narrow for her feet. As soon as she could hobble into an attorney's office she had filed divorce proceedings.

Neither did Thelma shed a tear when her second husband, Albert Half-Scar "the Moose", sent her to the Emergency Room with a broken jaw and three cracked ribs when she miscarried *his* child. She cried plenty then, to be sure, but it had nothing to do with her injuries. She called her attorney from her hospital bed and filed for divorce a second time.

Thelma had had moments of good fortune. She'd met Albert at a bar, but when you're a woman of a certain age, and you have aged beyond your years, and you have no use for church, where else are you *supposed* to meet men? Real men. It wasn't any dive either, but the Horny Goat, where some of Desert Gulch's prominent citizens went to wet their whistles. Thelma had had no reason to believe that she'd find another abusive man there. After all, wasn't the third time supposed to be the charm?

Charming was exactly the word to describe the Frenchman, although strictly speaking, Pierre wasn't French, but he was from Quebec. As far as the locals were concerned, that was the same thing. Pierre did have a charming accent and, more importantly for Desert Gulch, a lot of money. He'd come down for the winter warmth and sunshine for decades, as thousands of Canadians come to Arizona every year, but then eventually Pierre came to feel so at home in the Sonoran Desert that he decided to immigrate and establish a riding stable, possibly even a dude ranch, in the great American Southwest, the land of big skies and endless sunshine. That was precisely when he met Thelma.

So Thelma was Pierre's fast track to citizenship, nothing more. Pierre bought the land for the Busted Bridle, and together they built the business, but it was yet another marriage arranged in Hell. How much verbal abuse had she been subjected to before it dawned on her that the romantic sounds of French could cut two ways?

Every time Pierre screamed at her in the incomprehensible words of his native tongue, eyes bulging with rage, arms wheeling about like the rotary blades of a helicopter, her mother's words rang in her ears: "Stupid, clumsy Thelma. How could I have given birth to such a horrible, ugly, child? You're nothing but a spoiled brat. I wish you'd never been born!"

Mercifully, one day the eyes bulged a trifle more than usual and the arms whirled faster. Suddenly Pierre lurched forward and upward, as if attempting to become airborne. But then all movement stopped, and he crumpled to the floor. Within seconds, his eyes glassed over as the last breath of life was wrenched out of him by an eager Satan.

Most fortunately, Pierre's fatal tirade had taken place within the privacy of the couple's home, and not their business, because Thelma's immediate reaction was to dance a little jig of joy. Then she dutifully called the paramedics, and, after practicing a couple of grave expressions in the bathroom mirror, ran out to tell their employees that the "French cowboy" from Quebec was dead.

At last it was Thelma's time. The woman with eight toes and lopsided jaw was going to bloom like the Thelma that she was in the desert. The first thing that she did was change her surname name from LeBlanc (Pierre's family name) back to Dustrey, the name of her absentee father. The son-of-a-bitch would have to be a century old by now, but there was always a chance he might still be alive and looking for her, or that she might have siblings or cousins somewhere. The next thing she did was to enroll in the Creative Writing Class 101 at Desert Gulch Community College.

Imagine that! Stupid Thelma Dustrey had a brain after all. Of course the Senior Citizens Alive program, which allowed local residents over sixty-two to audit courses for free, wasn't exactly the same as being in college, but it did allow one to take actual college courses and have somewhat the same experience. For Thelma, that experience meant writing. Telling stories to herself had been her way of coping, and if she said so herself, she had become quite good at it. She knew that to be true, because she had a library card from the Desert Gulch Library and was such a voracious reader that at one point Miss Voss, the Head Librarian, thought it necessary to inquire about the armloads of books that Thelma took home with her every week. Miss Voss didn't know why the sight of so many books leaving and returning vexed her, but only that it was so unusual.

"I lose myself in them," Thelma said.

"I think that you've read every book in this library twice," Miss Voss said. "Did you ever think of writing one of your own?"

"Yes, ma'am. It's always been my dream to be a writer," Thelma said. "Ever since I was little I wanted to write. But my Ma called it 'scribbling' and a waste of paper. So I could only write the stories in my head. Anyway, I wouldn't know how to start. Besides, I'm too old now."

"Nonsense," Miss Voss said breezily. "Take some writing courses at the college. You're never too old."

"Yes, I am."

"Nah—uh, how old are you? Fifty?"

"Sixty-seven."

"Wow. I never would have guessed. You look really good. But you know, that means you would qualify for the Senior Citizens' Alive Program."

Thanks to Miss Voss, she finally started on the path to fulfilling her lifelong dream. Not that any of it mattered now! Assistant Professor Delbert Finkter had ruined everything. Assistant Professor Finkter was the caboose on the train of abuse that began with Thelma's mother and continued through husbands one, two, and three. The one really good thing that had finally come along in Thelma's life, the opportunity to bloom and become who she was meant to be—the chance to work through all the pain she'd experienced through the written word—that chance had been ripped from her soul, like a plant from the soil, by that demented little assistant professor.

When Thelma pulled into her parking spot at the Busted Bridle she was no longer bawling like a spoiled brat. Her pity party was long over. It was almost sundown—quitting time for her employees—and when the two women who worked for her came over to greet her, she even managed a cheery 'Hey.'

"Are all the hikers accounted for?" asked Thelma.

"Yuppers," said Misty. She was barely out of high school, so still had some life left in her.

"There were only two," Wanda said. "It's been too damn hot. They were together and stayed out less than an hour. No one took the mules out, and we had only eight burro riders all day. It's supposed to be even hotter tomorrow."

"Then you're getting a day off," Thelma said. "With pay, of course. Those temperatures are too high for man or beast." But not some men, she thought.

"Everyone's been brushed down and fed. We're ready for tomorrow." Misty talked about animals as if they were people, and treated them that way too.

"How was your class?" Wanda said.

Thelma managed a smile. "I got an 'A,'" she said. "Imagine that. My very first short story, and I got an 'A.'"

"No shit!" Wanda said. "But I thought you were just auditing."

"I am just auditing," Thelma said, fighting back more tears. "But the professor is a decent man, and he wants you to feel like you really are a college student, so he gives you an actual grade. He said my story, *Corpus Crispy*, was the best of the bunch."

"*Corpus Crispy*?" Wanda howled with laughter. "Is that the one you were telling me about in which the victim dies of thirst in these mountains because the murderer switched the trail signs? The watering hole in the dry stream bed way up yonder?"

"The very same story. Professor Stevens said it was a brilliant plot, even though it was unrealistic, because the watering hole that I described doesn't show up on the map that Jacob supposedly left behind."

"It's on our map," Misty said. "I know, because I've taken hikers up there to help them to look for the lost gold. But the water is a *long* way up there, most of it straight up, it seems."

Wanda patted Misty's arm. "That's a slight exaggeration, dear. But yes, dear, there is a watering hole on Black Canyon Trail, at the eight-mile mark. The other two trails—Narrow Canyon Trail and Badger Den Trail— are as dry as my tear ducts were when Thelma's mama passed. Otherwise, the maps we sell don't mean a thing."

Misty looked gobsmacked. "Honest? Holy guacamole," she finally squeaked.

"Wanda is wrong," Thelma said. "Those made-up treasure maps, and those three trails, they all mean hope for someone. They bring momentary happiness to a lot of people who might be having a bad day."

"And it is a lot healthier than sitting in a casino," Wanda said. "You have a better chance of finding the Dutchman's gold for real than striking it big at the slots."

The three women said goodnight, and Misty left, but Wanda stayed behind. "I know you just gave me a load of crap," she said.

"What?"

"You had a terrible time in class today, didn't you? We've known each other since third grade, and I can read you like a book. I know a storm is brewing inside you and something is about to break, but I just don't know what. Whatever's going on, I'm here for you, you know."

Thelma just turned and went into her house to rest. Shortly after the witching hour, Thelma gathered a flashlight and a canteen full of water and headed out into the desert. Since the night was as dark as the inside of her dead husband's asshole and as warm as a fat man's armpit, Thelma also packed a handgun. There was a chance that she might encounter a mountain lion, and she would undoubtedly run into packs of roving coyotes, but the biggest danger was stepping on a rattlesnake, as they came out at night to hunt.

***

On Monday, when Thelma went to class, she and the other students waited patiently for Assistant Professor Finkter to show. After half an hour, when he still hadn't made an appearance, the students began to drift out of the room. Thelma and the handsome blond man with riveting blue eyes were the last to leave.

"Hey," he said, on their way out, "I liked your story idea. And just between you and me, the guy's a prick."

Thelma didn't respond. She didn't have anything negative to contribute to the conversation either when Assistant Professor Finkter officially became a missing person. It wasn't until two weeks after the poor man went missing that the partial remains of a thoroughly dried-up corpse were found wedged in a crevice eighty-six feet below Standing Rock Peak, and forty feet below an active mountain lion den. Had this person jumped? Fallen? Were they pushed? Could they have been part of the lion's lunch that slipped away from her hungry cubs? Unfortunately, the difficult terrain made recovering the corpse impossible.

Later, when the summer heat had finally broken, and it looked like business for the Busted Bridle might pick up again, Wanda saddled up a mule. It was clear to Thelma that she intended to ride out by herself.

"What's up?" Thelma asked.

"It's time someone switched the trail signs back," Wanda said. "One crispy corpse is quite enough."

The Sultan Rules Mombasa

Annamaria Alfieri

Mombasa, British East Africa: 1912
Vera Tolliver put that dreadful early June down to her own failures. But truth be told, the sun was also to blame. She needed to have moved faster, thought more clearly. But the trade winds, which ordinarily cooled the equatorial island city, had failed and made way for a stewing heat that drugged the mind and annulled all but the most desperate intentions.

Vera's body had added its own impetus. The baby growing in her required warmth, she'd imagined. It seemed to like this cooking they were both receiving. In these past few days, it had begun to flutter about—a lovely, exciting sensation that she wanted to describe to her husband. But Justin was off to the north, investigating slave smuggling. And she had nothing to do but play the piano, write to her father, and visit with the only friends she had here at the coast—Bishop Peel's daughters, Virginia and Molly.

Until she met the Peel girls, Vera had failed to find a place for herself among the British in Mombasa. She may have been the wife of a handsome nobleman, but Justin was a second son without funds. He had decided to serve his king as a policeman—a way for him to stay in East Africa, which he had grown to love. And be near her, whom he had also grown to love. They had a lovely life here together. But according to British mores and customs, his work placed him, and her, into not much better than the servant class. Besides which, she was a Scottish missionary's daughter, born in Africa and had "grown up wild," according to the toney settler snobs.

Despite Virginia and Molly Peel's father being a lofty Anglican bishop, the two had befriended Vera, perhaps because life here on the coast offered few European girls to choose from. White settlers made for the high country around Nairobi, where this miserable equatorial heat dissipated in the rarefied air. The Peel girls needed someone like Vera.

At first she had been drawn to the older sister Molly, who was also twenty-one and of Vera's same stature—petite and slender, as Vera used to be. She was getting quite round now. She smiled to herself, deeply satisfied with her motherly condition.

As their friendship grew, though, Vera found true warmth and camaraderie with the tall, lanky, younger Virginia. They shared a lively sense of the absurd and a thirst for adventure that seemed completely absent from the more conventional Molly.

It was Molly, gasping, panting, and dripping, who rapped urgently at the door of Vera and Justin's government-issue bungalow late that morning. Without a hello, she poured out her outrage. "She has gone. And you must help me find her before she ruins her future. She is out of control."

Vera pulled Molly in out of the sun that beat on the front door as noon approached. "You are overwrought. Sit and tell me what has happened." It was just like Molly to judge too harshly everything Virginia did. And to appoint herself as main enforcer of the impossibly prudish standards of British society.

Molly pushed off Vera's hands and remained standing. "Have you not heard me? She has gone off on her own!"

Vera forced herself not to snap back. Molly was an alarmist. Poor Virginia, to have her sister always against her. She is too like me at sixteen, Vera thought, the sort of girl a mother always admonished her daughter not to be. But Virginia was not foolish.

"I am sure ... I don't think ..." Vera began. But no platitude would shoo away the affront in Molly's eyes. "When did you last see her?"

"When we went to sleep last night. She was gone before I awoke this morning." Molly's tone was that of a prosecutor describing a major crime.

Vera had to find a way to calm her. "But is that so awful? Really?"

"I was not concerned at first. I thought she had gone down to breakfast early, though she almost never awakes before me." Molly's put her fists on her hips.

"But Virginia was not in the dining parlor?" Vera asked, as patiently as she could manage.

Annoyance intensified in Molly's gray eyes. "Her place had not been occupied. Papa was reading the newspaper. I should have told him, but I did not. She has doomed herself and the whole family to scandal."

So like Molly to condemn at the first provocation. True, a girl as young as Virginia was not supposed stray an inch from home without parental permission. And no girl of sixteen ever went anywhere alone. Though Molly had once or twice half-heartedly lamented these rules, she rejected Virginia's every complaint about them. She treated Virginia more like her child than her sister.

Vera had sided with Virginia when it came to the oppressive dictums for British maidens. The Kikuyu girls she had grown up with were married and had children by the time they were sixteen. British girls were watched over like four-year-olds.

Secrecy had become Virginia's weapon. Vera was privy to what her young friend kept hidden. But she could not blurt it out now. It was not her secret to tell. Still, the possibility existed that Virginia *was* jeopardizing her future.

"Have you spoken to anyone else about this? If your parents find out, they will send her home to some awful English finishing school."

"No."

"And where are your parents?"

"Papa went to one of his endless clergymen's meetings, and mama is off visiting a parishioner in hospital."

"We must find Virginia before they realize she has gone," Vera said, taking her sun hat from the hook next to the door.

Molly hurried ahead to the corner. "If we do not find her this morning, will Justin find her and not tell mama and papa?"

Vera kept up with difficulty. The heat and the baby were slowing her down. "Justin is up in Malindi investigating a ring of slavers."

"But Britain has stamped out slavery," Molly said, without slowing her strides.

Vera felt as if she were in a foot race. "A bit slower please." She stopped to breathe. "You know as well as I that passing a law does not stop people doing the crime. We have the Ten Commandments, but many people are still wicked." She did not add what Justin had reported in utter frustration: that though the British administered here, the Sultan still ruled, and his subjects saw no sin in keeping slaves. Criminals among them shipped off boys and young girls—the most lucrative commodity—to the slave markets in Muscat. But this was not the sort of intelligence British women were supposed to have. The soaking sweat on Vera's back turned cold. She shivered off the thought. There could be no connection between that and Virginia.

"Truly, Molly," she said, "I don't think we will need Justin's help. We will both feel like fools when we find that your mother insisted on Virginia going to visit the sick." It was what Vera's mother would have done.

They neared the manse. "We will go in the back entrance, if you do not mind," Molly said, "to avoid my parents in the event they have returned. Perhaps Bani Kapoor saw Virginia this morning."

"Bani Kapoor?" Vera asked, catching her breath. She felt a little faint.

"Our Goan cook."

They found him in the kitchen, smoking a cigarette and stirring a pot, which as far as Vera knew was against Mrs. Peel's rule. She had forbidden him to smoke while cooking for fear the ashes would fall into the soup. He was squat and lethargic. And, when it came to their inquiries, completely unhelpful.

"Not see her." He shook his head.

"Did you hear anyone go out?" Vera asked.

"I sing while cook," he said, gleefully. "Not hear noises when sing. Know nothing."

They stole through the house and, from a side window, Vera saw Mr. Dingle, Mombasa's itinerant gardener, working near the fence that surrounded the cathedral across the road. She went to him.

With its domes and crenellations, the massive white church looming above them, like the city itself, had more a Middle-Eastern than a British aspect. Mr. Dingle, by contrast, was utterly English and totally unprepossessing. He doffed his hat and held it to his heart. "Good morning, Lady Vera, Miss Peel," he said. He always behaved like the gardener on a great estate in England.

"I wonder if you have seen my—" Molly began, but Vera clenched her arm to stop her and took over the conversation before their mission was given away. They needed to keep whatever Virginia had got up to out of British East Africa's overactive gossip mill. That lot of character assassins would think nothing of ruining a girl's reputation.

"What time did you arrive here this morning, Mr. Dingle?" Vera asked instead.

"Very early, my Lady. I brought flowers for tomorrow's service. At about six. I meet the sacristan early on Saturdays, before the heat can wilt the blossoms. I had some lovely white irises and some—"

Vera smiled and held up a hand to stop him from launching into an ecstatic lecture on garden blooms—Mr. Dingle's great passion.

"Was anyone else about?"

"Do you mean here on the cathedral grounds?"

"Hereabouts," Vera responded, with a sweeping gesture that included the manse but did not single it out.

Mr. Dingle paused and then shook his head. "Not that I recollect. A trolley or two went down the hill as I was coming up. Were you looking for someone in particular?"

Molly glared at Vera. "I do not see how we can ask about her without asking about her," she muttered. She turned to the gardener. "My sister Virginia seems to have left early this morning." After a pause, she added. "Not that she has done anything wrong. Umm … ah … I forgot to tell her something."

"Perhaps she is in the church, helping to arrange the altar flowers," Vera said, taking Molly by the arm and steering her in that direction. The most vexing thing about Molly was that she always treated Vera as if she, too, were a younger sister.

Mr. Dingle looked puzzled, but took up his spade and turned back to the beds along the iron fence.

"She is not in the church," Molly grunted through clenched teeth. "I looked there before I came to you. This is about *my* sister, you know."

It took two hands and all Vera's strength to pull open the massive door. "I know that," she said as calmly as she could. "But we must talk, and coming in here was an excuse to end that conversation." And to get out of the vicious noon sun.

Light poured into the church interior through high windows, but inside the stone kept the temperature ten blessed degrees cooler. Vera went into a pew at the rear of a side aisle to get off her feet and try to keep control of her temper. Losing it would only make matters worse.

"We've gone headlong into this, Molly. We must go back to why you are so upset. Is it only because you fear for Virginia's reputation? Or do you have some reason to suspect real danger?" Vera hoped her own growing concern would not show. Molly was het up enough.

Molly harrumphed. "I fear she is making terrible trouble for all of us. And so should you. If you were truly her friend, you would not want her to disgrace herself. She is foolhardy. She chafes constantly about how she must comport herself, wishing father was a shopkeeper instead of a bishop, because the daughter of a man in trade would not have to be so very conventional." She swiveled and gave Vera an accusatory stare. "She is more like *your* sister than mine."

Vera scowled. Really, what nerve! Vera had a mind to get up and leave Molly to solve the problem herself, if there truly was a problem. But her friendship for Virginia stopped her. What if something serious *had* happened? Worry trickled into Vera's heart. True, Molly was over-controlling, which often made Virginia rebellious. But suppose Virginia had taken a serious risk.

Guilt joined fear, chilling the skin on Vera's back. She had overfed Virginia's fantasies. Molly feared for the family's reputation, but Vera was beginning to fear for Virginia's *safety*. Vera had an inkling—no, more than that, a suspicion—about where the danger lay. And who might have taken advantage of Virginia's impetuosity. Vera knew where to find him.

"Listen," she said. "Let's have luncheon in the Ladies' Tea Room at the club."

Molly gaped. "Food? Now? Really?"

Vera took Molly's hand. "It is not about food. If you leave a message for your parents saying *we* went to the club, they will assume Virginia came too and not suspect anything. We will find out if anyone there has seen her. For all we know, we may find her there."

Molly pursed her lips. But she complied.

The bishop's own trolley was gone—taken by him to his meeting, no doubt. Propelled by native men, the contraptions ran on tracks that went up and down the hill to the waterfront, and helter-skelter along the narrow streets of the center. From this hour until close to sunset, they were the only sane way to get about. Theirs was steered at breakneck pace by a Swahili daredevil, who laughed at the way his two British passengers gripped their seats in fright.

The food would have been better at one of the European hotels, and the atmosphere more welcoming to ladies alone than that staid male bastion, The Mombasa Club, but it was the likely place to locate the man Vera had in mind.

They accepted the simpering welcome of the British matrons in the tearoom and took a table. Vera ordered a chicken curry and glass of lemonade and excused herself on the pretext of visiting the ladies' room—well, not really a pretext. These days, the baby left less space inside her and made such visits more and more frequent.

She took a detour to the front desk and asked if the man in question was in. The elegant, turbaned concierge gave her a bland, straightforward reply. "He has removed to quarters elsewhere."

This was not good news. Vera knew that Arvid von Finecke, the Swedish nobleman she sought, was hard up for cash—just one more impoverished European aristocrat, like the many pouring into East Africa, in search of a less costly version of the upper-class life they could no longer afford at home.

A guilty realization fell on Vera. In her sweet, naive way, Virginia had longed to find a handsome, gallant husband such as Justin. At a club gala, Arvid, with his golden good looks, had danced several times with the lithe and graceful and increasingly dreamy-eyed Virginia. The next day, Vera had recounted how her and Justin's love had blossomed after just such a dance. To Virginia, the description must have been an enticing fairytale.

What had then ensued seemed but a lark. Only Vera knew that Arvid and Virginia had exchanged more than pleasantries. Nothing sinful—just some billets-doux and private conversations snatched during walks with the three of them strolling through the town, with Vera pretending to examine the items on offer at stalls in the souk. Now, Vera saw clearly that what had seemed innocent, if somewhat clandestine, might have led to the girl's taking an ill-considered decision.

Vera rejoined Molly in the tearoom but kept her own counsel. Molly would become hysterical, which would be completely unhelpful. Vera had to do a little digging on her own before she brought up the possibility of an elopement. Such an event sounded romantic, but Virginia was only sixteen, and the charming Arvid could turn out to be much more of a blackguard Wickham than an honorable Mr. Darcy.

Their plates arrived. Molly pushed her food around without putting any of it in her mouth. "What good is this doing?"

Vera couldn't eat now either. "You are right," Vera said. She gulped some lemonade. "Let me sign for the meal, and we will go." She signaled the waiter. She needed to find an excuse for them to separate. "Where might Virginia have gone, if she went off on her own?"

"She does not go off on her own," was all Molly offered. "If she is not at home for tea, I shall have to tell papa."

"In the meanwhile, we need to look in as many places as possible. You walk to Boustead and Clarke's and see if she has been there shopping," Vera said.

Molly looked indignant. "You know how she dislikes going to the stores. I will look there and nowhere else. If I do not find her, I will go home. I am going to slap her when I see her."

"I will look for her in the souk," Vera said. "Let's meet at the manse at teatime. Perhaps she will have already returned home from whatever jaunt has caused all this upset."

They parted at the club entrance. Vera watched Molly go.

Dread inundated Vera's hopes. Arvid had moved out of his room. It might only mean that he had not been paying his bill. But she had to find him to assure herself that he and Virginia had not run off. Vera started toward the bazaar, but as soon as Molly was out of sight, she returned to the club and lied to the Indian at the front desk. "I am Mrs. Assistant District Superintendent Justin Tolliver, and I have received a packet from Arvid von Finecke's relative in Nairobi. I want to give it to him. Can you tell me where his new quarters are?"

"I know who you are, my Lady," the man replied with frosty courtesy. "It is not our policy to give out forwarding addresses of our members." His face turned to stone.

In an act that felt like rebellion, Vera smiled indulgently up at the foot-taller Indian and said, as haughtily as she could manage, "Certainly you mustn't ignore the rules for my convenience." She pivoted on her heel and marched out the door with as much regal bearing as the baby allowed.

She crossed over to the ancient Portuguese fort, which the British administration had turned into a prison. At the police desk near the entrance, she hoped against hope to find one of the chattier sergeants. Men of the force generally followed the gossip mill with great interest. But they told her nothing useful.

Head down, Vera turned away from the fawning sergeant who claimed to know nothing and said less. She cast about in her mind for another way to find Von Finecke. The sight of Justin's superior officer, District Superintendent Jodrell, jolted her out of her disappointment.

"Lady Vera," he said, as always observing the proper honorific for an aristocrat's wife yet managing to make it sound satiric. "I would not have expected to find you here on the threshold of the jail."

"I have just been lunching at the club," she said airily. "Perhaps you can tell me something I need to know." She fed him the fiction about a package for the missing Swede.

He backed away, signaling her to follow, and in the conspiratorial voice of one imparting a juicy tidbit, said, "Have you not heard? The blighter has completely bankrupted himself with his gambling. Evidently, as a desperate last resort, he appealed to his cousin upcountry, Baron von Blixen-Finecke to stake him passage home. But from what I've heard, he will get no help from that quarter. Blix is using his future wife's dowry to outfit a farm for growing coffee. His bride will arrive in a few months, and he hasn't a penny to spare."

Dismay weighed on Vera. Had the bankrupt Arvid convinced Virginia to run away with him? Oh, that would be awful.

Jodrell misread her. "Oh, no, my dear. You mustn't be distressed over him. Perhaps what you have in that package is something Blix sent him that he can hock."

"But I don't know how to find him," Vera said. "The club won't reveal where he went." She was beginning to feel desperate and feared that it showed.

Fortunately, Jodrell continued to assume that her dismay was for the handsome Scandinavian. "Please," he said. "He isn't worth your worry. You will find him in that rather dingy block of flats near the old port. Someone there will be able to tell you which one."

"I'll go at once," Vera said.

"Let me get you a rickshaw," Jodrell said. Then he turned back to her. "But you haven't got the package with you."

"I can fetch it from home on my way," she said.

As soon as she climbed into the rickshaw, Jodrell gave the boy a coin and the address of her bungalow and then disappeared into the fort. The second he was gone, Vera corrected the destination, and they bumped along at speed to the waterfront.

Vera rehearsed what she would say to Arvid, changing her lines every minute. What she wanted to do was hit him on his blond, handsome head with something extremely heavy.

The old Mombasa port had been abandoned for the larger, more modern one in Kilindini when the railroad was built. Now, the ancient anchorage was the precinct only of Arab dhows and small lighters that plied the coast. It was picturesque, if derelict, and carried an air of age-old mystery.

The building—stuccoed, with pretty, scalloped decorations along its three peaks—must have been lovely when it was first built. Now, with peeling and mottled whitewash, and tall weeds where flowers once grew, it appeared to be what it was—the last refuge of the down and out.

She did her best to convince the rickshaw boy to wait for her, but he flatly refused and rattled away with his contraption. She could imagine too clearly how Justin would scold her for coming here alone, even in broad daylight. But Jodrell hadn't objected. In a sense he had sent her here. Surely, if he knew it to be dangerous, he would not have suggested it.

She thought it best, however, not to enter the building without knowing exactly where inside she might find Arvid. Or Virginia. She prayed Virginia had not come to this baleful place. And she allowed regret at having fed the girl's desire for adventure and independence. She failed to convince herself that not even the headstrong Virginia would throw herself into the arms of a relative stranger.

The only people around were Arabs and Swahilis—a large group was gathered on steep steps that led down to the water's edge. At the bottom, a gangway stretched out to a stone column in the water. Some Arab men and women were moving along it and onto a makeshift gangplank to a dhow at anchor some fifty feet from shore. None of them paid her the slightest mind. She was trying to decide if it was sensible to ask them where Arvid von Finecke might be, when suddenly a tight knot of men halfway down on the steps parted and revealed him—his pale skin and his lithe form unmistakable. She moved tentatively to the top of the stairs.

At first he did not notice her. He was putting something into the breast pocket of his jacket. When he looked up, he was understandably shocked to discover her looking down at him.

"Lady Tolliver," he exclaimed. He swept off his sun helmet and reached out to take her hand and kiss it. His exaggerated courtly mannerisms annoyed her.

She kept her hands at her sides and ignored all courtesies. "What do you know about where Virginia Peel has gone?"

He gave her the shocked look of a moving pictures' actor. "Nothing!"

She studied his reaction to her silence.

He stammered. "Is there something … Has she …" His ordinarily perfect, witty English had deserted him.

He shrugged. "I am distressed," he said, more convincingly than Vera cared to accept. Those clear blue eyes held all the innocence of an infant. He gestured toward the building. "Let us get out of this awful sun."

It was the first thing he'd said that she liked. But, inside the tiny entryway, when he closed the door, she was suddenly blinded by the contrast between the darkness within and the blazing light outside.

"I am mortified, Lady Tolliver," he said, "to tell you of my condition."

Was it the acoustics of this small space or had his voice deepened? Its timbre sent a spider of fear across the back of her neck. She blinked, trying to compel her eyes to adjust. He was between her and the door. She forced out a strong voice. "I am aware of how …" She was about to say "foolish you have been", but a self-protective instinct stopped her. He was not the type to accept censure. Sympathetic understanding and flattery were her only weapons at this point. "… of how difficult things have become for you."

Those ingenuous eyes again shiny, despite the dim light. She refused to trust them.

"My dear sir," she said. "I am concerned only about my young friend. You cannot have missed how smitten she was with you, and understandably so. I was worried that she had left home to come to you."

"She is missing?"

"Yes." Her heart pounded, but she had to know the truth. "I insist you show me your room."

"It is empty," he said. "If you want proof, follow me."

Her hands shook with fear, but she followed him up a flight of stairs.

His room was a depressing hovel, but thank heavens, it contained nothing but a few piles of his clothing on the bed.

Vera did not know whether to be relieved or more afraid. "Have you, by any chance, told Virginia of your financial distress?"

"Yes. I confess that I did." He looked down at the floor, embarrassed, or perhaps feigning it. "I am aware of her affection for me and thought it only right to bid her good-bye. You see, I have no choice but to leave and start over elsewhere."

"How will you manage to travel without money?"

Those round, convincing eyes found hers. "A relative has given me the means for one last chance."

"Where will you go?"

His sculpted features turned crestfallen. "I have just arranged passage to South Africa on an Arab boat. The cheapest way. From there I have enough to reach Australia."

It was difficult not to pity him. Australia? Settlers up in the temperate highlands always spoke of it as a sort of purgatory. "When will you leave?"

"Within the hour. I would gladly accompany you home, but I must gather my belongings and be ready. My boat is expected at any moment. And will depart immediately." He turned and opened the door. "Please tell Miss Virginia that I wish her well. I made my farewells in my note, but I want her to know that I did not mean to lead her on with my attentions. She is a lovely, spirited girl."

"That she is," Vera said, and left.

Outside, she saw the dhow that had been loading. It was out, crossing the reef, tacking northward, its dark-red sail billowing, and beautiful against the brilliant blues of the water and the sky.

Drenched with perspiration, she dragged her increased weight for half an hour in search of a rickshaw. It made slow progress back to the manse. Her body wanted to lie down and nap. She told herself that she would find Virginia at home, having tea. Tea. She needed some badly.

She found Mr. Dingle pruning roses near the bishop's front door. He doffed his hat. "Lady Vera," he said, his voice anxious, louder than she had ever heard it. "Have you found her?"

Vera's skin crawled. "No, I have not." Her heart sank. The baby inside her fluttered as if it felt her terror.

Mr. Dingle burst into tears. "I did not think of it until after Miss Peel returned home, and I began to go over it all again in my memory. You asked if there was anyone else about early this morning. It did not occur to me then."

"What?" she demanded, grabbing his arm. "What did you see?"

He shook his head in despair. "I thought it was a Somali woman. With him. You know how tall they are. She is tall and slim, like them. I am very afraid, Lady Vera. It was that Swedish man. The handsome, blond one. In a trolley with a woman all covered in black. As some of them are. I could not tell who it was. In a trolley, the two of them, heading down to the port."

It flashed in Vera's anguish: The picture Dingle described. And the Arab women being moved along the gangway to the dhow. The something Arvid von Finecke had placed in his breast pocket. His sudden acquisition of the price of passage to Australia. The billowing red sail of the boat heading north.

Toward the slave market in Muscat.

Pale Yellow Sun

Richie Narvaez

The trophy was gone.

Señora Olga Lopez had had trouble sleeping. She had been anxious about the next day's meeting with Mr. Koch and his team of investors, a meeting that, if it went well—and of course it would go well, if she had anything to do with it—would save the Tamarindo Beach Golf & Country Club. And in turn the club and its tournament would bring tourism and wealth to help save her homeland—Puerto Rico, beautiful Island of Enchantment, which had been lingering in ugly recession for years.

Her thoughts turned themselves over and over and her body refused to relax. So she went downstairs to pour herself a healthy dose of brandy and milk and cut herself a thick slice of *flan.*

On her way down, she felt warm air penetrating the coolness of the house. Then she saw the backyard door was wide open. She could see the lit pool, its sloshing no longer muffled.

She knew immediately what had happened. And who had done it. She went to her office down the hall and saw that that door was open, too.

The crystal golf trophy was missing, of course. She cursed. For a long time. And then asked the Lord's forgiveness for her cursing. Still, she would not lose heart. Without the trophy, the deal with Mr. Koch was dead. But nothing and no one would stop Señora Lopez from making that deal.

She called her assistant, Luis. She told him what happened, and he screamed, because that's what he liked to do. He wanted to call the police, but she knew better. She told him to change the brunch meeting at her house to a lunch meeting at the resort. Mr. Koch would prefer that anyway—he could see the renovations and get red-faced with scotch instead of Bloody Marys. She told Luis to make sure to call the caterers and then to tell the construction crew to clear out of the conference room and then to make sure that someone cleaned up after them.

As for the rest, she would handle it on her own. This was a just an inconvenient but minor hurdle. She would get the trophy back.

At 6 AM, the maid brought her coffee. But when the chauffeur arrived soon afterward, Señora Lopez immediately put it down and went to the car. The day was heating up, and she was grateful that Alejandro already had the air conditioner blasting at full power.

She told him where they were going. She told him to take the 52 Expressway, because it would take them less than two hours to drive from San Juan to the southern side of the island, to Ponce. She would be back in plenty of time for the lunch meeting.

During the drive, she tried to sleep but couldn't. Starving, she ate a dozen candies, *pilones*, from a bag she had in her purse.

Ninety minutes later, they stopped in front of a single-story, concrete house painted mint-green and white. All the doors and windows were covered with metal gates. Señora Lopez had grown up in a house like this (a peach-colored one). She had known many houses like this. She told Alejandro to wait in the car. When she got out, the thickened morning heat hit her like a fist.

She went up the walkway, seeing soda cans and broken beer bottles all over the place. A horrible idea struck her. She looked closely. No, thank the Lord, it wasn't the trophy.

She stepped onto the porch and pressed the doorbell. She heard no bell ring, so she began to knock, and then bang on the door gate. Halfway through her second bang, the inside door swung open.

A young woman stood in the dim light of the entryway, behind the gate and the screen door. Maybe a teenager, maybe even a girl. In the shadow, Señora Lopez found it hard to tell.

"Good morning, miss," Señora Lopez said. Loud music came from inside the house, so she had to speak up. "I would like to see Idalia Lopez. She has done something very foolish, and I need to speak with her. I know she's here."

The girl or woman said nothing, so Señora Lopez began to repeat herself in Spanish. But the girl or woman said, "I heard you the first time."

"Please tell Idalia to come to the door."

"'Tell Idalia to come to the door', she says."

"I am her mother. I have a right to see her."

"She has 'a right', she says."

Señora Lopez was beginning to suspect this girl or woman was what they called "learning disabled."

"Miss, may I speak with your father?"

The girl or woman covered her mouth as she laughed, like a child would. Señora Lopez could see more of her now. She had long, black hair, straight. Over her thin frame, she wore a loose tee shirt and very tight, very short jeans. She could have been thirteen or eighteen or thirty.

"How about your mother?"

"I have no parents."

"Don't be ridiculous. Everyone has parents. No one comes from nothing."

"I'm not everyone." She laughed to herself again. "Who needs parents, really? They're super annoying."

Señora Lopez felt herself dripping with sweat. Although she was in the shade of the porch, the heat wave that had settled over Puerto Rico in the last few days had turned the air to steam. She wore a jacket over a polyester blouse and a skirt over stockinged legs.

"May I please speak to the owner of the home then, miss?"

"'Can I please speak to the owner of the home, *miss*?'"

"I can see I'm not going to get anywhere with you," she said. She hated having to deal with fools like this. Hadn't she worked hard all her life to get away from fools? "Could you please tell my daughter to contact me, miss? It's very important."

"Why?"

"Simple human courtesy, my dear. Is that so difficult for you to understand?"

"I no speak *inglés*."

"Oh boy." Señora Lopez threw up her hands and went back to the car, careful not to trip over any broken glass. Her driver popped out and opened the door, and she slid into the chilled air inside.

* * *

Right away she saw a red light blinking on the dashboard.

"What's wrong with the car, Alejandro?" Señora Lopez asked.

"I'm not sure."

"Not sure? The engine's overheating. You'll have to have it checked, but that can wait until after I get to the office," she said. "Let's get out of here."

They drove down the block of houses colored pink, orange, pastel-blue, grapefruit. She said, "This is terrible. Terrible! Idalia should have known better—she should have! You try to raise a daughter in this world, and see what happens. She was a beauty queen, you know? She won contest after contest, even when she was a little girl. Little Miss Ponce. Miss Teen San

Juan. But now this. Look what she's come to. All I can say is I hope I'm wrong, Alejandro. I know I'm not, but I hope I'm wrong."

"Yes, ma'am."

"The insurance company will just have to handle it. They'll pay to replace the trophy. That's all. I did my best. Take a left here, Alejandro. This street will get us back to the expressway faster."

"Yes, ma'am."

"Who am I kidding? We need that trophy today. Mr. Koch loves that trophy. He talks about it all the time. He was a pro golfer, you know. Yes, he lost the tournament here. Two or three times. But now he's rich enough to save our skin. And he's going to want to see that trophy, and touch it. Maybe he'll even want to buy it, so he can pretend he won."

Men were such fools, she thought. And what was her daughter doing, stealing the trophy? She would try to pawn it, of course, for ten dollars, five dollars. Or would she smash it out of spite?

"We have to go back," Señora Lopez told Alejandro. "Damn that girl—oh, I'm sorry, Lord, please pardon my language."

Alejandro parked in front of the house, and Señora Lopez let herself out. As she was walking up to the door, an older man in a doo rag and rotted jeans came out. He gave her a big smile filled with broken teeth as he passed and then said something vulgar.

Señora Lopez was too hot to communicate her disgust.

She got to the door just as the door gate swung shut. The same woman or girl stood there behind the screen, this time smoking a cigarette.

"Hello again," Señora Lopez said, trying her friendly voice. "I'm here looking for my daughter, Idalia Lopez."

"Are you? How super for you."

"Yes," she said. "My name is Olga Lopez. May I ask your name?"

"Awilda."

"Awilda. That's a lovely name. I have a cousin named Awilda."

"Everyone in Puerto Rico has a cousin named Awilda. It's a horrific name."

Señora Lopez's eyes widened. For a second, she—someone who had handled conversations with millionaires, with lawyers, with governors, with very important people—had no idea what to say.

"Well," she finally said. "That's very sad for you then. Now, miss, I have to know. Is Idalia Lopez here? Can you at least please tell me that?"

"This is not an office, and I am not a secretary."

"I'm just asking a simple question," Señora Lopez said. Beads of sweat were forming on her forehead. "You know, I could call the police on you people."

"You could. You have a cell phone, you have a fancy old car with a driver. He could even drive you to the police station. Do you need their address or do you know where it is? I could Google it for you, but I left my iPhone in my other house."

"You must think you're very amusing, Awilda. Tell me, who was that Mister Bigshot who just left here?"

"Why do you ask? Was he your cousin, too?"

"My daughter shouldn't be around people like that. I know she's here, but she needs to get out of here. I have to get her away from people like that."

"What do you mean by that exactly? People like what? Jehovah's Witnesses? People with bad teeth? Cubans? You should be more specific. My teachers always taught me to be more specific. Maybe they didn't do that with you. Did you go to public school?"

"Listen, I grew up around here, just a few blocks over. I knew plenty of people like that man, growing up. Those are not good people."

"You know, that could have been my father, and you just insulted him. That's not very nice."

"You said you had no ... never mind. It's like talking to a wall. Listen, let me ask you again: Is Idalia Lopez going to be here soon? Please, just tell me that."

"Did I not say that I am not a secretary? Do you see a desk in my lap?"

Señora Lopez gave the girl or woman a good, long look. No, she was definitely not a child, but she wasn't healthy, and hadn't been eating. This was not a healthy environment. There were smells coming from inside the house, something sour like vinegar, and then a stink like a skunk. She knew what all that was.

"Tell me, Awilda. Is there someone stopping you, is that it? Is there someone you're afraid of, that's not letting you give me answers?"

"You think there's somebody behind me with a gun, somebody making me a puppet? You've got a super imagination, lady."

"Fine then," Señora Lopez said, then she turned around and went back to the car. "I know how to deal with you people."

In Spanish, Awilda called after her, telling her to have a nice day.

"Drive to the nearest Banco Popular," Señora Lopez told her driver. "There should be one near the Parque de Bombas. It's ten o'clock. We still have plenty of time."

She felt warm and asked Alejandro if the air conditioning was on.

"I turned it off, on account of the car overheating. I can open the windows."

"Open the windows? God help me."

Alejandro rolled down the windows and, as he drove, a tentative breeze entered the car. Without the tinted windows, Señora Lopez saw a furious blue sky and the sun roasting everything, the pavement, the concrete, the street signs. Gray palm trees bent like old men into the road. The corpse of a dog bloated in the gutter.

At a stoplight, a man came up to her door with bags of *quenepas* for sale. She had finished her bag of candies and would have loved to have something sweet, loved to have popped the little green balls open in her teeth and suck out the sweet-sour pulp. But who knew where this *jibaro* had got them, or stolen them from, or how long he'd had them. No thank you.

Across the road was a water distribution center. A long line of people stood in the sun in front of a giant cistern. People were walking in the road, slowing down traffic. They carried plastic bottles and barrels. With the recent, lingering drought came strict water rationing and weekly cutoffs, and so the locals had to get water at places like this. Walking away from the cistern, a mother emptied a bottle of water over the head of her little boy, who giggled like an idiot. What a waste, Señora Lopez thought. They would need that water later. That mother is going to regret that.

There was no ATM near the Parque de Bombas, at least not one that looked decent. So they circled around the narrow streets packed with tourists. Finally, they found one in front of a supermarket. The unshaded area smelled of urine, and heat radiated off the stained and graffitied metal.

Señora Lopez withdrew five hundred dollars and immediately put the money deep inside her purse. Back in the car, she checked the time on her watch and then on her phone—almost eleven o'clock already! As she was holding her phone, it rang. It was Luis.

"Did you get it?"

"No," she said. "I did not."

"Are you really sure she took it?"

"Of course I'm sure. No one else would be desperate enough, stupid enough, to take it."

"But that trophy weighs thirty pounds. She's hardly in a condition ..."

"You'd be amazed what you can do in that condition, when you need money bad enough. She's lucky enough to have that pretty face, but not everybody's that fortunate. When you don't, you have to be smart and be fearless."

"She didn't have the keys to the house, right?"

"Not since I changed the locks, no. But she's been sneaking in and out of the house since she was little. She has a whole bag of tricks, Luis. Don't underestimate her. Did you call Mr. Koch?"

"Yes. He is not a happy man. But he did mention that he was looking forward to seeing the trophy!"

"Of course. If I am late to the lunch for any reason, tell him I have been delayed. Tell him it's a family emergency."

"He's not going to like that."

"Just make sure the scotch is on the table. And invite Analiz. She can chat him up; that will keep his mind off business. That's an easy fix, see? I should be there by one o'clock, God and traffic willing."

They drove back through the streets. At a stoplight near an underpass, one transvestite was shaving the legs of another, while a third fanned them both.

"I tell you, Alejandro, the things I have to go through, the things I have to do. This deal is very important for Puerto Rico. We bring in the millionaires at the resort, and they'll spend their money like water, and the money will rain down on everyone, I tell you. Everyone will get a little splash, and we won't have to see crazy things like this. These three have more hair than my cousin Raul."

Alejandro laughed and nodded.

"And my cousin Raul is a caveman." Señora Lopez allowed herself a good laugh that trailed off into a long sigh. "Drive a little faster, okay, Alejandro, please. *Ay*, and put on the air conditioner. I can't stand this heat. The car will be fine."

"Yes, ma'am," Alejandro said.

***

They'd only gone a few more blocks when steam starting billowing out from the front of the car. Alejandro got out and lifted the hood.

Señora Lopez stuck her head out of the car and asked him what was wrong.

"Coolant leak. I better take it to a mechanic now. If I don't, she might not make it back to San Juan."

"Oh Lord help me. And how long do you think that is going to take?"

"Not long. I think I saw a place by the highway."

"You think? I didn't see one. Are you sure?"

"I am sure, ma'am."

"Fine. Let me out here."

"Ma'am?"

"I'll walk to the house. It's really close. You get back as soon as you can to pick me up."

"Yes, ma'am."

"Are you sure you know where this mechanic is?"

"I think so. Yes. Yes, I do."

Señora Lopez threw up her hands in frustration and got out of the car. Again, the heat wrapped itself around her. She knew the way. Two blocks over from here.

She recognized a playground where she used to play for hours as a child. Now the rides were busted, trash everywhere. She used to take Idalia to parks all the time, taking time off from work. She wondered if Idalia remembered that. She wondered if that was worth anything.

Señora Lopez realized she was hungry and thirsty and that she should have stopped to get a little something. But she hadn't seen a *bodega* open, at least not a decent looking one.

When she came to the house, the woman opened the door before she could knock.

"*Hola*, Olga from a few blocks over. How super nice to see you again."

"Awilda," said Señora Lopez. She found she was short of breath. "I'd like to speak to my daughter, and I know she's inside. Maybe this will help." Señora Lopez put her hand against the screen, a twenty-dollar bill between two of her fingers.

"*Hola,* Señor Jackson," Awilda said. "Why don't you come in, señora?"

The young woman opened the screen door and gate and extended her hand. Señora Lopez put the twenty into her palm and stepped inside.

"*Bienvenidos.* I'm sorry, but our espresso machine is currently out of order," Awilda said. "And we don't have a bidet, but maybe I could find you a midget with a mouth full of water."

Señora Lopez paid no attention. The desolation of the room she'd entered was mesmerizing, even to someone like her, who had lived and seen so much. The room was lit only by the light glancing through the gated windows. Inside, the sour and skunky smells were much stronger. Cans, bottles, fast-food containers littered the floor, which was covered by a worn carpet that may once have been orange but was now the color of shit. There was no furniture, only an old boombox on the floor blasting reggaeton.

"Can you please turn that down? It's so loud I can't think."

"Of course." Awilda bent down and lowered the volume a barely perceptible amount.

Señora Lopez resisted rolling her eyes. She knew you didn't antagonize the enemy, you negotiated, you used honey. "Thank you, my dear. Now, can you tell me if Idalia Lopez is here?"

Seeing the young woman now, without the screen in her face, Señora Lopez realized that she was pretty. She also saw that beneath the short shorts, Awilda's legs were covered in a series of abscesses. They looked like a trail of bullet holes.

"You're very welcome. As to Idey, do you see her here? I don't," said Awilda, taking an exaggerated look around the small space.

"So you know her nickname then," Señora Lopez said. "Idey must be in one of the back rooms."

"Could be. I do not have X-ray vision."

"Very well," Señora Lopez said, digging into her purse. When she realized Awilda was watching her, she turned around and dug back in for the roll of money. Her hands were slick with sweat. She peeled off another twenty and gave it to the woman, who took it without looking at it. "Now look, miss ... Awilda. My daughter has been seen coming into this house many times."

"Ah, so you spy on your daughter? You have someone following her?"

"That is not your business, dear. I know what she does here. I know what goes on here."

"Oh, do you?" Awilda said. "You know what goes on here?"

"What's the point of talking about it? That's not what I'm here for."

"What are you doing here, then?"

Señora Lopez felt herself flushing. It had been a long, hot morning—if it was still morning—and she felt her patience evaporating.

"You ... you're a bunch of low-class people who sit around getting high." She heard her voice rise and could not stop it. "That's what's in this house. Low-class, sons of ... low-class *losers* wasting your lives. Ruining the town, the city, the whole island with your filth."

"And what are you doing with your life, señora? With your car and your chauffeur and your nice house in San Juan? Living the good life?"

"How do you... Ha! You don't understand," Señora Lopez said. "The world is falling apart, and this is part of the problem. You people don't see what's happening, you don't see how hard it's going to be to dig yourself out of this hell." The heat and stink of the room, the persistent boom of the music turned around and around in her head. "Oh Idalia. I have to take you out of here, don't you see? Can't you understand? I'm your mother." The room began to spin. "I feel funny," she said.

Her legs wobbled. She fell.

Down into a well of darkness. The little light in the room faded into shadow, and then nothing, and then a sound like a thud, and sour smoke and sweat and piss smell. And it was like she was sleeping, but it had no comfort and no release.

Then there was light, and above her was Awilda's face, which now looked very young, as innocent as an angel's.

"Ay, Señora Olga, come on. Don't you have a heart attack on me."

The stucco ceiling spun. The music still beat loud. But she was rising out of the well.

"I'm fine, *negrita*. Don't you worry. I just haven't ... I haven't eaten since breakfast, and all I had was a cup of coffee. I don't know how you can stay in here. It's so hot."

"I know. It's super hot. But I don't mind. You want something to drink?"

"I'm... I'm not sure."

"Don't worry. Your money buys you a soda."

Awilda walked over to a kitchen area and opened a refrigerator that looked new. She came back and handed Señora Lopez a can. Then she went over to the boombox and changed the music.

The can was warm and half empty. Señora Lopez put it almost to her mouth, but couldn't bear the idea of drinking it. She put it down on the floor.

The boombox was playing a pop song by Menudo. Its sweet, pubescent sound was like a shot of energy.

"Wow. That takes me back," Señora Lopez said.

"The song?"

"Yes. My daughter—Idalia—used to play her these songs back in the day, and we would choreograph our own dance routines and perform them in the living room. Every day. For hours. She loved it. Idalia was very young then. I was very young then, too. Although it hasn't been that many years."

"That sounds awesome. My mother—I did have a mother, a super-long time ago—she never would have danced with me. That's not the kind of relationship we had. She didn't hold my hand to dance. She gave me a fist."

"Oh my lord, I'm sorry to hear that."

"Don't be sorry. It's not your fault. It sounds like you loved your daughter very much."

"I did. I do. I was very tough on her, but that was the only way for her to learn how to make it in this world, you know. The only way."

They stayed still, listening, until the song ended.

Señora Lopez smiled at the young woman. "Listen," she said. "Young lady—Awilda. You're being very nice, and please know that I appreciate that. So please help me. I know my daughter is back there in one of those rooms. I know she is hiding from me. I want to go back there. I want to talk to her. I want to help her."

Awilda stood up and folded her thin arms across her breasts.

"I know. But I'm sorry to say that you can't. This place, well, it's like a club. A super-private club. You can't just go back there, to the rooms. You're not currently a member."

"What do you mean? Private club? This place? Look at this mess."

"Money only gets you this far. Back there, you have to belong."

Señora Lopez looked around her again. She was still on the floor, and she didn't have the energy to get up.

"Can I ask you a question, Awilda? And please tell me the truth. Did my daughter come here with something, something she was maybe going to sell?"

"You mean something big and super shiny?"

"Exactly! Yes. My God. You've seen it. It's a trophy. It's the trophy for the Tamarindo Beach Resort tournament. I'm a corporate officer there, at Tamarindo Beach. That's my job. It's Steuben Glass, the trophy ... do you know what that means? That means it's very expensive, and it's very important that I get it back. See, that was an old tournament, but it wasn't doing so well, decreasing attendance and what have you, so we're relaunching and rebranding, and we wanted to keep some of the tradition, so we need the trophy. And it was ... let's say it was *taken* last night, and the only person who could have taken it, unfortunately, is my daughter. She probably took it to buy drugs. She's been an addict since junior high school. She's never had any strength or courage. I tried to help her, God knows I tried, but her father was not around, and I had to raise her myself, you understand?"

"I hear you."

"So, is it here then?"

"Excuse me, Miss Olga, I thought you were here for your daughter."

"I am here for my daughter. I love her very much."

"But now it sounds like you're here for that trophy. Which is it?"

"I don't understand what the difference is," Señora Lopez said. She had to get back to San Juan—she was running out of time. "Now can I go back there, please?"

The young woman walked over to a corner and picked up a small Styrofoam ice chest. She put it in front of Señora Lopez.

"Like I said, it's members only. If you want to go back there, you have to be a member."

"Fine," she said, thinking of how much it would cost to make Mr. Koch and his investors happy, to save the resort, to save Puerto Rico. "And how do I become a member?"

From the ice chest, Awilda brought out a syringe and a tiny packet of pale yellow powder. "This is how."

"Are you crazy? I'm not going to do drugs."

Señora Lopez looked at Awilda. Who was now very serious. Who did now not look like a child or an angel. She wondered if she could push past her, hit her with one of the bottles on the floor. But that would be violence, and violence was for low-class people. Yet it would be easy—so many bottles around, and the artery under the ear is what you go for.

"Members only."

"Is that what my daughter uses?"

"Yes."

"Please, I don't want to."

"Then you have to leave. With your hands empty."

"I have more money," Señora Lopez said, reaching in her purse.

"This is not Disney World. You don't buy tickets."

"Please. I'm scared."

"Idalia was scared the first time. Now she's not scared at all."

The woman held out the syringe.

"The longer you wait, the longer it takes to see your daughter. Or your trophy."

It would be like sleep, she knew, like being curled up at the bottom of a very deep well. It would be restless, and full of things that were not real. It would be over quickly, but then she would yearn to go back to its deepness again, almost immediately. But she would beat it—it would be beaten—if she had anything to do with it. The hurdle was tall now, the obstacle a giant wall. But she had the courage, had the strength.

And God would forgive her for going backward in order to go forward. Nothing or no one could stop her now.

When Señora Lopez took the syringe, she was smiling.

The Logistics of Revenge

By Susan Froetschel

Our driver hit the brakes, ending the soothing rush of desert air into the Land Cruiser. Construction debris blocked the road for our convoy of aid workers, headed to a holding camp for refugees awaiting transfer to Zaatari—another day of promises and not enough food or supplies. I was on the logistics team, and even a short delay would add to the day's challenges.

The 4x4 heated up like a blast furnace, and Amy, the most experienced among us, was unnerved by the holdup. "Get us out of here," she ordered the driver. "Now! Do it now!"

Cursing in Arabic, the driver took a hard left. The tires left the road, grinding uselessly against the uneven soil. He put his foot on the gas, scraping steel against rock. As he shifted gears, three pickups approached, appearing out of nowhere.

The rest of our convoy scattered, and panic exploded inside our vehicle. Amy, in the front seat, turned on the driver with a string of unintelligible words.

"Stop that," another woman scolded. "He's doing the best he can!"

I kept quiet, alone in a strange bubble of calm. The morning sun was high, hitting the fields, rocks, and distant hills with a shimmering silver glow. Our driver was carrying a weapon, and the security checkpoint couldn't be more than a 3K-run away. Someone would see the commotion and intervene. Staring straight ahead, I reached into a side pocket of my backpack and shoved a burner phone down the back of my khakis.

Amy started pounding the driver with both fists. "We're being kidnapped, and he's helping!"

She was half-right. Six men with M4s, courtesy of the U.S., surrounded our vehicle and promptly shot the driver. Someone from our convoy behind us got off two shots before roaring off and abandoning us. Two men aimed rifles at Amy's wailing head. Another dragged us from the vehicle, shoving us to the ground and tying our limbs. Rough hands gripped my shoulders, took my ankles, and heaved me like a bag of trash into the back of the pickup.

The flatbed felt like an empty frying pan left on a hot stove, and I squirmed to avoid touching flesh to metal. Amy wouldn't let up. "You still have a phone, don't you?" She ordered me to call the base.

All I wanted was to shut her down. "Keep it up," I murmured, my lips tight. "And we'll end up like our driver."

Then I ignored her wild eyes and focused on the men. One man barked in rough Arabic as the others snapped at his commands. I glared, hoping to leave a question hanging in the hot morning air—What kind of men follow another's orders as though they were dogs? One of them studied me, suspecting I understood what was being said.

Two men climbed into the back of our pickup as the other vehicles took off. My head was suddenly covered in a dark hood. A moment later, Amy screeched. She was upset about more than a hood.

Then someone grasped my upper arm, tugging at the shirtsleeve and stroking the soft skin of my inner arm. A needle dug into my skin. My breath caught at the briefest moment of bliss.

"*Shaitan*," I hissed with contempt before letting loose with a hard laugh. A door slammed, and the truck roared along a twisting route. Blinded by the hood, I couldn't anticipate the turns or keep my balance. A fog descended, crystallizing my thoughts, and again I felt alone.

They'd drugged us to keep us quiet.

Taking a deep breath, I was grateful the hood hid how little I cared. Every reaction mattered. I pretended to sleep, letting my head sink to one side until it rested on the nearest shoulder—better there than bouncing against the side of the truck.

I had an idea of what the kidnappers were up to.

Aid workers are easy pickings for militants looking to collect quick cash. In the summer of 2015, the White House had dropped the threat of prosecuting families who tried to arrange ransoms, though everyone agreed the frantic payouts encouraged more abductions.

Of course, some families could not pay, and extremists had another use for those hostages. Aid workers, like audiences around the globe, had huddled around laptops to watch news reports of stoic men in orange kneeling on desert sand and their executioner ranting about a crusade. Our group had been mesmerized by the kneeling men who stared at the camera with sad and heavy eyes, at peace while waiting for the blade.

The news had showed less than a minute of footage. "They don't run or fight," a colleague had murmured in awe. "Why do they just kneel and wait?" another had asked, shaking his head.

One of the younger guys in our group had tapped away, searching for an unedited video. "The *how* matters more than *why*," I had snapped before leaving the room. The exhibition had left me squeamish, maybe because I wasn't sure whether the victims had been stoic or compliant. But the captors didn't need locks, chains, or doors. They only needed a steady supply of narcotics, and to keep their prisoners long enough so that nothing else mattered. They played with doses, maintenance most days, tauntingly close to nirvana on others, without knocking out the hostages completely.

Before long, nothing mattered but the next dose of heroin. And the last dose was the best of all.

One execution, not filmed, broke my heart. An aid worker and former U.S. Army Ranger. Analysts theorized that he had lashed out at the end, forcing the jerks to shoot him. He had beaten them at their strange game of control. Maybe he had known more about the drug than they did and tricked them into miscalculating on that final dose.

Journalists and government officials don't talk about how much heroin infiltrates ordinary cities and schools, military bases, and refugee camps throughout the region. And aid workers tend to look the other way. Entire societies are in pain, and there's a reason aid workers must be part mercenary, part missionary, part misfit. Maybe I was more misfit and mercenary than most, and I wanted to go down fighting. Escape was a little happy dream I could not afford.

The truck drove on as I drifted between sleep and drowsiness. Rough days were ahead, but that was a secret to keep for myself.

***

Night: Temperatures fell. My muscles curled tight, and I prayed for a bit of warmth. The truck made stops, the engine running, as if making deliveries. I didn't need a background in logistics and risk management to realize they were separating us. Amy struggled as they yanked her from the truck, demanding that we be kept together. Crying, she screamed my name. "Why didn't you ..."

A thud. Her voice went silent.

Better I was on my own, and when the truck stopped for the night, I was the last of my group. The truck didn't have to travel far, only a hundred or so kilometers, to reach any of five countries. My best guess was Syria.

A set of hands pulled me from the pickup, before pressing down on my shoulders and shoving me through an opening. I landed hard, groaning as the phone dug into my inner thigh. Only then did the hood come off, exposing more darkness. A stifling tent.

My limbs were sluggish as a man removed my shoes and used a knife to slice away my khaki pants and the sky-blue vest marking me as an international aid-worker. Left behind was my long-sleeved gray shirt, the socks, and two other small symbols of defiance toward the sensibilities of the land where we worked: a pink scarf with tiny, white skulls, and Italian underwear. The phone remained tucked in the taupe band of my panties.

An older man crouched in the doorway with a pile of cloth. The other one with the rough voice snatched it and tossed it at me. He spoke in Arabic, then English, demanding a name and the city where my family lived. On the spot, I made up a name and added that my parents were dead. He walked away, and the older man stood, closing the tent with a snapping sound.

Eyeing the door, I removed the phone and wedged it near the entrance. If the tent was a temporary hold, I could fall and retrieve the phone.

Only then, did I don the oversized *abaya* and *niqab.* The getup was stiff and scratchy. The headcover kept falling over my eyes, and I remembered young women at the camp defending their acceptance of the *niqab.* Men cannot spy on us, or pry with their eyes, they had confided. Better they cannot observe our disgust for them.

I did not waste energy quarreling that clothing did not provide a shield, that yards of black cloth couldn't hide which women endured abuse and which relished a display of moral superiority. The men would not forget that I was petite, blonde, and American.

The garment was unnatural, uncomfortable, and I felt like a witch. That notion of being marked as an ominous presence somehow made me feel better. I sat on the ground, waiting, and sure enough, footsteps approached. The young man with the rough voice entered the tent. Without a word, he grabbed at the *abaya,* thrusting the robe around my waist. Turning my head in disgust, I rallied all my strength. "*Shaitan!*" I screeched. "*Shaitan!*"

He didn't want others to hear and, lashing out, knocked the side of my head into the ground. Writhing backward, I shouted until my voice went raw as he kicked at my ribs.

No one came to help. Pressed against the canvas wall, I stared as he pulled out a needle.

I spent the night alone, sore, and adrift in memories, and hoped the man could not contact my family. My mother had died when I was six, and my father quickly remarried, snared by a woman who flirted and kept up with his drinking, convincing him that she held all the secrets for social success. With each passing year, it was made clear I did not fit in with her plans. And I did not need her now.

***

Day: I couldn't be sure how long I had slept when loud voices woke me. My bones ached from sleeping on the ground, and I held my breath, listening to arguing outside. I focused on tone more than words, wanting to know who was in charge.

Slivers of sunlight intruded into the tent. Standing to examine the walls, I almost fell over. Dropping to my knees, I took deep breaths and waited for the lightheadedness to pass before dragging myself about to check the tent's perimeter. Large enough for me to stretch out with a foot or two to spare in each direction, the tent was not well sealed, and sand pushed its way into every crevice. The canvas door was secured with a padlock through a grommet, and flaps covered two small mesh windows.

The air was close, and my mouth was dry. My insides twisted with cramps, and, despite the dry air, I was shaking and sweating in clothing that scraped against my skin. I reminded myself that my predicament could be worse. Much worse.

Slowly, I unzipped a window flap to peer outside. A small group of men did not look my way.

The older man, earlier so quiet, walked in circles, confused and howling as if in pain. The rough one laughed and waved an arm. The others followed him to a group of pickups, and the caravan left the compound.

Lifting the flap higher, I pressed my eyes against the mesh. A field of patchy, dry grass. A rock wall shielding the compound from winds, and perhaps overhead surveillance. A few makeshift buildings and broken equipment. The remnants of a farm.

The older man hurried inside a primitive stone structure and emerged with what looked like an empty cage. He placed it on the ground, plaintively calling "Holo ... Holo." Not looking toward my tent, he wandered out of sight.

Agitated, I again crawled about the tent floor. The phone was safe, and I found other prizes. Three worn wool blankets. A large and foul-smelling bowl for elimination. An empty cardboard box, and a copy of the Koran in Arabic. Some toilet paper and a plastic jug of water. I sucked the water gratefully, then poured some on the edge of my robe, pressing the cloth against my face to clean away the dust.

I had to find something to do or I would scream.

Underneath the tent's ground tarp and worn vinyl was hard-packed soil. Tugging at the canvas, I found a hole and groped for rocks, sticks, discarded metal, anything for digging. After finding a few sharp stones, enough to start, I worked throughout the day, keeping noise to a minimum while listening for footsteps. One stone broke. The others were small, better for scratching than digging. My fingers kept slipping, sand wedged under my cuticles.

Digging a shallow hole was an achievement, and I hid my phone away.

***

Night: The wind picked up, with odd bursts and scurrying noises. The tent was stifling, my skin sticky with a nauseating smell. Everything I touched felt gritty. Every swallow and blink scraped and hurt. I couldn't be sure how many days had passed, and my captors seemed to have forgotten me.

I reached for water, but the bottle was empty. Using some to clean myself had been a huge mistake, and I curled along the floor, eyes closed, trying not to obsess about quenching my thirst. Of course, it was all I could think about as I pressed the plastic against my lips.

Truck engines roared and then faded off into the distance. Sometimes the trucks went their separate ways, and sometimes the men left together as one. The engine noise, departing before dawn and returning at twilight, became a dependable marker of time. So were temperatures that left me hot and listless each day, shivering at night. I checked outside. No one was in sight, and while waiting for the sky to soften from gray to lavender and pink, I wondered if I was alone.

The outside air tasted like freedom. Though it seared my mouth, I gulped in more.

The older man delivered a bowl with cereal, nuts, dried fruit once or twice a day, but I wasn't hungry. My tongue was heavy, dry, and the thought of placing anything hard or crisp on it was unthinkable. Sometimes he brought a small bottle of water, and I refused to beg for more.

Behind me, the scratching noises became more insistent and distinct from the wind. Turning, I caught a movement near the doorway and the bowl of food. I lifted a window flap for light.

A small golden creature sat near the bowl, stuffing bits into its cheeks. A nervous hamster—I knew how he felt.

I crawled and reached out with one finger to stroke the hamster. The little creature, ears twitching, stood on hind legs and nuzzled against my finger. Stretching my hand out, I whispered, "Holo?"

Scampering into the palm, Holo seemed relieved by my soft murmurs.

I set to work, placing the little guy on a blanket and removing the phone from its hiding place. Reaching for my pink scarf, I chewed one edge with my teeth, eventually ripping the scarf into a pile of fluffy scraps and sprinkling them into the hole, along with shreds of toilet paper and a few pages from the middle of the Koran. Then I blocked the view of the arrangement from the doorway by folding two blankets into tight bundles and stretching out the third for me to sleep nearby. The hamster delighted in rearranging the bits before curling up into the hole to sleep.

I could make another hiding spot for the phone.

Watching the hamster's soft breaths was hypnotizing. It had been years since I had had the luxury of studying a pet for hours on end, and the feeling was bittersweet. A year before her death, my mother had surprised me with a calico kitten. Patches slept with me and followed me like a shadow.

Months after my mother died, my stepmother moved into our home and soon complained of allergies. After my father left for a business trip, I returned home from school. My cat was not waiting in the doorway, and I ran through the house, calling for her.

Then I noticed the bed, bowls, and litter box had disappeared. My stepmother flashed her poison smile. "We found a good home." It was all she would say.

I protested, screamed, and kicked at her bedroom door in fury. She refused more details, and I insisted on calling my father, but she got to him first. "She's too upset," the woman insisted. "Of course, we can't have her pestering the new owners."

That night, she began slipping me Vicodin, much as she plied my father with tumblers of vodka or bourbon. Anything to shut us up and keep us in control.

***

Day: My deep sleep broke as the rough man barked into tent's doorway, demanding my name. I struggled to sit up and shrug. Disdain does not transmit well from behind the *niqab*. "Laurie Davis," I repeated, acting drowsier than I felt. "From New York."

He wanted more—an address, a phone number. I paused, shaking my head and letting my voice break. "The ones who matter are dead."

Fortunately, I avoided glancing toward the hamster until after the man walked way. Not long afterward, the older man appeared in the doorway, delivering the same dry food and small amount of water. Typically, he didn't speak, but that morning he crouched to whisper, "You must give your name."

Blocking the hamster's nest, I insisted that they had my name. The man shook his head with a sad frown. "You could be free," he admonished. "Let him collect the money from your family. Otherwise..." He nervously looked outside the doorway. "For now, he thinks of you as valuable. A commodity. And you don't want to be traded away."

***

Night: Water and heroin did not come regularly, but the compound otherwise had rigid routines. With sunrise, one or all of the trucks left in a burst of noise, and the camp went silent. The trucks returned in the evening, and the men slept. I did not try to track the days.

After the trucks left, the older man often brought more water and food. My lips no longer felt like crinkled paper. It was a mistake calling me a commodity. Knowing that I was valuable made me stubborn.

Like Holo, I stayed awake at night and slept when the men left for the day. The hamster wandered off now and then, but returned each morning to his pink bed and the lid from a jug that served as his water bowl. I stored food in one of my socks, and trained him with frequent coos and tidbits. Hours with Holo distracted me from thinking about my family. But I had to sleep ... and that's when my stepmother's sweet torment resumed. More than once I opened my eyes with an awful feeling of having no place to hide, and then relief that the tent was not my childhood bedroom. Still, her deviously soft voice echoed, trying to convince others that she had my best interests at heart: I spent too much time alone, I did not know how to make friends, I balked at joining family activities. The woman had all the skills of a D-list actress, fawning when my father or grandmother was near, pretending to care while questioning my choices, micromanaging unnecessary clothes, chores, classes, and friendships. True enough, I nurtured her resentment as needed, once slipping into the dining room at night to chip a favorite piece of china, and sneaking into her closet to slash a pen against a silk blouse. I pretended to be dull and unmotivated while hiding in the library each day after school.

Any success for me propelled her fury. More than anything else, my stepmother resented the cavalcade of teachers praising my creativity and persistence for solving problems— skills I refused to display at home. Excellent grades undercut her many complaints—especially with my maternal grandmother, who had but one priority for her only grandchild, and that was to do well at school.

My stepmother did all she could to make my life miserable, and all pretense fell away one summer night after she insisted that my father show my grandmother items found in my closet: a glass pipe, tiny plastic bags, and burnt pieces of foil. Proof, my stepmother growled, that I needed protection and could not be trusted with my grandmother's small fortune. My father, stooge that he was, followed her orders, and my grandmother, sharing my unconditional acrimony, blamed my parents. If anything, the accusations prompted her to protect me with a trust fund that her attorneys assured was iron-clad and private.

My only goal was getting far away. I studied Arabic, worked hard in college, and volunteered for small non-profits before landing the job with the United Nations.

All my stepmother cared about was if I had a will and had named a successor for the trust. "Your father, of course," she advised. Smiling, I walked away, and had not seen her since.

Still, I could not escape thoughts of family. Families know one another's fears and secrets, and that's how my stepmother and I learned to torment each other.

Manipulating my captors who knew nothing about me was easy. Better that others resent me than the other way around.

***

Day: Searing heat made it impossible to sleep, and a headache hammered my brain. Gusts slapped the walls of the suffocating tent, but the hot winds brought no relief. Neither did the soft, scratching noises made by Holo, feebly digging to deepen his hole. The hamster did not do well in the oven of a tent, but knew enough to avoid the brutal sun outside. Focusing on the sounds beyond the tent, I thought I detected a faint rumbling in the distance, almost like a constant stream of vehicles on a busy highway.

I peered outside, and noted that only one truck was missing. The old man crossed into view, hurrying to unlock and load the oldest pickup. Three big containers, what looked like water, went into the back seat followed by a pack, a few boxes, and several rifles.

With one rifle slung across his shoulder, he ran toward my tent, and I didn't wait.

Bending, I scooped the hamster into my left sleeve. The burner phone went into the same sleeve.

Removing the padlock, the old man shouted for me to hurry. "We're leaving," he ordered, grabbing my right arm and pulling me along. Awkward in the *abaya,* confused about my first steps outside the tent since my arrival at the compound, I stumbled. "Hurry," he implored, and looked past me to the sky.

A towering wall of dark clouds stretched across the horizon.

Sky and land took on the colors of ruined film in yellow, amber, and red, and there was an unrelenting roar as bursts of sand and grit blasted every surface. Shielding our eyes, we ran to the loaded truck, and he shoved his rifle into the backseat and helped me climb into the front. Then he ran to the driver's side, getting behind the wheel and slamming the door. He searched a ring with numerous keys before placing one into the ignition and starting the engine.

Rubbing my burning, watering eyes, I asked where we were headed. He didn't respond. "Are we leaving for good?" I pressed, as a tumbling wall of sand was ready to surround the compound.

Shaking his head, he explained he was moving his truck to a more sheltered place. The farm belonged to him, and he would never leave. It became my turn not to answer. Instead, I used my right hand to clutch the cloth around the phone, allowing the sleeve to dangle. The phone stayed put as Holo wriggled into my lap. Gently, I cupped my hands around the hamster and lifted him up.

The man gasped. The animal wrapped its tiny front legs around my thumb, nodding before clambering back inside the sleeve.

"Holo," the man whispered with joy.

I cradled the sleeve and looked away, as if embarrassed or afraid. My pounding heart kept pace with the hamster's quick breaths. "The drugs," I said softly. "I'll get sick without them."

The old man didn't hesitate, leaping out of the truck and dashing back toward the stone hut as the cloud descended, obscuring details of the compound. He left the rifle and hamster behind.

I didn't hesitate either—gently shaking Holo away from the sleeve and placing him in the small compartment between the seats. I yanked my robe up to lunge into the driver's seat, releasing the brake, and gently pressing the accelerator to drift away from the other trucks. Then I cut the engine and, with a snappy click, locked the doors. Slouching low in the seat, I stared at the windshield and so many bits of sand tapping a tight little dance. I hoped the windshield would hold against the onslaught.

The storm consumed the compound. Scratching noises surrounded the truck, and I may have heard a voice cry out. I could only imagine the shadow of a man faltering around the group of trucks, trying doors, pounding at the windows, uncertain about which vehicle he had loaded.

Sandstorms can last minutes or hours. This one persisted, overwhelming the ability to see, hear, or feel and punishing any who did not take shelter. The man may have stayed inside the unprotected hut. But if he'd tried to return to his truck, eventually he'd have had little choice but to slump to the ground and shield his face from the abrasive force. Perhaps he'd crawled underneath one of the trucks and been buried in the sand.

Powdery dust infiltrated the truck, and the heat was unbearable. I dared not risk opening a window or starting the engine. Driving away from the compound was impossible.

The hamster was in the compartment, his breathing rough. I reached into the backseat for a container. Pouring water into my cupped hand, I held it near his mouth, but Holo turned away. I gently stroked him with my damp palm.

The blistering dust was too much, and eventually the creature stopped moving. I should have drunk some water myself, but I didn't want a clear mind. Instead, I retrieved the burner phone, pulling the case apart. The bag of powder was intact. Arranging a neat line along the dashboard, I pinched one nostril and took a deep and bitter breath, looking forward to passing out.

Never trust an addict.

Housecleaning

Greg Herren

The smell of bleach always reminded him of his mother.

It was probably one of the reasons he rarely used it, he thought, as he filled the blue plastic bucket with hot water from the kitchen tap. His mother had used it for practically everything. Everywhere they'd lived had always smelled slightly like bleach. She was always cleaning. He had so many memories of his mother cleaning something: steam rising from hot water pouring from the sink spigot; the sound of bristles as she scrubbed the floor ("Mops only move the dirt around; good in a pinch but not for *real* cleaning."); folding laundry scented by Downy; washing the dishes by hand before putting them through the dishwasher ("It doesn't wash the dishes clean enough, it's only good for sterilization."); running the vacuum cleaner over carpets and underneath the cushions on the couch.

In her world, dirt and germs were everywhere, and constant vigilance was the only solution. She judged other people by how slovenly they looked or how messy their yards were or how filthy their houses were. He remembered one time—when they were living in the apartment in Wichita—watching her struggle at a neighbor's not to say anything as they sat in a living room that hadn't been cleaned or straightened in a while, the way her fingers absently wiped away dust on the side table as she smiled and made conversation, the nerve in her cheek jumping, the veins and chords in her neck trying to burst through her olive skin, her voice strained but still polite.

When tea was finished, the cookies just crumbs on a dirty plate with what looked like egg yolk dried onto its side, she couldn't get the two of them out of there fast enough. Once back in the sterile safety of their own apartment, she'd taken a long, hot shower—and made him do the same. They'd never gone back there and, until they moved away, politely yet firmly rebuffed the neighbor woman's ongoing friendliness.

"People who keep slovenly homes are lazy and cannot be trusted," she'd told him after refusing the woman's invitations a second time. "A sloppy house means a sloppy soul."

Crazy as she seemed to him at times, he had to admit she'd been right about that. In school after school, kids who didn't keep their desks or lockers neat had never proven trustworthy or likable. It had been hard to keep his revulsion hidden behind the polite mask as he walked to his next class and someone inevitably opened a locker to a cascade of their belongings. He'd just walked faster, to get away from the laughter of other kids and the comic fumbling of the sloppy student as he tried to gather the crumpled papers and broken pencils and textbooks scattered on the shiny linoleum floor.

Take Josh, for instance. He'd been cleaning up after Josh for almost eight years now. Josh didn't appreciate the rule of "everything has its place, and everything in its place."

But he wasn't going to have to clean up after Josh again. Just this one last time.

Steam was rising out of the bucket, making his forehead bead with sweat. The hot afternoon sun was streaming through the big bay windows in the kitchen. No matter how low he turned the air conditioning, the room never seemed to get really cool. But heat and humidity were part of the price of living in New Orleans, like he always said, and the floor was a disgrace.

He lifted the bucket out of the sink after adding more bleach. The fumes made his eyes water, and his back was a bit sore. But the floor needed to be scrubbed. That meant hands and knees and a hand brush. It had been a while since he'd taken the time to clean it properly.

He poured some of the water onto the floor and watched as it slowly spread and ran to the left side. The tile was hideous, of course. He'd bought the house despite the green-and-white-and-beige patterned kitchen floor, faded and yellowed from years of use. It was one of those projects he figured he'd have time for at some point, either pulling it up and replacing it himself, or hiring someone to come in to do it. He'd been in the house now for five years and still hadn't gotten around to it. He pulled on rubber gloves up to his elbows, got down on his knees, and started scrubbing.

He liked the sound of the bristles as they scoured the surface. He'd gotten used to the ugly floor, he supposed, as he ran the brush over it, not really noticing it when he used the kitchen. Maybe it was time to do something about the kitchen. The window frames were yellowed from age, and the walls themselves, a pale green that sort of went with the ugly tiles, looked dirty. And as he looked around as he scrubbed, he could see other things he hadn't noticed before—the thin layer of grease on the stove top around the dials and timer; the filth accumulated under the vent screen over the stove; the yellowing of the refrigerator; the spots all over the black, glassy front of the dishwasher. The windows also needed to be cleaned.

"Your home will never look clean if the windows are filthy," he heard his mother saying as she mixed vinegar and water to use, "but a dirty house will look cleaner if the windows are clean. And you can't let the windows go for long, else water spots and the dirt will become permanent, and the dirt will also scratch the glass. And you can never ever rub away scratches on glass."

Should have put that on her tombstone, he thought with a smile as he dunked the brush back into the bucket and moved to a new spot.

Not that she had one.

"She'd be ashamed of this kitchen," he said aloud into the silence.

His iPod had reached the end of the playlist, and he hadn't stopped what he was doing to cue up another. He'd wiped dust off the iHome stereo system on the kitchen counter before starting the music in the first place. "But she didn't work full time, either."

That also made him smile. His mother hadn't worked nine to five, maybe, but she had worked.

She had always been very careful to make sure she wore gloves and a gauze mask when she cleaned, with her hair pulled back and tucked into the back of her shirt. Cleanliness might have been next to godliness, but she wouldn't risk her skin or her hair to do it. His earliest memories of her were of her brushing her thick, bluish-black hair that she always wore down before going to bed, putting cleansing masks on her face and creams on her hands. Her beauty rituals were almost as complicated as her cleaning habits. Every night without fail, she sat at her vanity and removed her make-up before putting on the mask of unguents that she claimed kept her skin youthful and her pores clean. When money was tight, she made it herself, from cucumbers and aloe and olive oil and some other ingredients he couldn't remember—but when times were good she bought the most expensive products at the most expensive department stores. Once the mask was firmly in place she brushed her hair exactly one hundred times, counting the strokes as she went. Once her hair was lustrous and silky, she retreated to the bathroom to scrub the mask from her face and rub lotions and oils into her hands, trim cuticles and file her nails. Her skin always glowed when she got into bed.

And she was always able to find some man willing to help out a pretty widow lady and her son.

"I do what I have to do" was all she would say when she went out for the evening, lightly scented, with minimal make-up applied—just enough to hide some things and draw attention to others. "Remember to not let anyone in if they knock, okay?"

She would kneel down beside him, or, when he was older, go up on her tippy toes to give him a kiss on the cheek.

He only met the ones who lasted more than a few dates, the ones who had money or might lead to something. He was never sure—still wasn't—what exactly she got up to with the men. She wasn't a prostitute, or at least didn't consider herself to be one. But she hustled the men somehow, got money and jewelry and presents from them, certainly enough for them to live on. She always had cash, never had credit cards. Sometimes the men would give her a car to use, but she never took it with them when they moved on.

Sometimes they moved in the middle of the night, in a rush, hurriedly packing everything they possibly could and heading for the station and catching the next train out of town. They never wound up anywhere that didn't have a train station or an airport.

She wouldn't ride the bus.

"Why do we have to change our names every time we move?" he'd asked her once, on a late-night train out of St. Louis, as the cornfields of Illinois flew past, barely visible by the light of a silvery half-moon. He was maybe nine or ten at the time, old enough to ask some questions, old enough to start wondering why they moved around so much, old enough to wonder why they had no family, no roots, no credit cards, no home.

She'd smiled at him, leaning down to kiss his cheek, smelling vaguely of lilies of the valley. "We don't want people to be able to find us, do we?"

"I don't even know what my real name is anymore," he'd grumbled.

She laughed in response. "I think in this next city you'll be David," she tapped her index finger against her pointed, cat-like chin, "and I'll be Lily. What should our last name be?"

They'd settled on Lindquist that time, for some reason he couldn't really remember now, and they'd chosen Pittsburgh as their new home, their new city, their new adventure.

They'd rented a little two-bedroom cottage in a suburb, and she'd put him into the local school. There was enough money, so they didn't have to worry for a while, and he liked it there. He liked the cozy suburb with the nice kids in the neighborhood and the nice teachers in the school and the friendly neighbors who liked to give him cookies when he brought them their newspaper up from the curb. He liked it there so much that he hoped they'd stay there for a while. He liked being David Lindquist. He was making friends, and sometimes, after he gone to bed and turned out the light, he'd pray to God—any god—that they'd be able to stay there, put down roots, and not ever move again.

They were there three months before she started getting itchy, when afternoon coffees with the neighbors and discussions about what was happening on *Days of Our Lives* and gossip about other women in the suburb began to bore her. She'd said they wouldn't have to worry about money for a long time, but he should have known better than to think she would become just another housewife, and that being the widowed Mrs. Lindquist who kept such a clean house and was raising such a nice son and always had time to listen to anyone who had a problem would begin to bore her.

She started going out in the evenings, after he'd gone to bed—she never said anything, always checked his room before she left. He would pretend to be asleep until he heard the front door shut, and then he'd look out the window and see her getting into the taxi waiting at the curb. Maybe it was because she had money socked away that she got so careless that time, that she didn't cover her tracks as well as she usually did.

It was three in the morning when a cry woke him from a dream about *Star Wars,* when he got out of bed and went into the living room where a big man he'd never seen before had his mother pressed up against the wall and was choking her. She was trying to get away.

He hadn't meant to swing the baseball bat so hard.

"You've killed him," she said finally, her throat raspy and her neck bruised from his thick hands. She staggered a bit as she stepped over to the body, kneeling down and feeling for a pulse in his neck. She looked up at him, her hair disheveled, her face wild. "I'm glad you killed him."

"We need to call the police—"

She pressed her index finger against his lips to stop him speaking. "We never call the police," she whispered, a half-smile on her bruised lips. "Never call the police."

She stumbled into the kitchen and came back with a kitchen towel. She wrapped it around the man's head, tying it into a knot. "Help me drag him into the bathroom."

The cottage had two bathrooms, one in the hallway that he used, and a private one off her bedroom, which he never got to use. It seemed to take forever, and the dead man seemed to weigh a lot more than he should, but they finally got him to the hall bathroom and into the tub. "There," she panted, "we can leave him there for now."

She pushed him back into the hallway, shutting the door behind her. "You can shower in my bathroom tomorrow morning. We need to clean up the living room." She laughed, a harsh, cynical laugh. "Thank God I didn't pick a house that's carpeted."

More of her wisdom—"never pick a home with carpet".

He stopped scrubbing, stood up, and dumped the dirty bucket of water back into the sink and reached for the mop. "I haven't thought about Pittsburgh in years," he said with a laugh. He dragged the mop through the bleach solution, wringing it out into the sink before mopping up more of the water. The floor where he hadn't mopped looked even dingier in comparison to where he'd already cleaned, and his back was already starting to ache a little bit. But now that he'd started, he had to finish.

"Always finish what you've started" was another one of her sayings.

He had come home from school that next day to find her sitting in the living room, coolly cutting up credit cards into a big mixing bowl sitting on the coffee table. A leather wallet was on the table next to the bowl, along with an expensive-looking gold watch and a man's ring, also gold. A wad of cash was on the other side of the bowl. "Nearly finished," she said, her tone almost gay as he shut the front door. She nodded towards the wad of money. "Two thousand dollars, David!"

He didn't say anything, just walked down the hallway to the bathroom. The door was open, but there was a horrible antiseptic odor coming from there that he had smelled long before he got to the doorway, where it was so bad his eyes watered. But the bathtub was empty.

"Caustic lye," his mother said from the end of the hallway, her hands on her hips. "You'll want to stay out of there for a few days."

"What—what happened to him?" He managed to stammer the words out.

"I told you, caustic lye," she replied, rolling her eyes. "Now do your homework. I'm going to start making dinner."

No one ever came looking for the man, and after a few more days of terror whenever he saw a police car or heard a siren, he began to settle back into life as David Lindquist. He never knew who the man was—he stopped at the library on his way home from school for a couple of weeks to look through the newspaper without her knowing, but there was never anything in there about him. It was almost like he'd never existed, and there were times he wondered if the man ever had, if he hadn't maybe dreamed hitting a man in the head with a baseball bat to stop him from strangling his mother. But then he would remember the sound of the bat connecting with bone, the way the skull had given, the gurgling sound the man made as he went down.

He hadn't dreamed that.

They left Pittsburgh at the end of the school year, saying goodbye to all of their friends and neighbors at a going-away barbecue, selling all the furniture and things and once again taking a night train. He didn't want to go—he was starting to grow, and he was starting to notice boys, and there was a boy in the neighborhood he really, really liked. But there was no arguing, no point in asking if they could stay longer. When she made up her mind to move on, she made up her mind, and that was that.

This time it was Atlanta where they landed, and she found a nice little house to rent in a quiet neighborhood.

It was in Atlanta that she found a man who wanted to marry her.

It was in Atlanta where he changed from David Lindquist to David Rutledge, taking the name of his mother's new husband.

He'd liked Ted Rutledge, who was a lawyer for a lot of big companies and had a huge house in a rich suburb. The house they moved into was enormous—six bedrooms, six bathrooms, and every room enormous and immaculate and beautifully decorated. She couldn't keep the house clean by herself, but a team of cleaners came in once a week to clean from floor to ceiling—and she watched them like a hawk, not tolerating any slacking or missed spots. Ted had a big booming laugh and always seemed to be in a good mood. But Ted also worked a lot, and even though she liked spending Ted's money, about six months after the wedding, he could tell his mother was getting restless again. He could see it in her eyes, the twitching of that muscle in her jaw, the way she sometimes stood in the window and stared out at the street across the vast expanse of the front lawn.

"Don't mess this up, Mom," he warned her one morning before he left for school. "This is a good thing, and we should make this work for as long as we can."

She'd just smiled at him and nodded.

"You never could trust in your own good luck, could you, Mom?" he said as he poured more water onto the kitchen floor.

He stood up and leaned backwards, his hands on his lower spine as it popped and cracked.

But she'd lasted much longer than he thought she would.

He was a senior in high school, straight-A student, letterman on the football and baseball teams (he didn't care much about playing sports, but it meant a lot to Ted), when he came home from school one day and found them both.

"They'd been fighting," he said numbly, still in shock, to the police officer who'd come in answer to his call, the call he couldn't really remember making. "I don't know about what. I know my mom was going out at night while he was at work, but he never seemed to mind. Not that I know about."

His new guardian, Ted's law partner, told him much later that it seemed like she'd killed Ted and then turned the gun on herself. He just nodded, the same way he nodded when he was told how much money there was and that it was probably best to sell the house and get rid of everything, all those bad memories. He just nodded and went to live with his new guardian until it was time to go away to school.

No one ever wondered about the deaths.

No one ever wondered if maybe it wasn't just a little bit strange that she'd waited until after her son went off to school before shooting her husband over his morning breakfast and then turning the gun on herself.

No one ever figured out that he'd walked into the kitchen that morning with one of Ted's revolvers in his hand, come up behind where his mother was sitting and fired the gun into Ted's face and, before she even had time to react, put it to her temple and pulled the trigger himself. No one ever wondered if he'd then taken the gun, put it into her hand and fired it again at Ted's chest, so she'd have powder residue on her hand.

No one knew that she'd caught him with a boy, seen him in the pool kissing Brad Brown, and that once Brad had gone home they'd both told him he was going to be sent somewhere 'to be cured.

Sometimes you have to make your own luck, like she always said.

He finished the floor and got back to his feet. The sunlight was already starting to fade a little bit, but the floor was finally clean. He glanced around the kitchen. Once the floor dried, he was going to have to come back in and clean some more, get those spots he'd been noticing. The grease on the stove back, on the vent, the spots on the front of the dishwasher—he couldn't just leave them like that. He'd never be able to sleep knowing the kitchen was so filthy. And he needed his sleep.

Tomorrow was going to be a big day.

He walked into the living room and gave the room a critical once-over. There was a cushion on the couch that needed fluffing, and the magazines on the coffee table weren't centered quite right. The TV screen shone in the sunlight, and there was no dust on any surfaces. He plumped the cushion and moved the magazines, fiddling with them a bit until they were just right, the perfect distance from each edge of the table.

He sat down on the couch and looked around. He loved this house. He was glad he'd found it, had made it his own. He'd carefully selected everything in the house, and everything was in its perfect place, as though it had been specifically made to go there. Ten years—it had been ten years since he'd bought the house, had moved in, made it his home.

And now it was all his again.

He'd miss Josh, of course. You live with someone for long enough, you're bound to miss him when he leaves, no matter how bad things had gotten between the two of you.

Josh had been like his mother, he realized, and that was part of the initial attraction. Josh was a hustler, with no family and no past, just like she was. Josh was good looking, with his green eyes and thick brows and bluish-black hair and slavish devotion to his appearance. And like his mother, Josh wasn't a whore. And they'd lasted for eight years, eight years with minimal strife, very few fights, very few disagreements. As long as Josh got to go to the gym and lie by the pool wearing the briefest of swimsuits and had money to buy nice clothes, Josh was very agreeable. There was enough money so that neither of them had to work, of course, and he didn't care if Josh wanted to go out to clubs at night. He didn't even care if Josh met people and slept with them, as long as Josh was there for him when needed. And he always was. Josh never pouted if he had to change his plans and stay home as directed.

He'd almost loved Josh, really. It wasn't even like he hated him, either.

He'd just tired of him, the way his mother had always gotten bored.

If he had to put his finger on the time when he'd decided it was time for Josh to go, he couldn't.

It was just one of those things, like his mother had always told him when she'd decided to move on.

This morning, when he woke up, he knew that it was going to be today. He just knew it, somehow, and that knowing was what made him think of his mother for the first time in years.

It felt right.

For a moment he wished he didn't have the ties—the house and the car and the credit cards and the bank accounts. He could understand her wanderlust now, the need to just leave and start all over again somewhere new, the need to be free from anything and everything, the ability to just pack some things and go, walk away from your current life. He was tied to this house now, he was tied to being David Rutledge, didn't know if he could just change his name and start all over again somewhere else the way she used to do.

It might not even be possible now, what with computers and cell phones and tracking and Homeland Security. It had been easy, back in the day, to change identities without too much fear of someone from the past tracking you down.

No, he knew it was a foolish thought—even if he moved away to some remote place in Central America, someone would be able to hunt him down if they were so inclined.

No one had ever suspected a thing about his mother and Ted, had they?

No one would ever suspect a thing about Josh, either.

Once the floor dries, he decided, then I'll use the lye.

The floor was now nice and clean, spick and span, gleaming.

Not one trace of blood had escaped his eyes. He'd gotten it all up.

No, no sense in taking the lye into the back bathroom now and tracking up that nice clean floor until it dried—not after all the effort he'd spent scrubbing it clean, like his mother always did.

Besides, it wasn't like Josh was going to get up and walk away from his resting place in the bathtub.

And no one was going to miss him, anyway.

It was going to be nice living alone again.

Someone's Moved the Sun

Jeffrey Siger

The light wasn't where it was supposed to be. It should be over there … in the east … coming through that window. I must be in the wrong place. But this was my room. I knew my bed. There was only one explanation: someone's moved the sun.

I should get up and start an investigation immediately. This was serious. Greek islands needed the sun to stay in the right place. It was hard enough keeping track of the moon, let alone the sun. Come to think of it, I vaguely remembered following the moon all over town last night. Or was it this morning? I better check the time. Now, where's my phone?

"Toni, are you in there?"

BAM. BAM. BAM.

"Stop pounding on my door, Niko, you'll wake up your other guests."

"You're not a guest. You're a pain in the ass. It's two o'clock in the afternoon, your mobile's off, and Stella's called me to tell you to get your butt down to the harbor. You were supposed to meet her there an hour ago."

I grabbed my pillow, pulled it over my face, and screamed. "*Fuck.*" I sat up. "Tell her I'm on my way."

"Yeah, like she'll believe it."

I heard Niko muttering to himself as he shuffled down the hall toward the hotel reception desk. I wouldn't really call it a hotel, more like a big house with a lot of bedrooms. I've lived here for the past five years, and at least once a week I'd either swear to leave or Niko would threaten to toss me out. During one of our ouzo-laden, soul-searching conversations, staring out to sea from the hotel's veranda, he told me our relationship was like a marriage—without any of the good parts. I had to take his word for that, because he'd been married for forty years, while I'd been blissfully single for every breath I'd drawn.

I swung my bare feet onto the marble floor and walked to the French doors at the far end of the room. Even in torrid mid-July the marble felt cool, but my room was shuttered up so tightly it had me thinking bathhouse. I yanked open the doors, and Meltemi breezes surrounded my body, flooding into the room to sweep it free of the stifling damp heat.

I stepped onto the balcony, stared out across a mat of fig and olive trees toward a sapphire Aegean Sea running off to meet an azure sky, and drew in and let out a deep breath. The old couple bent over at work in their garden a few meters away ignored me. They'd seen me naked many times before. At least that's what my nearly thirty-year-old body hoped was the reason.

No matter, *live and let live* served as the islanders' motto, and that suited me just fine.

But not Stella: she was all business, and punctuality served as a key virtue of her New York City upbringing. I'd lost that one—along with practically every other—bumming around Europe after turning eighteen, and promptly abandoning my disciplined upbringing as diplomat's child to pursue my long-held dream of setting the world on fire with my music.

For most, my sort-of artistic aspirations faded painfully quickly, which I guess explained why I was still on this island: I'd found a place that fed my habit every night. The only hitch was maintaining a proper day job to support my low-paying nighttime addiction.

And speaking of my day job, it was time to get my ass in gear and down to the harbor. I couldn't afford to lose *another* partner in the business, certainly not one as efficient as Stella. She'd married a local boy, Mihalis, she'd met here on holiday, but soon found her fantasy romance as difficult to maintain in real life as my performer's dream. We were a match made in business heaven: She needed a focus to support her sanity, and I needed an income to fund my insanity.

It took fifteen minutes of brisk walking in flip-flops along narrow, twisting, uneven flagstone paths to reach the harbor. Normally, I could make it through the maze of sun-bleached Cycladic shops and homes in ten, but with so many cruise-ship tourists standing every which way, taking photos of bright-white shapes adorned in painted woodwork of shiny greens, blues, and reds—often draped in purple, pink, and red bougainvillea—there was no way to make better time.

Stella was sitting under the blue-striped awning of a taverna near the southern end of the harbor, close by the farmers' market—or at least it would have been a farmers' market had I been there four hours earlier.

"Good morning. So happy you could join us, and dressed formally, no less."

I dropped into the chair directly across from Stella. I could tell she was pissed at me from the way she'd torn into my choice of tank top and cutoffs. "It's close to forty degrees— that's over a hundred for you Fahrenheit types. And what do you mean 'us?'"

"Until forty minutes ago, a prospective client sat where you just parked yourself. He left, saying he had some shopping to do for his wife, and told me to call him when you got here." Stella picked her phone off the table and punched in a number.

"Well then, his wife should be grateful to me."

Without moving the phone from her ear, Stella shot me her well-practiced frowning smile.

The broad-mustached, weather-beaten owner of the taverna sat leaning back against the front of a whitewashed building housing a toilet, tiny kitchen, and slightly larger dining room. Inside, the place was a favorite wintertime hangout for locals. He touched his nicotine-stained fingers to the brim of his fisherman's cap, and nodded at me. I nodded back.

"Toni is here now, sir." Pause. "Yes, the missing child was found safe and sound." Pause. "Of course we'll wait for you." Stella put her phone back on the table.

"Missing child?"

"What did you expect me to tell him? That you were sleeping off another drunken night on the town?"

"I was developing contacts, learning about the ins and outs of the sordid types who've come to prey on our island."

"Save that for the scandal rags and magazine folks who, for some reason, actually believe all that crap you feed them."

I held up my hands in surrender. "Okay, I give up. Just tell me what this guy wants."

"What most of our clients want. To get their stuff back from the lowlifes who break into their hotel rooms and vacation homes to rob them blind."

"Where's he live?"

"On the other side of island. Just past the windsurfers' beach, sharp right up the mountain. His house is at the top. Must have a terrific view."

"And a beacon to every thief on the island looking for a place to score."

Stella nodded. "He knows that. That's why he's had the head of the tourist police living in his guest house for the last two years."

"Ouch. This could get sticky."

"I already raised that possibility with him, but he's certain it's not an inside job."

"How can he be so sure?"

"I don't know. Why don't you ask him?" Stella stood and extended her hand toward a tall, well-dressed, fit-looking man in his early forties. "Mister Kleftis, I'd like you to meet my partner, Toni."

I stood and shook his hand. He checked me out as if he were about to buy me.

"You're not what I expected."

I smiled. "That's my secret weapon."

"Everyone says you're the best there is at finding lost things on the island."

"Who am I to disagree with everyone?" I slid my sunglasses up onto the top of my head."

"And blue eyes, too."

If he was hitting on me, I didn't care. If you're the blue-eyed, curly-haired piano player at a Greek party-island's most popular gay cabaret, you get used to that sort of thing—from all sexes.

"So let's talk about your problem." I pointed him to a chair between Stella and me. "What was stolen, when, and where?"

"Last night, a backpack disappeared out of the trunk of my car. I'd parked over by the yacht club." He pointed to the north end of the harbor. "When we got back to the car after dinner, the trunk was open, and the backpack gone."

"What was in it?"

"Things."

"What sorts of things?"

"Jewelry, some cash."

I looked off toward a small group of children chasing ducks along the narrow strip of beachfront ringing the harbor.

"What was the backpack doing in the trunk?"

"With all the break-ins on the island, I thought it safer to keep our valuables with us than to leave them at home."

I looked straight at him. "Don't you have a cop living in your guest house?"

"Yes, but he and his family were away last night."

Stella jumped in. "Did he know you'd be away and have the backpack with you?"

There was Stella, always dancing in with the obvious conclusion.

He looked at Stella, then at me. "Do you think he could have been involved?"

Stella started to answer, but I raised my hand to stop her. "Anything is possible, but I wouldn't jump to that conclusion."

"Why not?" said Stella, crossing her arms.

I softened my voice. "Because a Balkan gang has moved onto the island and reduced the art of breaking into cars to a science. They scout through parking lots on motorbikes scanning for what's in trunks."

"Scanning?" he asked.

I nodded. "They have the sort of high-end mobile scanners the Greek Coast Guard wishes it could afford to fight smugglers. Once they locate a target, they use an inflatable device the size of a credit card to force open enough room between a door and window to squeeze in a jimmy, pop the lock, hit the trunk release, grab the stuff, and take off. They work so quickly they never worry about car alarms."

"How the hell do you know all this?" he asked.

I smiled at Stella. "A lot of hanging out in the wrong places with the right people."

Stella didn't say a word.

"If the police know all that, how hard can it be to catch them?"

"The trouble is, the cops never find them with the stuff. No loot, no proof, no case."

"That doesn't make sense."

"This gang is patient. They bury what they steal inside abandoned buildings in out of the way places on the island and cover it over with cement. They'll come in the dead of winter, when no one's around, and dig it up and transport it back to the Balkans to sell there."

He shook his head. "I can't believe it."

"They know how the Greek system works. Out of sight, out of mind."

"Can you find my backpack?"

"If they opened it and found the money, I think you can kiss that goodbye. No reason to bury it, because cash isn't traceable even if you're caught with it. The jewelry, if it's unique, is probably buried."

"Maybe they'll try to sell it here?"

I shrugged. No reason to overly discourage a prospective client. "Do you have photographs of the jewelry?"

"Why would I have photographs?"

I watched his eyes. "For insurance purposes."

He smiled. "They weren't the kind of purchases one insures."

Like I thought, black money. Another patriotic tax-evader doing his bit to keep the Greek economy on its knees. "Well, get me as good a description as you can, and I'll see what I can do."

"What's your fee?"

Stella jumped in. "Five-hundred euros flat fee, plus ten percent of the value of whatever we recover."

"Sounds steep."

"A lot less than the taxes you owe on it," I said.

He nodded. "You're right." He reached into his pocket, pulled out ten 50-euro bills, put them on the table, and stood. "You know where to find me." He nodded and hurried off.

"A rather abrupt goodbye," I said.

"After your wise-ass remark about his black money, I'm surprised he didn't just walk away." Stella gathered up the money and shoved it into her bag.

"Nah, he wants that backpack too badly. I don't know what's in it, but for sure a lot more than he's telling."

"Think you can find it?"

"That's going to depend on what I pick up in the bar tonight."

"Pick up?" Her eyes twinkled.

"As in *learn*."

"Oh yes, of course." After flashing me a perky flutter of her eyes, she looked at her watch. Her perkiness faded. "It's late. I have to pick up Mihalis's mother from the doctor's."

"Can't he do it?"

She looked down. "He's fishing."

I nodded. Another reason to stay single.

***

I arrived at the bar around ten that night, and the bartender handed me an envelope containing magazine ads for expensive jewelry, with some pieces circled in red. That was it. No name, no instructions. Nothing to link it back to Kleftis should I be tempted to turn him into the tax boys for a bounty. A prudent way of handling things for those used to dealing with the untrustworthy.

Not that I could claim a holier-than-thou position on my own methods. Much of my success in the recovery business came from striking deals with the island's thieves for the return of my clients' property. My going rate was a 50-50 split of my fee.

Sure, it cost me half, but half was better than nothing, and getting the police involved could cost a lot more. It also worked out better for the crooks, because they didn't have to work through a fence, who would give them much less than I did. True, it wasn't a very dramatic or socially redeeming solution, but it worked out well for everyone.

But this Balkan gang's operation was different. I hadn't told my client or Stella, but the Russians were behind it, with a huge distribution network operating out of the former Yugoslavia. That made it highly unlikely they would settle for splitting my meager fee. Perhaps I could entice one of their local gang members into making a side deal, but that ran the very real risk of someone ending up buried alongside the backpack. Correction: Make that someone *me*. Nope, the risk of bloodshed was a definite no-no. Especially mine. I'd have to find a different approach.

I was deeply into my 1 AM set when an English woman at the bar started screaming for me to play *New York, New York.* She'd been coming here for years, spending a month every summer at the beach working on her all-over tan, and most of the rest of her time in our bar trying to find someone to show it off to in private. I never understood why she looked for guys in a gay bar, but she insisted the straight guys she hooked up with here were classier and more sensitive than the sort hanging out elsewhere. Tonight she was with a guy I pegged as one of those foreign day-laborers who dressed up as a ship-owner at night to chase after tourist girls, a longstanding and hallowed tradition on the island.

"*Toni*, play the fucking song already," she shouted.

"Don't worry, Annabelle, I'll get to it."

She staggered off the stool and headed straight for me, a drink clutched loosely in her hand. She leaned in across the piano and whispered, "Please, Toni, you got to play it for me. This guy I'm with really wants to hear it, and I told him you're a friend of mine."

I kept playing. "I am a friend of yours, Annabelle, which is why I don't think you should pay much attention to him."

"But he's a big spender."

"Buying you a drink doesn't make him a big spender."

"He's promised to buy everyone in the bar a drink if you'll play it now."

"Really?" I looked over at the guy. He smiled and raised his drink to me.

It was a tough bridge from my *Man of La Mancha* medley into Annabelle's request, but I did it in a manner I'm sure their composers would have appreciated. I felt I owed it to the poor girl to show her that her Don Quixote was a phony.

No sooner had I hit the familiar first bar than her new boyfriend yelled out "Drinks for everyone," and dropped the biggest tip of the night into my tip jar. So much for a piano player's legendary people instincts.

On my 2 AM break, they crowded around me at the piano, and boyfriend began bragging about how successful he was. He'd tipped me big time, so I listened. Not that I cared, but piano players who like to eat learn to be flexible. When they worked their way around to probing each other's dental work, I lost interest, picked up my client's envelope, and studied the ads.

A minute or so later, boyfriend took a break for a sip from the drink he'd positioned precariously along the top of the piano. "Hey, what's that you're looking at?"

I held up one of the ads.

He squinted at it. "You like that sort of stuff?"

"A friend does."

"I can get that shit for you for a good price." He looked at Annabelle and preened.

"Yes, he can get you anything you want."

"For sure." He took the page from my hand. "In fact, I can get you these two circled pieces tonight."

"Not tonight, honey," cooed Annabelle. "We're busy."

He leaned over and kissed her. "Yeah, not tonight, but tomorrow, first thing."

"Sounds great," I said. "Where and when?"

Annabelle pressed her head against his chest. "My place, but not early."

He put his arm around her and squeezed. "Yeah, not early."

They left around four. I called Stella ten minutes later. She answered, screaming "Where are you?" When I said the bar, and what I wanted, she realized it wasn't Mihalis on the other end. Embarrassed, she gave me Kleftis's number without even asking why I wanted it at such an ungodly hour.

Next, I called the client, woke him up, and told him where, when, and from whom he could recover his stolen jewelry. All he said was "Wrong number" and hung up.

***

Early morning banging on my door was becoming a habit. "Stop it, Niko, I don't have to be anywhere this morning."

"It's not Niko, Toni. It's Annabelle."

I looked at the clock. 10 AM. Way early by island standards. "Just a minute." I pulled on a pair of shorts and a tee shirt and opened the door.

Bright daylight was not kind to Annabelle, even less so with the remnants of mascara streaked down her cheeks, her hair a bird's nest, and a plum-red bruise across her forehead. I pulled her into my room. "What happened to you? Did that bastard beat you up?"

She shook her head. "No, he didn't touch me. It wasn't him. Two men broke into my room just before dawn."

My heart skipped three beats.

"They grabbed him, and when I tried to stop them, one threw me into the wall. I hit my head and passed out. When I woke up everyone was gone. I thought it was a nightmare. But it was real." She touched her forehead.

"What happened after you woke up?"

"I called the police, and they told me to stay put. It took them two hours to get there, and then they didn't believe a word I said. They figured I'd brought a guy home for a good time and got more than I bargained for." She lowered her head. "It didn't help that I couldn't give them more than his first name." She burst into tears.

I put my arm around her shoulders. "I understand. Some cops can be pretty insensitive when it comes to this sort of thing."

"I didn't know who else to turn to. I knew you lived at Niko's, so I came here."

I patted her shoulder. "You did the right thing." I handed her a bottle of water and pointed her to a chair by the French doors. "Take a sip."

I waited until she'd finished drinking. "Did you recognize any of the men?"

"No."

"Can you describe them?"

"No."

"Did you hear anything?"

She shook her head. "No. The police asked the same questions. It happened so quickly, and I was unconscious practically the whole time they were there."

I sighed. "I guess it wouldn't have mattered anyway. They probably spoke in Greek."

She shook her head again. "He didn't speak Greek. Only Russian and English."

"How do you know that?"

"I heard him tell them …" She raised her head. "My God, I thought I was dreaming. I must have heard it when I was unconscious."

"Do you remember anything else?"

She squeezed her eyes tightly shut. "A backpack. They wanted to know about a backpack."

"What about the backpack?"

She kept her eyes closed. "They asked if he knew where it was and what was inside."

"What did he say?"

"That he didn't know what they were talking about." She opened her eyes. "I can't remember anything else. They must have taken him away."

"I want you to stay here until I get back."

"Where are you going?"

"To ask some questions."

"I should come with you." She started to stand.

"No. I think your friend is mixed up in some really bad stuff, and the only reason you weren't taken was because they thought you were just a girl there for the night. If they suspect you know what you just told me, you'll be in big danger."

Her head drooped, and she started to cry again. "I want to go home to Sussex."

"That might not be a bad idea, but not quite yet. Let me see what I can do." I lifted her chin with my fingers. "Okay?"

She sniffled. "Okay."

That seemed to calm her down. Now to figure out how to do the same for myself.

***

Traffic out of town was light. Sun-worshipers had already made it to the beach and late-night partiers were still sleeping off their hangovers. With no wind and the tarmac shimmering in the midday heat, my motorbike had me feeling like a lamb on a spit. Which, considering where I was headed, might not be such a bad comparison.

The narrow road up to Kleftis's place was where Stella said it would be, with a sharp drop off to the right, and a composition of just enough loose dirt and rock to discourage the curious. It split into two at the top. To the right lay a church, to the left a slightly better one-lane road running between two high, stone walls. I went left.

The road opened onto a broad flagstone parking area. Two men stood waiting for me. I knew I should have fixed the noisy muffler on my bike. A man built like a bulldog put up his hand for me to stop.

"This is private property."

"I'm here to see Mister Kleftis."

"Is he expecting you?"

"Just tell him Toni's here to see him."

He spoke into a walkie-talkie, stared at me, and said, "Mister Kleftis will see you in the garden." He pointed toward a stone archway on the near side of a one-story, white stucco structure that appeared to float across much of the mountaintop.

"Wow. Is that the house?"

Bulldog ignored my question and pointed again toward the garden.

I found Kleftis on the other side of a patch of olive, palm, and lemon trees, sitting under a grape arbor, staring down from his beige-and-brown mountain perch toward a bright blue-green bay.

"Pretty nice place you have here."

"Thank you. My wife and I like it. Please, sit." He pointed to a chair across from him. "So, to what do I owe the honor of this visit?"

"It's not this visit I'm concerned about. It's a visit made at dawn today to an address I'd given you at four in the morning."

"I have no idea what you're talking about." He gestured the 'no' the Greek way, with an upward jerk of his head.

"Did you at least recover the backpack?"

"What backpack?"

"Oh, I get it. Well, no more reason for me to stay here and bother you."

He smiled. "Thanks for stopping by. I'm glad you understand how things are."

I smiled. "Sure, and I hope your wife will accept my apology."

"My wife?"

"Yes, I wrote her a letter apologizing for not recovering her stolen jewelry, but because I'm sure she has so much, I included the pages you so kindly sent me. I'm sure she'll figure things out."

His smile disappeared. "Where's that letter?"

"Safely tucked away."

He reached for his walkie-talkie.

"Nah, I don't think you want to call in your buddies. Going after a likely illegal Russian is one thing, going after me with all my friends knowing I'm up here isn't going to work. I won't be so easy to make disappear."

"What do you want?"

"What we agreed on. Ten percent of the value of what I recovered."

"You didn't recover shit."

"You know, I don't really care what actually was in that backpack that drove you to come to me, rather than to the cop who lives in your house, but I'm sure you know people who'd care quite a bit. So, if you want to make paying my fee a big deal, and risk getting those folks all worked up in the process, go right ahead. It's your business, not mine."

He clenched one hand into a fist and reached for the walkie-talkie with the other.

Maybe I'd pushed him too hard.

He shouted into the walkie-talkie, "Bring me my briefcase," then sat silently glaring at me.

Bulldog brought him a black alligator briefcase and immediately left.

Kleftis popped the lock on the case, reached in, and handed me a thick stack of 100-euro notes. "Are we done?"

"I wish I'd worn pants with bigger pockets. Do you happen to have an envelope?"

"Get the fuck out of here?"

"One last thing. Where's the guy who was taken?"

"He's off the island. Now get out of here before I change my mind."

I hustled back to my motorbike and sped away, almost hitting a cement truck coming up the hill head-on. I had to turn around and go back up the hill to give the truck room to get by.

The driver stopped beside me.

"Hey, Toni, how you doing?"

"Great, Panos. Haven't seen you in a while. Where are you headed with this load?"

"Some big-time Athens contractor tight with the government honchos who award building contracts wants to put in a new patio. He told my boss he's expecting some important guests and needed it poured today."

I nodded. "See you around." I wonder how Sussex is this time of year.

***

After convincing Annabelle to cut her vacation short and spend the time back home reevaluating her process for choosing men, I called Stella and asked her to meet me at a quiet beach taverna just outside of town.

I told her everything that happened, because if anything went squirrely, she'd be as much at risk as I.

"So what do you think was in the backpack?" she asked.

"Cash for sure, likely a lot of it. My guess is it was intended as a payoff. And there must have been something that revealed what it was for, perhaps a government contact."

"I'm glad we don't know."

"Me too."

"But what about the jewelry? Why was that there?"

I smiled. "I guessed right. I figured any guy who has bodyguards and a cop living on his property must also have a safe. So why not keep whatever he was worried about in the safe? The jewelry tipped me off. His wife doesn't trust him— apparently for good reason—so he was afraid to put anything in the safe that she might find."

"Like her jewelry?"

"That's the point, it wasn't her jewelry. It's probably something he intended giving a girlfriend, but whatever the explanation, he didn't want his wife finding it. That's why I made up the story about the letter. It's why he paid us."

"What happened to the guy who disappeared from Annabelle's?"

"I think a lot of his friends will be asking that same question. Which is why Annabelle's on a plane back to Sussex."

"You think he was part of the Russian mob?"

"I'm not about to start asking questions on that subject, but if he was, and they figure out what happened to him, I wouldn't want to be Kleftis."

Stella nodded and kept looking out to sea. "You know, with all the nights Mihalis has been spending away from home, I'm thinking maybe I should remodel the house, do something to keep him with me."

I shook my head. "I don't think redecorating will keep him around."

"I was thinking of something more concrete, like a new patio."

I laughed. "That's funny."

She kept staring out to sea. "I didn't mean it to be."

"Oh."

The Freemason Friends

Timothy Williams

Canada, Fall 2015

Létitia was not going to call.

In the weeks since Anne-Marie had arrived in Canada, she had heard from her daughter just once—an indistinct message on the voice mail, saying that she would be in touch and that the children were dying to see their grandmother. Anne-Marie knew she was wasting her time and that Létitia would never be in touch.

Anne-Marie tried to concentrate: a Danish film on television, while outside, beyond the sash windows, the afternoon clouds grew darker with the threat of snow.

She could understand people watching Scandinavian noir in the heat, in Arizona or in Guadeloupe, where you longed for zero temperatures and biting air in your lungs. Here on Lake Ontario, the low, grey skies of northern Europe were no more appealing than the encroaching darkness of a Canadian winter.

She shivered. Anne-Marie hated the last months of the year; even more so now she was retired and had no regular work to occupy the empty days.

She wished she were somewhere warm: sun, good food, children's infectious laughter.

"Come to Toronto," her daughter had said in September. "Maman, the children would love to see you and, for once, you can relax. Get away from Paris and stop fretting over Fabrice. There's nothing you can do. Your son and his wife are going through a difficult time, but they're both adults, and they must sort out their problems. Get on with your own life. Spend three months with us. The cold has its charm, you know. We can take the girls to Quebec, and if you really want, my husband and I can invite Fabrice and his wife. We can pay the air fare."

"How is your husband?" Anne-Marie had asked, but Létitia had merely laughed.

On the television, the detective in the knitted sweater spoke in Danish. She sounded strange, as if from an alien world.

Anne-Marie read the English subtitles.

Short of making a scene, there was little chance of seeing her two grand-daughters; there never had been. Anne-Marie hated the way her daughter went back on her promises, but to remonstrate would only make things worse.

At least over one thing, Létitia was right: life went on, and it was time Anne-Marie got on with hers. Getting away from Paris and leaving her son's marital problems behind her had been a good idea.

Anne-Marie now watched the television and frowned in concentration. A murdered girl had been found outside the city. The woman detective appeared obsessed by the death.

Danish police procedure was different from Anne-Marie's professional experience as a French magistrate. And perhaps that was why she was not concentrating, why her mind wandered, why she kept thinking about the past, about the Caribbean, and about the years in Guadeloupe.

People get killed everywhere, she told herself; in hot climates just as much as on the cold shores of the Baltic.

Darkness, cold, the woolen sweater, the obsession, the northern angst—it was unreal: alcohol-fueled, depressive, and dour. Anne-Marie needed the sun.

Just as she turned the television off, the computer began to blink as if in answer to a silent prayer.

Someone was calling her on Skype.

***

The Dominican Republic

The plane from Toronto touched down on time, but border control in the Dominican Republic was punctilious and unbearably slow. Anne-Marie lost her place in the immigration line because she had not paid entry tax. She went back to an unsmiling woman who took ten American dollars and, without a word, gave her a printed chit. Then she queued for forty minutes before being processed by another unsmiling woman, this time in uniform. Finally, Anne-Marie stepped out of the airport into the hot, damp evening.

A woman in a shift dress held a card with the scribbled name "Anne-Marie Laveaud".

Luz was young and friendly. She had the high cheekbones, dark eyes, and tanned skin of an Amerindian.

They shook hands.

Luz spoke no French, but in broken English indicated there was a taxi waiting for them. They climbed into the back of an SUV. Anne-Marie stared through the tinted windows as the car left the airport and drove towards the city. Bright lights and low buildings, palm trees and heavy traffic.

"*Emigración golondrina*," Luz said, laughing. "You're a snowbird, and you come here for the winter."

"I don't live in Canada but was visiting my grandchildren in Ontario. I'm in Santo Domingo to see Dolores."

"Dolores is good," Luz remarked.

After twenty minutes they left the highway, took a slip road and then stopped in a side street in the old part of Santo Domingo. There were parked cars and motorcycles along the curb. Low houses, old and run-down, were protected by iron gates and grills over the glassless windows.

Anne-Marie paid the driver with her remaining dollars, and Luz ushered her through a gate, unlocked another iron gate, and then pulled back a bolt on a third one.

A fat woman got to her feet with difficulty.

Deep wrinkles, the flesh of her jaw loose. Anne-Marie did not recognize her friend immediately. Dolores had grown very big.

Beneath the bare bulb hanging from the ceiling, the two women embraced. Dolores smelled of lavender.

They held hands. "So good to see you, Anne-Marie."

Luz asked if Anne-Marie cared for coffee.

"Please."

"I'm so glad you could come," Dolores said. "I'm safe here. Two doors down from the Haitian Embassy, and nobody knows where I am."

"Safe?"

"Luz's Rudy's friend—my son's girlfriend—and she's studying at the university. Nobody's going to look for me here."

"Why should anyone look for you?"

"In Guadeloupe I'm wanted for murder, Anne-Marie. Didn't Luz tell you?"

***

Guadeloupe, French West Indies

Fabrice had always had good teachers in Guadeloupe, but things changed when Létitia went to high school in Baimbridge. Létitia was not a brilliant pupil, but she was hardworking and determined. Like her mother, she was never afraid to speak her mind and, at times, spoke too freely when silence would have been wiser.

A couple of years before taking her Baccalaureate, Létitia joined the editorial staff of the school newspaper. She wrote several articles about school discipline; nothing iconoclastic, but her French teacher took umbrage, assuming wrongly the articles were directed against her. Once, following a perceived insult, the woman had marched Létitia to the headmaster's office. Until that moment, Anne-Marie had had a good relationship with the *Monsieur le proviseur,* a light-skinned mulatto with a pink, round face and a potbelly that pushed against his crocodile-skin belt.

Anne-Marie contacted the headmaster and demanded an explanation. From then on, there was a chill between Anne-Marie and the school. Whenever Anne-Marie went to a parent–teacher meeting, the principal, instead of chatting about his years in law school, studiously ignored her.

Fortunately for Létitia, her last two years at Baimbridge were enjoyable, thanks to the friendship with a new girl in her class. Ludivine Salcède was, like Létitia, of mixed parentage, and in next to no time the two teenagers were as close as sisters.

Anne-Marie became a friend of the girl's mother. Dolores Salcède had glistening black hair and a lithe, graceful figure. In another life, she could have been a dancer in the cabarets of Buenos Aires. In those days—twenty years ago—Dolores taught Spanish and was married to a successful dentist. She was the mother of Ludivine and a younger brother, Rudy.

The two families went to the beach at weekends. Fabrice, who normally spent time with old friends, was always happy to come to the beach when Ludivine was there.

After Létitia went to university, first in the Caribbean, then in Montpellier, Anne-Marie saw less of Dolores, although her friend would occasionally phone to chat.

They were difficult years for Dolores, who worried about her son's stumbling progress at school. Rudy was a late reader and by the time he got to high school, he was gravely lacking in motivation. On two occasions, he had to repeat his year and, in time, started hanging out with the wrong set. One morning Dolores phoned Anne-Marie to say that she had discovered her son was skipping classes to spend the day in the ghetto at Lauricisque. At seventeen, he was smoking marijuana. Yet, Dolores said, the more she worried about her son, the more Rudy resented her concern.

The headmaster at the Baimbridge lycée was a man called Jean Marie, who had been at school with Dolores's husband. They were both Freemasons, and on hearing of Rudy's errant behavior, Jean Marie had suggested Rudy should attend his lycée, where, as a favor, he would personally keep an eye on him.

So Rudy changed schools.

Rudy Salcède disliked the headmaster intensely and resented the exaggerated discipline Jean Marie wanted to impose. Yet strangely, for the first time in his life, Rudy started enjoying school. Being the oldest pupil in his class gave him confidence and, with motivation, he found the work easy. His classmates looked up to him. He was elected class representative and, much to everyone's surprise, did well at the end of his first year. The teachers appreciated his attitude.

Dolores still found cigarette papers in his pockets, but no longer worried about her son. Rudy seemed to have found his way.

***

Santo Domingo de Guzmán, Dominican Republic

"I haven't seen you in nine years," Dolores said.

"When Létitia left to get married, there was no point in my staying on in Guadeloupe."

"That doesn't stop you from staying in touch with your friends."

"I came as soon as you contacted me."

"Your son gave me your Skype address, Anne-Marie."

"Really?"

"He says you've become a recluse."

"My children are adults. They have their own lives to lead."

"He says you never see the grandchildren."

Scratchy merengue on a distant radio. In a corner, Luz sat on a small chair, her arms wrapped around her knees, a look of contentment on her copper face.

"What were you doing in Canada, anyway?" Dolores shivered, "How can anybody want to live in a place like that? All that snow."

"Tell me who you've been murdering, Dolores."

***

Guadeloupe, French West Indies

Rudy was one of the few pupils who went to classes at the lycée until the very end of the last term. One morning, in late May, just days before the Baccalaureate, Jean Marie stopped him at the school gate. The headmaster, potbellied and threatening, glowered as he placed a hand on Rudy's chest, abruptly stopping him in his tracks. He asked Rudy where he thought he was going. Rudy replied. Jean Marie then asked why he was wearing his jeans low on his hips and why his hair was not combed.

"There are no rappers here, young man. This is not the Bronx. This is my school, my lycée; it is not a ghetto," Jean Marie shouted, his face flushed with indignation.

Rudy's parents had told him to be polite, so he said nothing, and, looking down, tried moving past the headmaster into the school premises.

The reaction was unexpected and painful: the headmaster grabbed Rudy's jeans by the belt and forcefully pulled them upwards. "You dress properly in my school."

There were witnesses, and two girls corroborated the headmaster's claim that Rudy had hit Jean Marie. Rudy maintained that he had simply pushed the man's hand away—a reflex action. According to Rudy, Monsieur Jean Marie had stumbled backwards and had fallen to the ground.

Rudy was immediately expelled from the school and for several days, Dolores and her husband worried their son would not be allowed to sit the Baccalaureate. In panic, Dolores phoned Anne-Marie, asking if she could help. "You're an investigative magistrate. You have powerful friends."

Anne-Marie phoned several people. Freemason friends of friends intervened at the educational authority and, over the headmaster's remonstrances, Rudy was allowed to sit the examination, alone in a separate examination hall, with a lone invigilator.

Rudy did well, and the following September he went to France. A few years later, he graduated with a degree in psychology.

***

Santo Domingo

"Many people I could have killed over the years, but there's no blood on my hands."

"Why do you want no one to know you're in The Dominican Republic?"

"You remember Jean Marie?"

"The headmaster with the potbelly?"

"Yes. Two months ago, Jean Marie was found floating face down in mangrove."

"What's that got to do with you? Your son left school ten years ago."

"They found his car hidden in the mangrove. My identity card was on the front seat."

***

Guadeloupe

The airport, the city, and the encroaching mangrove swamps grew bigger as the ATR banked. Skyscrapers and slow-moving traffic along the Pointe à Pitre bypass appeared like a picture from a geography book. The airplane flew over the hospital and leveled off. There was a high-pitched ping as the safety belt/no smoking light was turned on.

Anne-Marie tried to relax.

Seen from the sky, Guadeloupe was small. In a New World dominated by the capitalists to the North and the Spanish-speakers to the south, the French island of Guadeloupe beneath the plane looked insignificant. An anomaly: French, isolated, and self-absorbed. Yet, for the eighteen years that Anne-Marie had lived there, the island had never felt strange to her—no more than Bordeaux or Lyons or Besançon. The two wings of a butterfly, transfixed against the blue of the Caribbean waters, had been her home. This was where she had worked and where she had brought up her children.

***

The steward wished her a pleasant stay, and Anne-Marie stepped out of the airplane into the Perspex tunnel leading into the terminal. A long walk, and then there was a wait at immigration.

"Schengen, Schengen," a Haitian shouted, while the uniformed officer looked away in boredom.

There was an even longer wait for the bags.

Sniffer-dogs and the two men at customs glanced briefly at her as she wheeled her luggage through the sliding doors and out into the concourse.

Bienvenue en Guadeloupe!

Welcome to Guadeloupe!

Nou kontent vwe zot!

The concourse was full of people. A man in slacks and a white shirt open at the collar stepped out of the crowd and placed his hand on one of her bags.

Anne-Marie's frown vanished. "Rudy!" she said, and they hugged.

"So glad you could come, Anne-Marie."

"You look wonderful," she said, smiling at the handsome young man.

***

When Anne-Marie woke, it was still dark. Three o'clock in the morning in Guadeloupe. It was hot and sleep eluded her. She tried to empty her mind, but her thoughts kept returning to the past. After half an hour of tossing and turning, Anne-Marie threw off the bed sheet, went downstairs, and wandered around the flat.

Anne-Marie had lived here for nearly two years before moving into a small villa in Gosier, where she had spent the last three months of her second pregnancy. She had always known her ex-husband had kept the flat as a pied-à-terre in Pointe à Pitre but until now she had never been back.

The cupboards and refrigerator were well stocked, yet the place felt empty. Unlived-in and soulless. The dust on the television and the bookshelves stuck to her fingertips. She found a shaving kit in the bathroom, and in the small bedroom where Fabrice had once slept, she came across sanitary towels in a drawer.

Anne-Marie had never seen the photograph before, but she recognized it immediately. September 1980. It must have been taken by one of Lebel's gendarmes at the Hotel Fontainebleau. The telephoto lens had caught Anne-Marie in profile. The photo was in a grainy black and white and was quite flattering. Her chin was resting on her son's head, and he was sitting on her lap.

Looking at the photograph, Anne-Marie could almost feel Fabrice's hot skin and the sand caught in his hair.

That same evening, thirty-five years ago, the gendarmes had arrested her husband.

***

"There was no need to leave," Rudy said.

"Nobody knows Dolores is in the Dominican Republic, staying with your fiancée."

"Luz? My fiancée?" Rudy laughed and shook his head.

"Dolores will be arrested if she comes back here to Guadeloupe."

"Arrested for what?"

"I spent two days with her. Your mother's a frightened woman."

"My mother has a tablet, and she's been calling people on Skype. The police know where she is—but they're not going to arrest her, because there's no proof. Why would my mother want to kill Jean Marie? Any problem she had with him was ten years ago, when I was at the lycée. She's never seen him in all these years."

"Why was her identity card on the driver's seat?"

"If you want to kill someone, the last thing you do is take your identity card along." He clicked his tongue. "Mother's making herself ill."

"She likes being with Luz. She's safe."

"Luz's a nice girl," Rudy said, "but I want my mother to come home."

"Are you saying she's being set up?"

He shrugged. "Killers don't go around with their driver's licenses. Particularly when they're middle-aged ladies."

"She's asked me to help her."

"My mother's panicking for no reason."

A pleasant breeze filled the apartment. They were sitting on the balcony, drinking coffee made with instant chicory and milk powder. Rudy had brought a couple of flakey croissants that Anne-Marie heated in the microwave.

"I don't see how I can help her."

"Mother doesn't need help, Anne-Marie—not yours, nor anyone's."

"If it wasn't her, why was her license found in the car?"

"He was only sixty-three when he retired last year. People like Jean Marie don't retire early, but there'd been complaints. After nearly forty years of him mistreating pupils and teachers, somebody had finally written to the educational authorities at the Rectorat."

"I complained to the Rectorat when there was a problem with Létitia."

"That was twenty years ago and back then the man was untouchable, protected by the unions and the Freemasons.

Now there are social media and Youtube, and kids at school have mobile phones and can film anything. A video of Jean Marie touching a pupil got onto the Internet, so his friends at the Rectorat decided the time had come for him to retire."

"That's when he was murdered?"

"Guadeloupe's politically sensitive. Having Jean Marie running the biggest lycée suited everybody. He imposed discipline, the parents were happy, and the pupils got on with their studies. I loathed the man, but thanks to the discipline at Baimbridge, I got my Baccalaureate and was able to go to university. The guy was a bastard, but people weren't going to complain. A boy slapped around, a girl touched inappropriately, a few lewd insinuations? The lycée's on the edge of the projects, and there's a lot of weed and crack in circulation beyond the school gates. Jean Marie kept the place safe. People willingly overlooked his peccadilloes."

"Why kill him?"

Rudy shrugged. "Jean Marie didn't want to retire, so, to sugar-coat the pill, the Rectorat promoted him. Good for him, because he would get a bigger pension. Personally, I was pissed off. Without the intervention of powerful friends ten years ago, Jean Marie would have prevented me from taking my exams, and I wouldn't be here now, chatting to you, in nice shoes and a Lacoste shirt. Personally I was delighted when I heard on TV he'd been murdered."

Rudy smiled broadly and handed her a newspaper cutting.

The Interregional Directorate of Judicial Police (DIPJ) has been entrusted with a murder enquiry following the discovery yesterday of a dead body in the mangrove under the Gabarre Bridge near Lauricisque, Pointe à Pitre. Rope had been used to tie the arms and wrists behind the victim's back. The victim has not yet been identified.

On Tuesday evening, members of the Lauricisque Kayak Club saw a partially submerged body in the brackish water of the Cul-de-Sac Marin. The instructor immediately alerted the fire brigade, and divers were called in to retrieve the corpse, which was in an advanced state of decomposition. A piece of cloth had been tied around the man's 'neck and a piece of rope fastened the victim's arms and wrists. The nature of the knots would indicate that death was not self-inflicted. An autopsy will determine the cause of death, but the examining medical officer observed signs of drowning, which suggests the victim was still alive when he entered the water of the mangrove.

Yesterday evening, investigators had still not identified the victim. A man of West Indian ethnicity, about sixty years old and well nourished, he was wearing a short-sleeved shirt and trousers, but no shoes or socks. Although the body had been in the water for several days, identification is now imminent.

Anne-Marie handed back the cutting, which Rudy folded and placed in his wallet.

"His wife thought her husband was in Martinique. Then the SUV was found in the mangrove not far from where his body washed up. Mother's ID was found on the front seat."

"How on earth could a woman like your mother kill a big man like Jean Marie?"

"Nobody believes my mother killed anyone."

"Then why is she in hiding in the Dominican Republic?"

When Rudy smiled he looked like his mother, but younger and healthier, with smooth, soft skin. "The police phoned her, and she was summoned to the Commissariat in Pointe à Pitre, but instead she took a plane and went to see Luz. She feels safe in the Dominican Republic."

"Without an identity card?"

"With her passport."

***

Lafitte was a few years older than Anne-Marie. From Roubaix or Lille, he had entered the police after a brief career as a professional cyclist and later he had captained a veteran team. He looked fit. Anne-Marie wondered if he had taken up cycling again. Or even give up rum. His short hair was snow-white.

He still spoke with a hint of a northern accent. "I haven't touched a drop of alcohol since I met Martine," Lafitte said, in answer to her unasked question. "She was my wife's nurse and, at the age of seventy-two, I became a father for the first time."

"Congratulations," Anne-Marie said, surprised by her own sincerity.

They went to a Haitian restaurant opposite the La Croix projects.

It had once been an old wooden shack nestling against the cliff face where once you could buy greasy *bokits*, hamburgers, and beer until late into the humid tropical night. The wooden walls and the corrugated roof had been renovated and where there had been plastic chairs, there was now a dining room with wooden furniture, white tablecloths, and air conditioning.

They ate conch and rice.

"Dolores Salcède didn't murder him," Lafitte said. "Physically, she couldn't have pushed him into the mangrove."

"Perhaps she wasn't alone."

"*Scientifique* went over the car, and I'm merely telling you what I've been told. I retired ten years ago, but I still have friends in forensics. You know something?"

"What?" Anne-Marie asked, and she could sense in the pit of her belly the same irritation she had always felt in Lafitte's company. The man was both unbearably earnest and very sly.

"I loved my job, and working with you was a pleasure, even if you were a hard taskmaster, but I was never as happy as I am now. Life's good."

"Congratulations."

"You should come back to Guadeloupe, Madame, back to the sun and the warmth. What do you want to do in France?"

"I've just arrived from Canada."

Lafitte laughed, showing teeth that were too brilliant to be real. "Jean Marie had been to a ceremony at the Rectorat honoring his contribution to education in Guadeloupe. He was flying to Martinique for another award ceremony. Everyone thought he'd left his car at the airport, and that's why his wife didn't raise the alarm for over twenty-four hours. The SUV was found partially submerged in the mangrove. The PJ think Jean Marie had been tied to the steering wheel, and then released before he drowned. However, his arms were still tied together."

"'A lot of hard work for a killer."

"Killing is hard work," Lafitte said and, for a moment, Anne-Marie's mind reverted to the Nordic television series and the anxious detective in the knitted sweater on the outskirts of Copenhagen. "The murderer pushed him into the water."

"Why?"

Lafitte shrugged his shoulders and smiled. "Hardly the sort of thing a fat lady is going to do, no matter how much your friend wanted to get even."

"But Dolores' identity card was in the car."

He nodded. "Precisely where the investigators would find it."

"That's what' she was scared of?"

"Dolores Salcède hated Jean Marie, and she had a motive, but I'm told she had an alibi. If she'd really killed him, she must have had an accomplice."

"What motive?"

"Madame Salcède was furious at the promotion Jean Marie was getting at the end of his career. The honors and the golden handshake."

"A lot of people were furious. He wasn't a nice man, but they didn't all murder him."

"You know about power better than me, Madame le juge. For twenty years, Jean Marie was useful to his colonial masters. His behavior was inappropriate, and people knew he touched the pupils. But Guadeloupe is France, and France is the land of Dominique Strauss-Kahn, where politicians are pimps, and where we taxpayers subsidize Hollande's bodyguard during his sordid midnight trysts. Powerful men can do as they please with impunity. Liberty, equality, impunity.

"Jean Marie should never have been a headmaster," she said, "but he was recruited by the politicians at a time when France needed to show this island was run by blacks and not by white colonialist masters sent from the mainland. He would have made a perfect sergeant major. A dull, unimaginative man who terrified both pupils and parents, but he did run a tight ship.

"Jean Marie was a socialist, and it suited our regional president to be seen as his friend and mentor. Then, a few years ago, people started talking on Facebook about his violence, collecting information about the man. The Rectorat went into damage control, but parents wanted to know why the *proviseur* talked to pupils about menstruation and why he was touching the girls. There was pressure from the ministry in Paris, and it became clear to his friends at the Rectorat that his time had come. The best way to get rid of him was an early retirement and a golden handshake. Madame Salcède was furious—and she said as much on Facebook."

"Being furious doesn't make you a murderer."

"Of course not."

"Why would Dolores be a possible suspect?"

"On Facebook she had announced she was going to kill Jean Marie."

***

The Dominican Republic
Anne-Marie stepped out of the airport into the hot, damp evening.

Again, Luz was wearing a shift dress. She gave Anne-Marie a kiss on the cheek and smiled as they made their way to the waiting taxi.

"How was your journey?" Out of character, Luz appeared talkative. "How's Rudy?"

Anne-Marie stared through the tinted windows as the car drove towards the city. Bright lights and low buildings, palm trees and heavy traffic.

"I told Rudy you wanted to see him, Luz."

"Rudy's a good man. We're friends, but he doesn't love me. Dolores thinks we are *novios*. She wants me to marry her son, but it will not happen."

After twenty minutes they left the highway and took a slip road to the Zona Colonial.

"Dolores is a good person," Luz remarked. "She's unhappy about Rudy."

Anne-Marie paid the driver with her remaining euros, and Luz ushered her through the three gates.

Dolores got to her feet with difficulty.

***

"Nothing."

Dolores frowned.

"Jean Marie took many secrets to the grave, and that suited everybody. With an open-and-shut case, perhaps his murderer would have been arrested, and there would have been a trial. But an unsolved killing suits all the people who had protected him over the years. Too many skeletons in the cupboard. Even the ministries in Paris were informed of his violence a long time ago, but they never did anything other than push him towards retirement. 'Murder by persons unknown'—it's better for everybody." Anne-Marie smiled.

Dolores relaxed.

"Nobody in the police believes you murdered him. Your identity card stuck on the dashboard? A bit too unsubtle, even for the *Police Judiciaire*."

"I wasn't the only person who hated him."

"Go back to Guadeloupe now, Dolores. You've nothing to be afraid of. His Freemason friends need to protect themselves. The *Police Judiciaire* will go through the motions of interrogating you. You wrote on Facebook that you'd kill him, but you have an alibi. Can a middle-aged woman like you really have overpowered a man like Jean Marie?"

Scratchy merengue on a distant radio.

Luz served coffee and then disappeared from the small kitchen.

Anne-Marie drank slowly. She said, "Rudy killed Jean Marie."

Despite her bulk, Dolores sat back sharply in her seat. She frowned, staring at her friend, and Anne-Marie could remember how she looked all those years ago, when Rudy was causing his mother anguish, and Dolores would try to explain the situation to Anne-Marie.

"Rudy hadn't seen Jean Marie in years."

"You helped him. It was your idea."

Dolores laughed. "Me?"

"I don't know what happened, Dolores. Perhaps you should tell me. You'd been posting on Facebook for a long time, gathering evidence against Jean Marie. Something you discovered must have tipped the balance. I don't know what happened, but I know your identity card was placed carefully where it wasn't going to be overlooked. It wasn't an accident. Somebody wanting to embarrass a much-loved teacher? Not very likely, I'm afraid." Anne-Marie shook her head. "Jean Marie hurt you, and he hurt your son. You needed people to know that justice had been done."

The round face crumpled, and Dolores started to cry, squeezing her eyelids while large tears ran down her cheeks. She looked like an unhappy, oversized child.

***

Dolores accompanied Anne-Marie to the airport, and it was at the last moment, on the long concourse, just before their final hug, that Dolores finally spoke. "You see," she said, as around them passengers hauled luggage and headed for the airline counters, "it was when I saw on TV he was going to be decorated that I realized I was not going to have grandchildren."

Anne-Marie smiled and frowned. "Grandchildren?"

"It had all been in vain. Everything."

"I don't understand."

"Jean Marie was friends with my husband, and the man believed that friendship gave him carte blanche to insult my son. Rudy told me how Jean Marie had always humiliated him. He'd told my son he wasn't a man, that he was little better than a larva, and that he would never have wife and family because no woman would ever want a loser like Rudy.

"Rudy was hurt—he cried in front of me—but for me those insults were an excuse. Rudy's such a good-looking boy, and he has got so much to offer, and he's a good person but …" She made a gesture towards the door. "He was close to Luz when she was studying in Guadeloupe, and they're like brother and sister. I knew that, but I put it down to the insults from Jean Marie. Insults that Rudy in time should and would get over. Then watching Jean Marie on the local TV one evening in September, preening himself and saying how he had devoted his life to the education of the youth in Guadeloupe, I realized it was all lies."

"And?"

"All lies that I'd been telling myself. Lies that suited me. Lies that were easier to deal with than the truth. My son is not interested in women, and instead of thinking it was something Jean Marie had said that handicapped my son, I had to face up to the fact that my son was gay. I was never going to be a grandmother. Worse still, I had to face up to the fact Rudy could never bring himself to tell me the truth about his feelings."

An announcement in Spanish and English told passengers that boarding had started for Air Canada flight 770.

"For years Rudy never told me the truth, but I was to blame because I was no better. For years I never told Rudy the truth, either."

"What truth?"

"One day in Pointe à Pitre, Luz and Rudy took me to lunch, and we started talking about Jean Marie's retirement, and Rudy laughed. He told Luz how he had nearly failed his Baccalaureate. How he had struck the headmaster and how he had been expelled, and how it was the Freemasons who had put pressure on the Rectorat and how he had sat his exams all alone in a big hall with just one invigilator."

Air Canada Flight 770 to Toronto …

"Freemasons? What Freemasons? I had to tell my son the truth, and so I finally did. To both him and Luz."

"What truth?"

"When my son was at the lycée, I was an attractive woman and after all my husband, Rudy, and I had been through, I was not going to see my son denied his Baccalaureate exam. So, in the headmaster's office, I got down on my knees. Those were the days before Jean Marie's prostate problems. I can still feel his stubby little penis in my mouth."

***

Canada

The Airbus dropped out of the blue sky and entered thick grey cloud. The plane hit turbulence, and the flight attendants buckled themselves into their seats.

The wet skies of the north, the encroaching darkness of a Canadian winter.

She shivered, but forty minutes later, when she stepped onto the concourse and heard the delighted screams of her grandchildren, and when she saw the broad, proud smiles of Fabrice and Létitia, Anne-Marie knew she was glad to be back in the cold.

There was nowhere else she would rather be.

Spirits

Michael Stanley

It had been another scorching day in New Xade, with the temperature passing 100 degrees and not a trace of moisture. Usually things cooled off at night in the Kalahari, as the sand threw the heat back at the sky, but for weeks it had been stifling at night as well. Constable Ixau lay naked on his bed, trying to catch the breeze from an old desk fan on the table opposite him. Being a Bushman, heat and dryness didn't usually bother him, but the persistent drought was upsetting. *It's a bad time,* he thought. *People are worried; people get angry. There will be trouble.*

Just then there was a hammering on the door and a woman's voice calling him.

"I'm coming!" he yelled, turning on the light. He pulled on a T-shirt and shorts and jerked open the door.

"Q'ema! What is it? What's the matter?" He'd recognized her at once. How not? She was the most attractive girl in the village, and all the young men sought her attention. Ixau had a secret longing for her, but he was much too shy to do anything about it. But tonight she wasn't pretty. She looked as though she'd been crying.

"What's the matter?" he repeated.

"It's my father! He's ... you have to help me. Please. I'm so worried and scared. Can you come at once?"

Ixau wanted to tell her it was all right, that he'd take care of the issue. But he was flustered, and he just stood in the doorway and looked at her.

"He's … I don't know. He's on the ground. Writhing. Saying mad things." She hesitated. "There's blood running from his nose."

Ixau felt icy fingers touch his spine. Everyone knew this was a sign that a man had entered the spirit world, the sign of the shaman. Indeed, Q'ema's father, Gebo, fancied himself as just that, but people laughed at him behind his back and gave him no respect—particularly after he'd promised to bring rain, with no result. Still, these were not matters to be taken lightly. If Gebo had gone to the spirit world, perhaps he couldn't get back? These things were known. Ixau felt the icy fingers again.

"I think a spirit has him! An evil spirit," Q'ema said, as though reading his thoughts. "Will you come? You must come!"

Ixau pulled himself together. "Have you been to the clinic?" When she shook her head, he added, "We must get the nurse. She won't be at the clinic now, but you know where she lives. Go and fetch her. Maybe your father is sick. I'll go to him right now. Don't worry, it will be okay."

She gave him a grateful look and turned to go, but he called after her. "Perhaps you should call N'Kaka too. After you call the nurse." She nodded and disappeared into the night. There was no real Bushman shaman in New Xade, but N'Kaka was old and respected and knew things. If there was indeed a spirit, he might know what to do.

***

Ixau walked quickly to the house where Gebo lived with his daughter. He found the man on the floor with his back propped against a table that had been knocked onto its side. He was breathing fast and, as Q'ema had said, there was blood on his face. When he turned to Ixau, the constable saw a glassiness in his eyes that reminded him of the trances he'd seen brought on by drugs. Maybe Gebo had been trying to communicate with the spirit world and had taken too much? Perhaps that was it.

"Gebo, it's me, Constable Ixau. Are you all right?"

The older man stared at him blankly.

"Where is Q'ema?" Gebo said at last. "I heard her calling in the other world, but she wasn't there."

"She's coming with the nurse. And N'Kaka."

"That old fool? What does he want?" He tried to stand, but couldn't manage. He held out his hand to Ixau, who pulled him to his feet. He staggered, and Ixau had to steady him. Then he grabbed Ixau and shouted, "They're coming for Yuseb! You have to stop them! Yuseb ..." His eyes rolled back and he collapsed, and Ixau had to drag him to a chair, where he slumped, unconscious.

Ixau felt panic. Was the man dying? Should he give CPR? He remembered the brief course he'd done in the police college, but hated the idea of putting his mouth to Gebo's bloody face. He checked his wrist and could feel an erratic pulse. Relieved, he decided to do nothing and wait for the nurse.

Suddenly the small room was full as Q'ema, N'Kaka, and the nurse burst in. The nurse pushed Ixau aside and started examining the unconscious man. N'Kaka tried to peer over her shoulder, but she pushed him away too. Q'ema started to cry.

"I helped him up, and he seemed okay," Ixau told Q'ema, "but then he started shouting something and passed out. I carried him to the chair."

"What?" N'Kaka growled.

"He passed out and I—"

"No!" N'Kaka interrupted. "What did he say?"

What had Gebo said? Ixau wondered. A good policeman would remember. Something about Yuseb? Something about someone coming for him. He told N'Kaka as closely as he could recall.

N'Kaka liked neither Gebo nor Yuseb, who didn't show him the respect he felt he deserved. "It's the spirits who speak through Gebo," he said. "They're angry with Yuseb because he doesn't show them respect. He's in grave danger." He nodded with satisfaction.

Q'ema had stopped crying. "What about my father? Is he all right?"

N'Kaka shrugged. "They are finished with him now."

The nurse looked up from her patient. "Yes," she said to Q'ema. "Once the drugs wear off. What did he take?"

Q'ema looked at the floor. "What he takes to visit the spirit world. He was going to beg for rain, I think. He said they could help if they wanted to."

There was a groan, and Gebo eyes fluttered.

N'Kaka snorted. "He's a fool. They won't listen to him. He has no power. They took him and chewed him and spat him back to us." He turned away and left without another glance at Gebo.

"Help me get him to his bed," the nurse said. "I'll bring him something. He'll be fine in the morning."

"Yuseb," Gebo muttered. "They are coming ..." He groaned again.

Ixau knew his duty. Although he was scared, he knew he must check on Yuseb. He would first fetch his knobkerrie even though it wouldn't help him against powerful spirits.

***

As Ixau walked, his eyes darted all around. He was grateful for the moon—not full, but bright in the cloudless sky. As he approached Yuseb's house, he focused on the path, looking for any unusual tracks—perhaps baboon or hyena prints, because shamans and spirits often used these disguises. I don't really believe in such things, he told himself, yet he scanned around the path intently. But only human footprints—most of sandals made from cut-up car tires—led to Yuseb's dwelling.

When he came to the house, he stopped. The door was slightly ajar and the window next to it was broken. There was no glass on the ground, but if it had been hit from the outside that would be the case. He called out to Yuseb, but there was no response. He called more loudly and thought he heard something. He was glad of his knobkerrie as he pushed open the door and entered quietly.

The house was just one large room, with a table and some rickety chairs, a gas stove, a few cupboards, and a bed. Yuseb was standing next to the bed, wearing only a pair of underpants, looking very angry. "What are you doing in my house? In the middle of the night!"

"I called," Ixau said. "You didn't answer. I thought—"

"I was asleep! Do you know how late it is?"

"It's a police matter," Ixau responded, trying to sound important. "I'm investigating ..." His voice trailed off. He wasn't really sure what he was investigating.

Yuseb waited, looking suspicious.

"I was informed that there might be a problem here. That you might be in danger. Then I saw the door open and the broken window."

Yuseb snorted. "The window's been broken for months. Kids. As for the door, have you noticed how hot it is? Is it against the law now to have the door open? Get out of here! I can look after myself. I don't need you and your stick."

Ixau felt he was missing something. Perhaps if he was a real detective instead of a barely-trained community constable, he would have a clever question. Suddenly he was angry. It was late and he always rose at dawn. His night had been ruined for nothing.

"Goodnight then," he said and walked out leaving the door ajar.

***

The next day, Ixau looked in at Gebo's house. As he'd hoped, Q'ema was also there. She thanked him sweetly for what he'd done and told him that her father was better, although he had yet to rise. She invited him to sit outside under the tree and offered him tea. "It's a little cooler there than inside," she said, smiling. Ixau accepted and smiled back.

While he was waiting for the tea, probably the last person Ixau wanted to see arrived.

"You!" Yuseb said, walking up the path.

Ixau politely rose to his feet and waited for Yuseb to offer a formal greeting.

Yuseb ignored him. "Where is she?"

Q'ema appeared with the tea on a tray.

"What are you doing with him?" He waved a finger at Ixau.

"We're having tea," she replied. "Do you want a cup?"

"Where's your father? I want to see him right now."

"He's unwell. You mustn't bother him."

Yuseb ignored her and shoved past her to reach the house. Ixau jumped to his feet and stopped him.

"She said Gebo wasn't to be disturbed."

Yuseb glared at him, but gave way. "I'll be back."

Q'ema apologized for the scene, then quietly poured the tea while Ixau watched her.

"Call me if he causes you any more trouble," Ixau said, feeling good.

***

After that visit, Ixau sought out Little, his best friend. They were very different: Ixau was conservative and shy, while Little was full of fun, and particularly partial to practical jokes.

Little slapped Ixau on the back. "What have you been up to, my friend?"

Ixau told him about the events of the night before, expecting Little to shrug it off with a wisecrack. But he was surprised. Little looked somber. "I don't like it," he said. "I think

Gebo's playing with fire. If he continues, maybe he'll get badly burned."

Ixau shrugged. Then, cheering up, he told Little about Q'ema.

Again, Little slapped him on the back. "Well done, getting her attention! Even *I* haven't managed that," he concluded modestly. "She likes that Maki—stupid, pretty boy—and Yuseb is after her too. He's always nagging Gebo about it, and since Gebo owes him money he has to listen."

Ixau wondered how his friend picked up all this gossip.

"But Q'ema will make her own choice," Little continued. "She's headstrong. I bet she picks Maki." He looked at friend. "You're in with an outside chance, though."

Ixau laughed and felt his face getting hot.

***

That night, yet again, there was no letup in the heat, and not a sigh of wind. Ixau's fan squeaked and squealed, and he wondered if he could somehow oil it. He touched the casing and was alarmed by how hot it had become. He turned it off hastily. At once the stillness and heat of the night closed in on him, and all he could do was lie on his bed and hope he could sleep.

He was wakened by the wind. The curtains were flapping wildly, and he could hear sand being hurled against the outside wall, like some creature trying to get in. He leaned out to see what was happening, and immediately his nose and mouth filled with fine sand.

Reluctantly, he closed the window and tried to get back to sleep. But with no air at all now, his room was stifling. He tried the fan, grateful for even the hot breeze, but its squeaking and his worry about it burning out kept him awake. About half an hour later, the wind dropped and everything was as before.

And half an hour after that, Q'ema was banging on his door again.

This time she was hysterical, claiming the spirits had attacked her father or even killed him. Maybe N'Kaka was behind it: he had powerful spirit allies and disliked her father, she gabbled. Or maybe there were no spirits, and it was Yuseb.

Ixau just nodded, put his arm around her shoulders, and then hurried her towards the house. When he saw Gebo, Ixau caught his breath. This was much worse than last night. Not only was Gebo's nose bleeding, but there was also blood all over him. He was wearing a yellow, plastic rain jacket, unbuttoned, and old khaki shorts, both of which were stained with dried blood.

"We went to bed early," Q'ema told Ixau. "Both of us were tired after last night. I was asleep right away. Then I thought I heard grunting and scrabbling noises and my father's voice. I couldn't hear what he was saying, but it was something to do with Yuseb. I was scared, but I came out quietly and found him like this!" She started to sob. "I tried to lift him, but he's too heavy, so I left him there."

"Was he alone?" Ixau asked. He was on his knees, checking Gebo's vital signs.

She nodded through the tears.

"He's alive," Ixau said, gently pulling the raincoat loose. "And I can't see any wounds." He stood up. "We have to get him to the clinic, then maybe drive him to the hospital in Ghanzi. I don't know where all this blood's come from."

He washed his hands in the sink.

"I'll get the nurse," he continued. "And bring the police car and a stretcher. And another man to help. Will you wait with him?"

She nodded, but looked scared.

"I won't be long."

***

Half an hour later they had Gebo at the clinic. As they carried him in, one of the men dropped his end of the stretcher, and the shock aroused Gebo. He started shouting about Yuseb and about spirits and shamans. Then, apparently exhausted, he lapsed into a fitful sleep.

None of it made sense to Ixau, but he had a suspicion that Yuseb was deeply involved in whatever was going on. He was determined to find out what that was, and the sooner the better. Once the nurse had decided that there was no need to rush Gebo to Ghanzi, Ixau collected his knobkerrie and headed off.

He walked up to Yuseb's house, announced himself loudly, and banged on the door. Once again there was no reply. Ixau banged again. "It's the police!" he shouted, rather enjoying himself. When there was still no response, he shoved the door open.

Although the light was off, there was enough moonlight to see Yuseb. He was lying on the floor naked. The first thing that registered with Ixau was that Yuseb's throat had been torn out, leaving a gaping, bloody hole in its place. His face was disfigured by deep, vertical scratch marks. His mouth hung open, and his eyes stared blindly.

Ixau shook so badly that he dropped the knobkerrie as he backed out of the door.

***

Ixau had been very shaken when he called the Ghanzi Criminal Investigation Department in the middle of the night. They had taken him seriously, and the next morning they sent Sergeant Segodi with a forensics guy, as well as a constable with a pickup to collect the body. However, forensics turned out to be a waste of time. Fine sand from the dust storm had blotted out everything.

A tall Motswana, Segodi towered over Ixau and the other Bushmen. As he sipped his bush tea, he looked around Ixau's office with approval. The desk was clean and clear except for a few neatly stacked files. Segodi disliked anything that was untidy, including unexplained dead bodies. He had already decided what had happened to Yuseb; it was only the details he needed to fill in.

"Obviously he was attacked by a wild animal," he told Ixau. "What do you have around here? Lions?"

Ixau shook his head. "I've never seen a lion here, sir. In the Central Kalahari Game Reserve there are lions, but they don't come out here." In fact, Ixau had never seen a lion.

"What do you have? Leopard? Hyena? They can be dangerous if cornered. Maybe Yuseb came back and it was in the house. You said he leaves the door open. And a leopard could get through the broken window anyway."

Ixau considered that. It didn't seem right. "Why would it go in the house?" he asked. "There *are* leopards—sometimes they take a goat—but why go inside the house?"

"Perhaps he had some meat or something that attracted it."

Ixau nodded. He supposed that was possible, but he didn't think it likely. Another thought occurred to him. "Maybe a baboon? We had some around a few weeks ago, looking for water. The dogs went for them, but baboons are vicious. One dog got too close and the baboons tore it apart."

Segodi nodded. "Baboons," he said thoughtfully. "That's a good possibility. The big males are aggressive, and their teeth are really something." He paused. "Have you got a firearm?"

Surprised, Ixau shook his head. Police in Botswana didn't carry guns.

"I have a rifle in the vehicle. I'll leave it with you, and some ammunition. You better warn people to call you if they see any wild animals. Especially baboons. It's probably the drought and shortage of food that's getting to them."

Ixau nodded slowly, worried because evil spirits often took the shape of baboons or hyenas. But he kept that to himself.

He cleared his throat. "There is one thing you should know, sir. There's a man called Gebo who lives here. The last two nights he's been raving about Yuseb being attacked by evil spirits. I don't believe in such things, of course, but last night he had blood on him. The shamans do that sometimes in a trance. Bleed, that is." He hesitated. "That's why I went to see if Yuseb was all right."

"Where was the blood? Was there a lot?"

"On his face and clothes. Quite a lot."

"You're not sure it *was* a baboon, are you?"

Ixau shrugged. "They sleep at night. And make a big mess if they get into your house."

"What else could it be?"

Ixau shrugged again. "Maybe a leopard ... I don't know, sir. But how did Gebo know?"

Segodi frowned. It was a loose end, and he didn't like loose ends. "We'll do this by the book. I'll send the body for autopsy in Gaborone. And we'll interview this Gebo. But I'm leaving you that rifle, and you'd better keep it handy for baboons. Or leopards. They say that once they taste human flesh they become man-eaters."

Ixau nodded, although he thought that was lions, and Yuseb hadn't been eaten as far as he could tell.

***

Q'ema answered the door and showed them into the living room where Gebo was propped in a chair. He seemed fine, but his eyes wandered, as did his mind. The interview was painfully slow: Ixau had to translate for Segodi, and Gebo's answers were often confusing, forcing Ixau to dig further. Q'ema sat quietly until she was asked a question, and her answers agreed with what she'd told Ixau the night before.

After half an hour, Segodi summed it up. "So he was here all night, didn't take any drugs or alcohol, but had visions and saw spirits." He snorted. "His daughter slept through most of it, but woke when she heard him shouting, apparently to himself. What do you make of it?"

Ixau was cautious. "He may be a *seer*, Sergeant. Maybe he saw the future. Maybe he saw something attacking Yuseb."

Segodi raised his eyebrows at that, but didn't comment. Instead, he turned to Q'ema. "Do you have the clothes your father was wearing last night? With the blood?" She understood enough Setswana to respond, "I washed what Father wore. Only not yet his jacket." She rose and returned from the back room with the yellow raincoat that Ixau had seen the previous night. It was still crusted with blood.

Segodi stuffed it into a plastic bag he'd brought with him. "Give her a receipt for it," he told Ixau. "And write this up. I have to get back to Ghanzi." He stalked off without another word.

***

After he'd finished the report, Ixau had a chance to think about what had happened. He was attracted to the sergeant's simple explanation—a wild animal's frenzied attack—but it didn't seem right. His mind jumped to spirits who took animal form. That's what N'kaka believed. Ixau told himself this was nonsense—old Bushman tales were no longer relevant in the sad world of New Xade. Other possibilities also nagged at him. Who were Yuseb's enemies? Perhaps someone else who wanted Q'ema for a wife? He decided he should pay Maki a visit.

When Ixau reached his house, Maki was just walking up with his goats.

"I'd like to ask you some questions," Ixau said.

Maki nodded. "Okay. But I have to water the animals first. We've been looking for grazing in the bush. There was no water. And precious little food for that matter."

He turned his back on Ixau and ran the tap into a water trough. The animals jostled each other to drink. Clearly they'd been without water for several days.

"Where did you go?" Ixau asked after Maki had stuck his head under the tap to wash the dust off his face.

"Into the bush. There." Maki pointed vaguely to the east.

"Why?"

"I can't afford to buy them food! Everything in town's been eaten. I had to take them out. I've been there for three days. Last night I was caught in the dust storm. I thought I was going to join the ancestors, but the goats found a spot behind a sand hill, and we huddled there."

Ixau hesitated, not sure what else to ask.

"What's this all about?" Maki asked.

"Yuseb. He was killed last night. Maybe a wild animal. Maybe something or someone else. I thought you might know something."

There was no doubt about the shock on Maki's face. "Yuseb?" It was almost as if he'd expected bad news, but not this. After a few moments, he burst out, "Why would I know anything? I was in the bush. What happened to him?"

Ixau told him, then asked about Q'ema. Maki looked angry. "She likes *me*! Yuseb wants her and tries to use the money Gebo owes him to buy her. Gebo wants her at home looking after him, so he won't agree. But she wants me."

They talked for a little longer, then Ixau left. Everything Maki had told him struck him as true. But he had a feeling there were things Maki hadn't told him that might be important.

***

A few days passed, and no one spoke of anything but Yuseb's death. The explanations became progressively more fanciful and often more scary. N'Kaka held court, and everyone flocked to him for advice. If there *was* an evil spirit about, who knew what it might do next? Ixau was worried about that too. He was trying to put these thoughts out of his mind when Little burst into his office with Old Marta.

"Old Marta has a story to tell you," Little announced. "I told her that she must come immediately. It's really important."

The old woman glanced around the office and sat down opposite Ixau.

She nodded. "I'm here to tell you something, but I'll have some Rooibos tea first."

Once the tea was ready, she said, "Gebo went to see Yuseb the night he was killed."

"Gebo? But—"

"I saw him."

Ixau took a breath. "You'd better tell me the story from the beginning."

"I woke late that night. Ever since my last child, I have to go to the toilet all the time. The nurse says—"

"Yes, yes," Ixau interrupted. "But what did you see?"

"I thought I heard something and looked out of the window. Gebo was walking past towards Yuseb's house."

"How did you know it was Gebo?"

"He was wearing that old raincoat of his. The yellow one. I suppose he thought there was a storm brewing. The wind had already started."

"Did you speak to him?"

She shook her head. "I was on the toilet and looked out of the window. I thought it odd that he was out so late. What was he doing? Where was he going? That's what I wondered."

"Did you see where he went?"

Again she shook her head. "I went back to bed. When I heard about the terrible things that had happened, I wondered if Gebo had been possessed by an evil spirit or was under the power of a shaman." She shuddered theatrically. "I talked about it to my friends, and one spoke to Little, and he said I must tell you."

Ixau felt a momentary irritation that she hadn't come to him at once.

"What time was this?"

She shrugged. "Late, but before the storm."

Ixau asked her several more questions, but she had nothing to add. Eventually Ixau wrote a statement for Marta to sign with a cross. She finished her tea and left.

Little slipped into the chair she'd vacated. "You realize what this means?" he asked. "Gebo killed Yuseb! I wouldn't be surprised if the whole story about spirits was just an act. Or maybe he *is* possessed. Who knows what he'll do next? Even hurt Q'ema. We must arrest him at once!"

"I'll speak to my superior officer," Ixau said. "He'll instruct me what to do."

Ignoring Little's pacing about the tiny office, he phoned Ghanzi CID.

Segodi listened to the story without interrupting. Then, after a pause, he said, "Well done, Constable. This is *very* important evidence. I have some information also. I spoke to the pathologist in Gaborone. He told me that he's almost certain the wounds on the victim are not from an animal. The slashes on the face are too sharp for teeth or claws, and he thinks the throat was cut out, not ripped or bitten. And Forensics thinks the blood on that jacket is Yuseb's—it matches his blood type. We'll have to wait for DNA tests to be sure, but with your witness we've got enough to bring him in. Can't figure out a motive though."

Reluctantly, Ixau told him about the money and the fight over Q'ema.

"Interesting," Segodi responded. "Keep an eye on him. I'll head out there now with a constable."

***

Ixau explained to Gebo what was happening, and then the constable from Ghanzi sat with him in Segodi's Land Rover. Gebo looked shocked, but didn't create a fuss. Next, Ixau told Q'ema that they needed to search the house and that she should pack a bag for her father. She objected and argued, but eventually did what he'd asked. Ixau tried to reassure her but she brushed him aside.

Then he joined Segodi going through the drawers and cupboards.

"She your girlfriend?" Segodi asked.

Ixau shook his head. "Just someone I know, sir."

Segodi glanced at him. "But she came to *you* when her father was supposed to be ill that night."

Ixau was about to respond, but then he lifted some cleaning cloths in a drawer and saw the knife. It was a hunting knife, and there were brown stains where the handle held the blade. He called the sergeant, who came over and carefully lifted the knife by the tip of the blade using one of the cloths. They were both sure that they'd found the knife that had killed Yuseb.

***

Slowly, things returned to normal. There were no more events and the arguments now revolved around whether Gebo had killed Yuseb out of anger or drugs or whether he'd been possessed and forced to perform the fatal act. N'Kaka was the main proponent of the second argument, warning anyone who'd listen to be careful lest they suffer the same fate.

Gebo maintained his innocence, despite the raincoat stained with Yuseb's blood, the knife with its telltale traces, and Old Marta's evidence. No one believed him.

Q'ema spent her time with Maki. She listened to Ixau's reports on her father, but was very distant. At first Ixau thought it must be because she blamed him for her father's arrest, but then he started to wonder. Why *had* Q'ema come to him that night? Her father was raving or unconscious—clearly ill. Why not go to the nurse? Or to her boyfriend, Maki, if she needed support? Or even to N'Kaka, if she believed her father was possessed? Why to a shy policeman she hardly knew?

And Yuseb. Would he have let a man with whom he was on bad terms approach him in the middle of the night with a hunting knife? While he was naked? The night before he'd been wearing underwear. Of course, the killer could have removed it, but why? On the other hand, there was an obvious reason why a man would remove all his clothes.

And the raincoat? Why had Q'ema washed everything, but not that? It was a plastic coat—easy to rinse out. And the knife had been poorly hidden and still obviously stained with blood.

He had another talk with Maki, this time over a few beers, and discovered that Maki had been told to be away for a few days, and who had told him.

He visited Old Marta and asked to use her toilet. It was then Ixau realized he'd been played for a fool.

At last, with a heavy heart, he went to talk to Little.

***

The next morning Ixau found Q'ema alone at the house and asked her to join him for a walk. She said that it was too hot, but agreed, provided it wasn't far. After several minutes, when it was clear that they were walking towards Yuseb's house, Q'ema stopped.

"Where are we going?"

"This is far enough," Ixau said. They'd reached Old Marta's house. "I want to show you how lucky you were." He paused. "The moon was up there." He pointed behind them. "So it was at your back and quite low by then. Old Marta saw you from her toilet window, which faces the street." He pointed it out to her. "If the light had been better, she would have realized it wasn't Gebo walking past, alone, in the middle of the night."

"What are you talking about? Marta saw my father. She said so. Do you think she made a mistake?"

"There is Yuseb's house right ahead. Did you have anything on under that raincoat? Probably not. You offered Yuseb for free what he was trying to buy from your father. All you had to do was get him close enough. You knew it would be easy to clean the blood off your body afterwards. You'd have plenty of time with your father drugged. Easy to slip that coat on him too. I suppose you also told him the stories about Yuseb, so he'd think he'd heard it from the spirits. People are susceptible when they're scared, drugged, worried."

"You're mad, Ixau! I'm going back now."

"Yes, let's go back. What I can't work out is why you did it. You could just have gone off with Maki."

Q'ema swung on him. "That's what you think because you're a man! Because men have choices. Women here have no choices. They own nothing and have to do what the men—husbands, fathers—tell them. My father wouldn't even let me marry. He wanted me at home for his servant!"

She tried to hurry on ahead of him, but Ixau easily kept pace.

"Leave me alone!"

Ixau grabbed her arm. "No, Q'ema. You used me. It was more than luck, wasn't it? First me falling for you, then being seen by Old Marta from just the right angle, then the dust storm. What did you get to help you, Q'ema? Maybe N'Kaka knows. The ancestors certainly know. So, when he joins them, your father will also know, and be very angry. You'll *never* be free of him. Or from the ancestors. All of them. Can't you sense their anger already? I can."

She turned on him. "My father? He didn't only want me at home for a servant! You and your ancestors can go to hell!"

They'd reached her house, and she tried to close the door in his face, but Ixau forced his way in. But then he stopped dead.

"Oh, my God. The ancestors are all around us here. Oh God." Ixau turned as if to run from the house.

Q'ema looked at him, shocked. "I don't hear any ..."

The wardrobe at the back of the room started to shake. Ixau spun round to look at it, and Q'ema turned too, horror written all over her face.

The cupboard door opened a little, and a white, skeletal arm reached towards them. Q'ema screamed and rushed from the house.

The cupboard door opened fully, and Little climbed out, his arms caked in white clay.

"That was a good joke," he said, but he sounded doubtful. They could still hear Q'ema's screams.

"We must take her to Ghanzi now," Ixau told him.

***

Some days later Gebo came back. The police van dropped him at his house with the same bag Q'ema had packed for him several weeks before. He stood in the dirt road watching the dust build up behind the van as it accelerated on its way back to Ghanzi. Then he picked up his case and walked into his empty home.

News of his return spread quickly, and several people made their way to his house: his friends with small gifts—a bottle of beer or a few cigarettes—to ease their consciences. Even N'Kaka went, but he didn't take a present. Soon the house was too small, and the group settled outside under a thorn tree. Gebo said little but drank the beer he'd been given, while his friends told him that they'd always known that he wasn't responsible for killing Yuseb. They admitted they'd believed him possessed by an evil spirit; no other explanation had seemed possible. Gebo nodded, seeming to accept that.

"Yes," he responded. "Indeed an evil spirit was to blame. I *saw* these things."

N'kaka nodded.

Word that Gebo was back soon reached Little, and he searched out Ixau and told him.

"I don't think I'll go there now," Ixau said. "Perhaps later, when Gebo is alone."

Little shook his head emphatically. "People will say you're ashamed. You, who were responsible for finding the real murderer, and also for getting Gebo released."

Ixau hesitated. "Sergeant Segodi thought it was a leopard. I could've said nothing about Gebo or Q'ema."

Again Little shook his head. "You did your job! That girl was mad!"

Ixau didn't respond, but hauled himself to his feet, and the two of them headed for Gebo's house.

Ixau hadn't expected to be welcomed, and he was right. As they approached, the talking died away. Gebo said nothing until Ixau greeted him respectfully.

"You! You dare come here? You're to blame for all this!" He spat the words at the constable.

"I apologize for arresting you. I made a mistake."

Gebo brushed that aside. "Don't you know what you've done? Without your meddling, everything would've been all right in the end."

"But Q'ema—"

"You're such a stupid fool!" Gebo interrupted. "*She* was the one possessed. I'm a *seer*, and that's what I *saw*. I just didn't understand it at the time. If you hadn't meddled, the spirit would have left her. She could have had her life."

Ixau stepped back, as if he'd been slapped.

"My life is over anyway. And so is hers!" Gebo was shaking with anger.

Ixau wanted to explain that this was nonsense, but the words jammed in his throat. He looked around at the faces—some shocked, some curious, some even hostile. Little started to say something, but N'Kaka interrupted him. "It is as Gebo has said," he stated firmly. "Gebo *saw* this, but not clearly. As if reflected in a muddy pool."

"Get out of here!" Gebo shouted. "You—" He hissed a name that Ixau wouldn't throw at his worst enemy.

"Just you wait a minute!" Little began, now as angry as Gebo. But Ixau stopped him from speaking further. "Come," he said to Little. "They live in a world that no longer exists."

Ixau turned and walked away. After a moment's hesitation, Little went after him.

There was dead silence until the two young men were out of sight. Then everyone started to talk at once.

The Man in Prampram

Kwei Quartey

After decades of service all over Europe, Patrik Blom developed a medical condition called cryoglobulinemia. When the weather was cold, as it was so often in his native Sweden, abnormal proteins in his blood thickened and closed off his blood vessels. The result could be as mild as mottled skin or as severe as kidney failure ... or death.

So Blom had decided to relocate to Ghana, which has a hot climate and excellent beaches. Since cold weather could kill him, he had no intention to return to his frigid homeland. The second, and no trivial motive, was that police authorities all over Europe had been trying to hunt him down for years.

Blom had abhorred the dust and bludgeoning noise of Accra, so he moved to Prampram, a beach community thirty miles east of the capital, and built himself a fine house. That was before too many Americans and Europeans started to follow his example.

March was Ghana's hottest month. Were it not for the mitigating ocean breeze at night, it would have been impossible for Blom to sleep. He could only use a ceiling fan, because an air conditioner might drop the ambient temperature too low and provoke his illness.

The day he met the beautiful woman, he woke at seven in the morning and went for a thirty-minute run. After his shower, he dressed and emerged from the side door of the bedroom directly onto the shaded back porch, where Kojo the houseboy brought him his customary breakfast of a bowl of fresh fruit, two soft-boiled eggs, and four slices of buttered toast with Made-in-Ghana pineapple preserves on the side. As he ate, he took in the peaceful, unobstructed majestic view of the cyan Atlantic Ocean. The waves were fringed with churning white foam as they broke and ran up the tawny sand in an infinite cycle. Sometimes, when Blom thought back to childhood summers swimming with his brother Markus in the Swedish Archipelago, he laughed at what they had considered 'warm water'.

Around nine in the morning, Blom and Kojo strolled to the shore for the fresh catch of the day—red snapper, tuna, and grouper. The fishing canoes came in slowly. They took form as they came closer—long, hand-carved vessels with pointed sterns and bows, two or three muscular fishermen in each. As they came into shallow water, the fishermen hopped out and ran their canoes up onto the shore. Piled on the bottom of each was the overnight fish haul.

Market women wrangled with the fishermen over the price until they got what they wanted. They filled their metal pans and buckets, and someone nearby helped lift the loads onto their heads. Together, Kojo and Patrik bargained with a fish seller, Patrik, mixing English with his bad Ga-Dangme. Once upon a time, the fishermen would have inflated their prices because he was a white man, but after the decade he had lived in Prampram, they knew him too well to try that.

Blom spotted someone that took his attention. And his breath. About fifty meters away, farther up on the sand, a young Ghanaian woman was also buying fish. She was tall, very dark, with glistening, smooth skin, and not a trace of sweat in the already brutal heat. She had long, braided hair that flowed to her shoulders, and she wore a bright yellow blouse that contrasted shockingly and beautifully with her blackness. Blom was transfixed as he watched her for a good long minute. As she finished her transaction, he snapped out of his trance and made his move. "I'll be right back," he told Kojo.

***

She was already leaving when he caught up with her. Up close, she was even more flawless than from a distance.

"May I take that?" he offered, holding out his hand to her purchase wrapped in a plastic bag.

She inclined her head to one side. "Depends," she said. "Are planning to give it back?"

"I am," he replied. "Unless you would like me to cook for you."

Her eyes flashed, and she smiled, a set of brilliant whites behind soft, plump lips. Kissing a black woman was like nothing else in the world, and in his mind he felt her mouth.

"Certainly an unusual offer, Mr. ..."

"Blom," he said. "But call me Patrik, please. And you are?"

"Rowena. Pleased to meet you." She held out her hand, but he kissed the back instead of shaking it. She was surprised, but pleasantly, and she laughed lightly. "Such a gentleman. Where are you from?"

"Sweden."

"I've always wanted to go there."

"Really?" He smiled. "May I walk with you ... wherever you're going? Or would that be improper of me?"

"No, not at all. Come along. It's not far. I'm staying with my friend Janet for a couple of days. I live in Accra."

They strolled, side by side. In Prampram, one never needed to hurry. Rowena told him she had visited the town only once as a small girl, long before people started building fancy beach houses and gated properties selling for tens of thousands of dollars.

Blom told her how much he loved Prampram. "But I'm afraid it's going to be ruined by all this," he said, gesturing at a nearby development of six identical homes sitting on land that still had not been cleared of wild brush. In the opposite direction was the Pointe Coconut Beach Resort, with its rows of beach chairs and tables under clusters of palm trees.

"Will the build-up drive you away?" she asked him.

"I don't know," he said a little sadly. "I don't want to leave."

They walked on.

"Do you go back to Sweden from time to time?"

"No, I don't. Not much reason to return. I'm retired, divorced, and estranged from my ex-wife and children."

Rowena said nothing to that, but sent him a look of empathy, which made him smile inwardly. He found her utterly beguiling.

"What did you do before you settled in Ghana?" she asked.

He shrugged. "Civil servant," he lied. "Tedious government work."

"Is that what drove you away from Sweden?"

"No," he said. "The cold weather did."

***

Two weeks earlier

On the second floor of the Criminal Investigations Department in Accra, Detective Sergeant Adwoa Tagoe sat with her boss, Chief Superintendent Nas Opoku. He was an odd-looking man with a high, shiny forehead and a jutting chin that looked like an outcrop of rock.

"Interpol believes they have finally tracked down a man they've been trying to catch for more than ten years," he was saying. "They say he's a master of disguise." He moved his laptop over so she could click through the headshots. "See what you think. They claim all of these men are one and the same."

Each image had a corresponding name underneath it. Patrik Blom; James Windsor; Helmut Schlein; Emmanuel Carlberg; Andre Blix; Conrad Freeman. Windsor and Carlberg had mustaches and beards, but the others did not. Green-eyed Blix had a shaved head, while Carlberg, with hazel eyes, had a full head of hair. Freeman wore thick, unappealing glasses, and Schlein sleek, modern eyewear. Blom was lean, but Windsor was chubby.

"If these are all the same man," Adwoa said, "he's a magician."

"They say he uses prosthetics in his cheeks, colored contact lenses and other devices to change his appearance," Opoku said. "He has many forged passports and false birth certificates. Most of the names are made up, but Blom, Carlberg, and Blix belong to deceased individuals. The Swedish authorities think the guy who stole those identities is a man now living in Prampram under the name 'Patrik Blom'."

"What's Blom's real name?" she asked. "Or don't they know?"

"As far as they can gather, he was born Johan Skog. Besides passport fraud and identity theft, he's now been linked to assassinations in Sweden, Finland, Estonia, Germany, and Greece over a period of almost twenty years. Some were standard political killings—prime ministers and so on. Others appeared to be personal vendettas, like the murder in Finland of the CEO of Nokia about ten years ago."

"Then this man Skog in Prampram is dangerous," Adwoa said. "If he really is Skog."

"That is the question," Opoku said, nodding. "Is Blom actually Skog, and is Skog the man they want? We need to find out if there's enough evidence to issue an arrest or search warrant."

She sat back. "Where do I come in, sir?"

"We know Mr. Skog has … um … a weakness for … uh … beautiful Ghanaian women." Opoku seemed to be choosing his words carefully, and he wasn't looking directly at Adwoa. "That is his Achilles heel, and we are going to use it to our advantage. No male can easily gain access to his house. On the other hand, if you play it right, you can … um …"

"'Seduce' my way in, sir?"

Opoku cleared his throat. "Something like that." He pulled a folder out of his left-hand drawer. "Here are your documents. Your name is Rowena Tagoe. This is your voter's ID, driving license, and, in case it comes up, your passport."

She examined them, not much liking the name Rowena. Ironic that she would have false papers just like Johan Skog did. Or whatever his name was.

***

One week earlier

The room was warm, softly lit and peaceful. Markus Skog held the bone-thin hand of his mother as she lay in a hospice bed in Stockholm. Her voice was so weak that he could barely hear what she had just said. "What, Mama?"

"Where is Johan?" she whispered through parched lips. Her white hair was as light as a wispy summer cloud.

"He's in Africa, remember?" Markus told her.

She turned her head toward her son with almost all the energy she had left in her tiny, cancer-wracked body. "When is he coming?"

Markus's heart was rent. "Mama, he won't come. I've talked to him many times."

She gazed at him with a new fire in her eyes. "Then go and fetch him."

"What, Mama?"

"Go to Africa and bring him back. I want to see him before … before …"

She drifted off to sleep.

***

The Hunter

Alvar Koski was fifteen. He and his father were on the way to Ruka, one of the best ski resorts in Finland. As Ukrit, the chauffeur, drove and Papa did some work in the backseat, Alvar gazed eagerly at the cold, white landscape. For a moment, he turned to glance worriedly at his father. He was the CEO of Nokia. Was it true a lot of people hated him? Alvar put it out of his mind. He didn't want to worry about that right now. It was a time to be happy.

Snow had begun to fall, making the music in the car sound soft and insulated. As they came to a junction, Ukrit slowed the Audi to a stop. Alvar heard the muffled sound of a motorcycle pulling up on the right-hand side, next to Papa. Alva looked and saw a man all in black astride a sleek machine.

"Oh," Alvar murmured in awe. "Papa, look—"

His father never had the chance. The window beside him shattered with a pop, and he crumpled sideways, a bullet through his skull.

***

His father's murder had left a jagged laceration in Alvar's soul, and the wound was still raw. He could still feel the warmth of his father's blood splattering the side of his face, as if it had happened only hours ago. He had waited for the police to catch the killer, but they never did, and so Alvar vowed to personally hunt him down. He began the moment he turned eighteen and received his sizeable inheritance. He didn't need to earn a living the hard way. His investments made money for him. He could travel anywhere he wanted, and he could hire the best of Europe's private investigators. Their sole function was to find the assassin, and he paid them to see, hear, and say, nothing more.

The first tip didn't come for more than a year after Papa's death. A London PI had picked up the trail of a suspect called Andre Blix. Alvar traveled quickly to London, but Blix had disappeared before the wheels of Alvar's private jet had even touched down. Nothing happened for several more months until an alert came in from Corfu that a Helmut Schlein, a vacationing German businessman, bore a resemblance to Blix. But again, the lead evaporated.

After years of dogged, painstaking work, Alvar had found out that the killer's real name was Johan Skog. He went by several aliases, each with a corresponding disguise. Again and again, just when Alvar thought he had caught up with Skog, the trail went cold. Once, Alvar arrived at a bed and breakfast in the French countryside where Skog was reportedly staying. Sig Sauer in his right hand inside his jacket pocket, Alvar knocked on the door with his left.

The housekeeper opened the door. "Oh," she said with regret, when Alvar asked for Skog. "*Il est déjà parti!*"

Alvar had missed Skog by one day.

Now, after a decade of resolute searching, Alvar had traced Skog to—of all places—Ghana. The Swede was living there as "Patrik Blom" in a beach community called Prampram. Like bees to nectar, Americans and Europeans were flocking there to build expensive beachfront houses.

You can run as much and as far as you like, Skog, Alvar thought, but as long as I'm alive, I will be right behind you.

***

In the evening, the man known as Patrik showed Adwoa—the woman known as Rowena—around his house, which had four bedrooms, five bathrooms, a pool in the back, an unparalleled view of the Atlantic, and a thoroughly modern kitchen where Patrik spent a lot of time cooking and eating. She noticed the safe in his bedroom and wondered what was in it.

They sat at the bar overlooking the beach. She drank wine while he had scotch in a shot glass.

"So much space in your home," she said to him. "Don't you ever get lonesome?"

"I do, sometimes," he said. "But not tonight, because a most beautiful black woman has joined me."

"Thank you, my dear."

He threw back the rest of his whisky in one gulp and put down the glass with a sharp crack on the counter. She poured him another.

Later on that night, he was inebriated and morose, leaning against her on the sofa and talking about how his dying mother had not loved him.

"But you must go back to see your Mama before she passes," she said coaxingly. "You have but one mother."

He grunted and groped for more scotch on the side table, but she moved the bottle gently away. If he had any more, he might fall asleep, and she didn't want him to do that yet. She had to keep that loosened tongue working.

***

In his room at the Mövenpick Hotel in Accra, Alvar plotted. He had spent one week carrying out reconnaissance in Prampram to be sure the intelligence was correct. A few discrete inquiries was all it had taken to confirm that Patrik Blom lived in the two-story, white-and-tangerine mansion about half a mile along the beach from the house Alvar had rented.

With a powerful pair of binoculars, he observed his target. Skog was a man of set routines. On Monday mornings, he went jogging for about thirty minutes, after which he had breakfast on his porch. Predictably, around nine, he went to the shore with his houseboy to buy fish. Around seven in the morning Tuesday through Friday, Skog swam, impressively, far out to sea and back. He accessed his secluded beach through a padlocked gate in the wall encircling the house and the back garden. A good amount of shrubbery grew alongside the wall—enough to conceal an assailant.

***

Skog had a bad hangover when Kojo knocked on his bedroom door to check on him. He sat up and groaned, his head pounding. What had happened last night? He had been with Rowena in the sitting room, but now he was in his bed with his shirt open. Had they had sex? He didn't think so. He had been too drunk to perform. What had they talked about, and why had he drunk so much? As he got slowly out of bed, he panicked. *What had he told her*? He felt ill, went to the bathroom, and threw up. He took a shower and felt better.

His phone rang as he came out of the bathroom. Markus was calling from Amsterdam. Johan's heart sank. He had forgotten: his brother was en route to Ghana.

***

It was already warm and muggy by six-thirty that Thursday morning. Alvar had thought the sea breeze would cool the air a bit, but apparently not. Lying under the bushes against the wall near the back gate of Skog's house, Alvar sweated profusely underneath his black clothes. He was covered from head to foot—even his hands were gloved—so no one would see his white skin. He cursed under his breath. How was it so fucking hot in this goddam place? He agreed that winters in Scandinavia dragged on too long, but this heat was utterly ridiculous.

Two minutes to seven. Alvar caressed the Sig cocooned in his palm. A few minutes past the hour, the gate squeaked open. He tensed. Through the leaves and branches, he saw Skog emerge with a towel draped over his shoulders. He was wearing green trunks and sporting goggles and snorkel. He looked around for a moment, and then came toward the bushes. Alvar's heart stopped. *He's seen me.* But instead, Skog dropped his towel on the ground in a heap and bent down to undo his sandals. His head was only inches from Alvar's, but this was not the time to make a move. Skog would jump back and Alvar would miss the shot.

Now the Swede stood up and moved away from the Finn, adjusting his snorkel and goggles. Alvar rose up and emerged from the shrubs. Skog started and turned toward him. Alvar got within two meters and raised the Sig. Skog put his hands in front of him defensively and uttered, "*Nej* ..."

Alvar shot him twice in the face, and Skog dropped like a stone. Then Alvar ran. The motorcycle was waiting where he had left it. He leapt on and sped away, his heart and his mind racing. It was like a dream, but he had done it.

I did it. He was high on endorphins and his insides were screaming with joy.

***

When Adwoa, Nas Opoku, two police constables and two SWAT officers blasted their way into Patrik Blom's compound to take him in, they first found Kojo cowering and weeping in a corner of the kitchen.

"Where is your boss?" Opoku yelled. "Why are you crying?"

Adwoa knelt down beside him. "What's happened, eh?" she asked, more gently.

One of the constables ran in from outside. "Please, sir," he said to Opoku. "You should come. We've found a body on the beach."

Johan Skog, aka Patrik Blom, had a bullet through his forehead and another through his upper right jaw. Oddly, his snorkeling set was still on his face.

Sergeant Adwoa Tagoe arrested an incoherent Kojo for the murder of his boss, even though they couldn't find the weapon anywhere. But Chief Superintendent did find Johan Skog's passport in a drawer in the office.

***

Mama Skog's breathing was labored. She had hours to live at the most. Her eyes fluttered half open, barely enough to see her son.

"Johan," she whispered. "You came back."

She lifted her hand slightly off the bed, and he brought his face down so she could stroke his cheek—the feather touch of a ghost.

"I'm sorry," she said. "I did love you, Johan. I just didn't know how to express it."

Her eyes drifted closed again, and she appeared to stop breathing. The hospice nurse was nearby. Johan looked up at her, and she nodded with an encouraging smile.

"Forgive me," Mama said, coming awake and surprising him. She still had life left.

He stroked her skeletal hand. "I do, Mama." A lump rose in his throat.

She sighed softly. "Where is Markus?"

Even in her final minutes, she could distinguish her sons from each other. They were fraternal twins and often mistaken for one another. Johan didn't have the heart to tell her Markus was dead—shot in Prampram by an unknown assailant. Johan was certain the bullets had been meant for him, not his brother.

***

The brothers had stayed up all night listening to the sound of the waves crashing on the shore, drinking and talking about life and death. At last, Markus had persuaded his brother to return to Sweden with him.

In the morning, Markus wanted at least one swim in the warm Atlantic before he and his brother departed. Johan, who was packing his bags, laughed at his brother with his snorkel set. "You won't see that much, you know," he told him. "Water visibility around here is awful. And Markus, be careful of the rip tides."

"Of course," Markus said, cockily. "I'm as strong a swimmer as you, remember?"

And off he went. After a few minutes, though, Johan felt uneasy and decided he should join his brother and keep an eye on him. The Atlantic was a wild beast, plenty different from the Swedish Archipelago.

As he reached the gate to the beach, Johan heard two gunshots and instinctively dropped to the ground. Then a motorcycle tore off into the distance. Johan opened the gate a crack. His brother lay dead in the sand, a red halo expanding around him.

Kojo would be in for work in about thirty minutes. Johan moved quickly, the way he knew how after all these years. He left his own clothes and passport and took his brother's instead. And then he was gone.

***

Chief Superintendent Opoku tried to reassure Detective Sergeant Adwoa Tagoe that she had done good work, but she was full of regrets and doubts. If she had arrested Johan Skog that night, he would have been still alive. And as for Kojo, she couldn't even think he had murdered his boss.

Skog had wanted to make love to her that night. She held him up as he staggered to the bedroom with her. Hammered, he flopped onto the bed. "C'mere," he said.

She sat next to him, opened his shirt and caressed his hairy chest with a feeling of revulsion.

"Make me hard," he slurred.

"Tell me more about Mama," she said soothingly.

"Nothing to say," he growled, reaching for her breast.

She stopped him. "We'll do that in a little while. Tell me more about Mama. What did she call you?"

His hand dropped. "Stop teasing, Rowena," he muttered, his eyes closing. "Stop being such a goddamn bitch."

He began to snore lightly.

"Johan?" she said.

"Mm?" He started and lifted his head to look at her with some puzzlement. "Don't call me that," he said, and went back to sleep.

He had responded to the name. *Or had he?* He might have, but Adwoa wanted something more solid than that. She went into his office and hunted through the drawers of his desk, hoping to find a fake passport or two. She was disappointed. Nothing. He had a safe, but it worked by fingerprint recognition, so she had no chance of breaking into it. Adwoa went back to the bedroom. Patrik—Johan—had turned over onto his stomach, she'd noticed a mole on his back.

The dead man on the beach didn't have that mole.

But Opoku dismissed her fears. He wasn't even going to have the house fingerprinted. He was satisfied. An international fugitive was dead, and they had the culprit. The weapon? Well, they would keep searching. Meanwhile, the Chief Superintendent was looking good and headed for a promotion.

***

"Markus Skog?" the cute Ivorian hotel receptionist asked, looking up at him from his passport with a smile.

"Yes," he said pleasantly. "That's correct."

"Welcome to Côte d'Ivoire and Bassam Beach Resort," she said. "How long will you be staying?"

"For quite a while, I expect," Johan replied. "I like beaches, and I like hot weather."

The Cigarette Dandy

Barbara Nadel

He was known only as the Cigarette Dandy. Referring to himself in the third person, he would say things like, 'The Cigarette Dandy is feeling very well today,' or 'The Cigarette Dandy thanks you most kindly.' Old and heavily moustachioed, he was thin, neat, and very, very smart. Even more than the silver cigarette holder that forever hung from his lips, the Cigarette Dandy wore clothes that were the height of chic—provided one happened to be living in the nineteenth century. A three-piece, all-wool, night-black suit, a wide fedora, and an astrakhan coat, plus shoes that gleamed with fresh polish. As poised as a model, he was usually to be found sitting in the small tea garden in the Imperial Ottoman cemetery on Divanyolu. Inspector Cetin Ikmen of the Istanbul Police had known him all his life.

But now the Cigarette Dandy was dead.

* * *

'I took him bread and tea every morning,' the young man said. Sitting on the ground between two rows of tomato plants, his hands shook as they attempted to hold the cigarette that Ikmen had given him.

It was only 10 AM, and already the city was melting in the heat. Ikmen had to squint to look across the garden at the tiny building that had been the Cigarette Dandy's home.

'How long had he lived in the shed?'

The policeman had never known where the old man slept until now.

'A year.' The young man, who was called Ismet Oz, looked up. 'He told us he used to live in the gardens beside the city walls at Yedikule. Said the gypsies had let him stay there for decades.'

Most of the centuries-old market gardens at the foot of the city walls had been requisitioned by Istanbul Municipality for new housing. The gypsies who had once tended them were long gone. Ikmen felt how strange it was that someone as fastidious as the Cigarette Dandy had lived there.

'How did he end up here?' Ikmen asked.

'He turned up,' Ismet said.

A lot of people knew about the small vegetable garden that a few young environmentalists had established in the trendy district of Cihangir. In the eighteen months since it had been inaugurated, it had become a popular feature of the area.

'He didn't ask anything from us. He just wanted a place to stay. We fed him because we wanted to.'

'When did you last see him?'

'Yesterday, early evening.'

'Was he alone?'

'Yes. He always was.'

'What did you call him?' Ikmen asked.

'The Cigarette Dandy, same as everyone.'

'Sir, the doctor would like to see you,' his sergeant, Kerim Gursel, interjected.

'OK.' Ikmen put a hand on Ismet's shoulder and told him he'd be back in a little while.

***

It was stuffy in the tiny shed. In addition to the body of the Cigarette Dandy, there were several bags of fertiliser, various garden implements, and the stout figure of the police pathologist, Dr Arto Sarkissian. An ethnic Armenian, he was also Cetin Ikmen's oldest friend.

'I don't actually remember when I first saw the Cigarette Dandy,' the Armenian said, as he removed one set of plastic gloves and put on another. 'I think that I may first have heard stories about him from my father.'

'He was old when we were children,' Ikmen said. 'Or rather he always seemed old to me.'

They both looked at the deceased. His eyes closed, the Cigarette Dandy looked entirely at peace. He could have died naturally—if it hadn't been for his hands. Rather than hanging from his wrists, they lay on the table beside him, each one roughly ripped and mutilated.

Although the floor of the shed was covered in blood, Ikmen had to ask, 'Did he bleed out?'

'Oh yes,' the doctor said.

'And because he couldn't have done that to himself ...'

'He was almost certainly murdered.' Arto cleared his throat. 'Whether anything else was involved, I won't know until I do the post-mortem.'

Ikmen frowned. 'Anything else?'

The doctor winced. 'It was poorly done.'

***

The Cigarette Dandy's identity card gave his date of birth as 1st January 1915, which meant that he was one hundred years old. Not even Ikmen had expected that. What he had also not been expecting was the old man's real name.

'Pierre Yildiz,' he said. Then he repeated, 'Pierre?'

Kerim Gursel opened Ikmen's office window and Ikmen lit a cigarette. Smoking had been banned in indoor public spaces in Turkey since 2009. The Cigarette Dandy had naturally disapproved.

'Maybe his mother was French,' Kerim said.

'What, in 1915? We were at war with France. That's highly unlikely.' Ikmen looked again at the old man's battered identity card. 'Pierre Yildiz, born 1st January 1915 to Mehmed and Nilufer Yildiz. His mother wasn't French!'

'And yet the Cigarette Dandy spoke French,' Kerim said.

'Turkish as well,' Ikmen said. 'I heard him.'

Thinking back to his encounters with the Dandy, Ikmen was aware of the fact that the old man had only ever spoken Turkish when he'd had to. Ikmen had never had a conversation with him in anything but French. Even the name 'Cigarette Dandy' referred to a uniquely Gallic phenomenon. The cigarette dandy, Ikmen had once read, had been as much a feature of nineteenth-century Parisian culture as absinthe or the Folies Bergère. Basically, they were elegant men who didn't need to work and who considered cigarette-smoking both a vocation and an art. Even for a smoker like Ikmen, that was outré.

Ikmen's phone rang. It was his friend and colleague, Inspector Mehmet Suleyman.

'Is it true that the Cigarette Dandy is dead?'

'I'm sad to say that it is.'

Suleyman sighed. 'Another one.' he said.

Ikmen didn't understand, unless he was bemoaning the demise of yet another Istanbul eccentric or if Suleyman knew something that he didn't.

'What do you mean, "another"?'

'Ottoman relic,' Suleyman said. 'My father's cousin last week, now the Cigarette Dandy.'

Mehmet Suleyman came from a vast, aristocratic family related to the deposed Ottoman royal house. Most of his relatives were Prince or Princess something-or-other.

'What have your lot got to do with a mad old man who smoked all the time?'

'He spoke excellent French, Cetin,' Suleyman said. 'Everyone at the Ottoman Court spoke that very precise version of the language. My father was always of the opinion that the Dandy was some sort of aristocrat.'

'Haven't you got enough relatives?'

Suleyman laughed.

'And anyway, his name is Pierre,' Ikmen said.

'Pierre what?'

'Pierre Yildiz. Born 1915.'

'God! Pierre Yildiz?' Suleyman said. 'We were at war with France ...'

'Precisely,' Ikmen said. Then he turned the old man's identity card over to check his religious affiliation. 'Oh, and apparently he was a Christian. And he was murdered.'

'Murdered? Why?'

'I've no idea.'

***

No one at the elegant French Consulate on Istiklal Caddesi knew anything about Pierre Yildiz, although a couple of the Turkish employees knew of the Cigarette Dandy. The Consul General was quite taken aback.

'That is so very anachronistic!' she told Ikmen over coffee and madeleines. 'How bizarre.'

When he left the consulate, he switched his phone on and found that he had a message from Dr Sarkissian. 'Meet me at the Cihangir Garden as soon as you can.'

It was walking distance, so Ikmen took off his jacket and walked briskly. But even though he was careful to walk in the shade, he was still dripping with sweat by the time he turned off Istiklal at the Galatasaray Lycée, or the 'posh boys' school' as he called it, to walk down towards Cihangir. As he entered the garden, he lit a cigarette.

Accompanied by Ismet Oz, Arto Sarkissian stood beside a middle-aged man who was looking, very seriously, down at the ground. When he saw Cetin Ikmen, the Armenian called him over and introduced him.

'This is Dr Guven,' Arto said.

Ikmen shook his hand.

'He's a botanist.'

'That's nice.' Ikmen didn't feel that he needed a botanist to tell him what was, and was not, a tomato plant.

Arto Sarkissian led him away from Ismet Oz and the botanist and said, 'There was poison in Pierre Yildiz's system when he died.'

'What kind of poison?'

'Alkaloids—atropine and hyoscine. He'd ingested dried mandrake root, which is why I called Dr Guven,' he said. 'If it was grown here, then there may be more.'

Ikmen asked, 'What does mandrake root do?'

'It's a narcotic. Its provenance goes back thousands of years. In the past it was thought to have magical properties and was used in pain relief and sometimes as an anaesthetic. Unsurprisingly, the Cigarette Dandy had advanced lung cancer.'

'So it was self-administered?'

'Possibly. He may have been ill for some time; cancer tends to grow slowly in the elderly. But the amount in his stomach was considerable, so he may have intended to kill himself. For the moment, however, we have to find out whether he grew it here and whether there's any more on the site. If kids got hold of it and found out it induces hallucinations ...'

'I see.'

The city was awash with illegal narcotics. What nobody needed was another substance hitting the streets.

Ikmen watched the botanist stroke leaves and reveal flowers. 'So he took this root, and then his hands were ripped off?' he asked.

'Yes. Cause of death was loss of blood, but with that much alkaloid in his system he would have died anyway.'

'So someone murdered him as he was committing suicide?'

'Potentially, yes. Although whether he knew he was committing suicide or not is a moot point. If he'd been using mandrake root as pain control for some time, he may not have realised how much he was taking. Forensics have found traces of the plant in his tea glass but, so far, the rest of his shed is clean.'

'Murder weapon?'

'Nothing,' he said. 'Although I don't think we're looking for a knife, at least not a sharp one.'

Ikmen remembered the jagged edges of the Cigarette Dandy's severed hands and how the flesh had, in places, been almost torn from the bones. 'So if it's not a knife—' he began.

'Some sort of clawed instrument,' the doctor said. 'I'd almost go so far as thinking maybe he was attacked by an animal of some sort. But that's absurd. Any animal that could do that to a person would completely destroy him.'

Cetin Ikmen shook his head. Why would anyone, or any thing, rip off the hands of a dying man?

***

There was no plot of mandrake plants in the Cihangir garden. Wherever the Cigarette Dandy had got his archaic narcotic from was a mystery. Local pharmacists knew how to obtain synthesised alkaloids, but actual mandrake root was unknown to them. Not even the herbalists in the Spice Bazaar, who claimed to be able to cure almost anything, had any in their considerable pharmacopoeias. Could the old man have prepared the plant himself? But if he had, from where had he obtained it?

Ikmen was chewing on the end of a pen and trying not to drift off to sleep in the midday heat when Mehmet Suleyman walked into his office. Kerim Gursel was out, so the two men were alone. Suleyman shut and locked Ikmen's office door and offered him a cigarette.

He sat down. 'Cetin, didn't you tell me that the Cigarette Dandy used to live in one of the gypsy gardens in Yedikule?'

'Yes, but they're long gone,' Ikmen said. 'I doubt whether even the hardiest mandrake could survive urban renewal on that scale.'

The old market gardens by the city walls, together with the gypsy residential district of Sulukule, had not been so much flattened as completely destroyed.

'Gonca told me her family used to grow mandrake,' Suleyman said. 'The gypsies used it for all sorts, including purging and toothache. But it also gets you high and so, of course, some of them just wanted to get a hit. She says her family doesn't grow or use it now. But she knows a woman who still does.'

'A gypsy?'

'Yes. Gonca doesn't really do people outside the Roma community.'

'Except you.'

He smiled. Handsome and unfailingly attractive to both women and men, Inspector Mehmet Suleyman had been conducting a passionate affair with Gonca Sekeroglu, a gypsy conceptual artist, for years. At least ten years his senior, she was the only woman who had ever been able to stop Suleyman from straying.

Suleyman said, 'She's a witch.'

'Like my mother.'

'Yes, and no. Papatya *hanim*, unlike your mother, is a witch who does harm,' Suleyman said. 'She'll get rid of your lover's husband, make a dancing girl fall in love with you, poison your dog. She apparently breeds mandrake plants as pets. She believes they're not plants at all, but little people who scream when you pull them out of the ground.'

'Makes sense ... if this was the thirteenth century,' Ikmen said. 'Mandrake plants, it is said, do make a sort of screaming sound when they're pulled from the ground. Papatya *hanim* sounds like someone I should meet.'

'I'll get Gonca to arrange it,' Suleyman said. 'Papatya *hanim* lives in Sulukule.'

'Sulukule? How? Hasn't that area been "developed"?'

'Oh yes, but even when businessmen tear down a district and then rebuild it in order to extend their property portfolios, they leave the local witch's house alone.'

***

Sulukule wasn't the rackety district that Cetin Ikmen remembered from his childhood in the 1950s. Then the streets had been alive with flower sellers, dancing girls and musicians. A lot of raki had been consumed in the small tavernas that were on every street corner back then, where stories were told of ghosts, dead ancestors, and tragic lovers. As he looked around at the silent streets of poorly constructed new houses, Ikmen wanted to weep.

'Who lives here?' he asked.

Gonca shrugged, then she said, 'Mainly Syrian refugees.' She was a tall, dark woman with thick, hennaed hair down to her ankles. Closer to Ikmen than Suleyman in age, she was nevertheless the light of her lover's existence. As they walked down the middle of a silent, potholed road, Suleyman held her close.

'Weren't "nice, pious" families meant to move into these houses?' Ikmen asked.

'Yes, but look at them.' Gonca laughed. 'Would you move in here? Our people wouldn't live here even if they could afford it.'

But Papatya *hanim* had stayed. Ikmen didn't know how Gonca had set up this meeting with the witch, and he knew better than to ask. Still, he couldn't help feeling that she had to be lonely. They turned a corner and walked up a steep track parallel with the Byzantine city walls. Ikmen gasped for breath and sweated.

'We all knew the Cigarette Dandy,' Gonca said.

'Including Papatya *hanim*?'

'Especially her,' the gypsy said. 'Back in the old days, they could often be seen whispering to each other. The Cigarette Dandy knew that the gypsies would keep his secrets.'

'What secrets?'

She smiled. 'Ask Papatya *hanim*,' she said. 'If she likes you, then maybe she'll tell you.'

***

They stopped in front of a mud-and-breeze-block shack, typical of the old Sulukule. With its thatched roof and crumbling chimney, it looked completely out of place on a street full of empty, faux-Ottoman houses. Gonca knocked on the ill-fitting front door and called out, 'Cuneyt *bey*!'

'I thought we were coming to see Papatya *hanim*.'

'Cuneyt *bey* is her son,' Gonca said. 'She may be a witch, but not even Papatya *hanim* can stop time. She's very old.'

A man, probably in his sixties, opened the door. He had bare feet and carried a tambourine. To Ikmen, who remembered such people, he looked like a street entertainer in the old days. He looked at Gonca and, without speaking, moved away from the door into the shack.

Ikmen recalled peeping out from behind his mother's skirts to look into the homes of Sulukule gypsies over fifty years ago. If Papatya *hanim* place was anything to go by, they hadn't changed. There were still chickens running about on the floor, still dried herbs and cuts of meat hanging from the roof, very little furniture or light, lots of smells—some plant-based, some animal. His mother, an Albanian folk-healer, had always said that only the gypsies really understood magic.

Despite the heat, there was a fire burning in a makeshift grate beside a large, iron-framed bed. Gonca walked over to the bed and spoke to its occupant.

Ikmen turned to Suleyman. 'Out of your comfort zone?'

The younger man fanned his face and brushed invisible dust from his expensive suit.

'Papatya *hanim* will see you now,' Gonca said.

There was stuff on the floor that could have been anything. Some of it crunched, some of it squelched. Ikmen tried not to think too much. When he got to the bed, he saw a tiny woman with a red face surrounded by what, at first, looked like dolls. Closer inspection revealed that they were actually mandrake roots.

The old woman smiled. 'I knew you'd come a-knockin' at some time, lovey,' she said to Ikmen.

Witches, in Ikmen's experience, often claimed prior knowledge of current events.

'Gonca tells me that you knew the Cigarette Dandy, *hanim*.' he said.

'Yes, dear,' she said. Then she looked up at Suleyman. 'Is that Gonca Sekeroglu's young man?'

'Well, er, yes ...'

The old woman looked at Gonca. 'Very handsome,' she said. 'Well done, darlin'!' She turned back to Ikmen. 'And a prince too! Him, not you,' she said. Then she laughed. Then she stopped. 'Pierre *effendi*.'

'Pierre Yildiz,' Ikmen said, 'was the Cigarette Dandy's real name. Gonca *hanim* tells me you know his secret. Was he your prince, Papatya *hanim*? The sultan of your heart?'

The term '*effendi*' would only be used by the old in reference to either an Ottoman prince or someone who was very greatly loved. Could Suleyman's father possibly be right about the Cigarette Dandy? Had he really been a member of the Imperial family?

'I'm dying.'

'We all are, *hanim*,' Ikmen said.

A surprisingly strong hand took hold of his neck, pulling his head close to her face. She whispered, 'No, I am dying *now*.

As you watch me, my body is shutting down. By tonight I will have gone.'

He looked into her eyes, which were, unusually for a gypsy, bright blue, and he knew that she was telling the truth. 'How?'

She let him go. 'Don't you want to know how the Cigarette Dandy died?' she asked. 'That's why you've come isn't it?'

'Yes—'

'Well, there are a few conditions you'll have to agree to,' she said.

Ikmen frowned. 'We don't make deals, *hanim.*'

'Don't you?' She looked up at Suleyman. 'You do. You make a deal with yourself every day. You say, "If I am faithful to Gonca *hanim*, I will let my body do everything it desires to her".' She fixed him with her eyes. 'Things so dirty—'

'What sort of deal do you want to do, *hanim*?' Ikmen cut in. He'd seen the blood drain from Suleyman's face as well as the fury rise in Gonca's eyes.

'Firstly, I want you to promise you will allow whoever took the Cigarette Dandy's hands off to go free,' she said.

***

'He knew he was dying,' she said. 'He was disappointed it was cancer. He said to me, "They'll all say it was because of smoking." He didn't want that. It was his art form.'

'It *was* because of smoking,' Ikmen said. Everyone except the old woman was dripping with sweat. 'May we have some water, please?'

The son poured some from a pitcher in the corner. Whether it had originally been bottled, Ikmen didn't ask. If it had come from a tap, he'd soon know about it in this weather.

'Yes, but you must know how he actually died by this time, dear,' Papatya *hanim* said. 'Poison.'

Ikmen said nothing.

'He did it himself at a time of his choosing,' she said. 'In spite of the fact his church teaches that suicide is a sin.'

'Which church?'

'He was a Catholic, like his mother.'

Ikmen frowned. 'His mother was called Nilufer. Hardly a common French name—'

'There was one thing about his death that did worry him, though,' she said. 'And that was the possibility that he might be buried alive.'

'Buried alive!'

'Christians worry about that,' she said. 'They tell stories about it. They keep their dead for days, sometimes weeks before they bury them.'

In Islam, burials were quick. The soul was believed to be in torment until the body was underneath the ground.

'But that wasn't good enough for Pierre. He wanted his hands cut off so there could be no chance of survival.'

'He wanted that?'

'Yes,' she said. 'He even held his arms out for it.'

'You were there?'

'I was.'

'With the person who ripped the Dandy's hands off?'

'Yes,' she said. 'Now will you swear you will not imprison him?'

***

There was no shade in the little yard behind Papatya *hanim's* shack. The ever-dour Cuneyt *bey* didn't speak as he led Ikmen and Suleyman down a path towards some outbuildings. Noises, muffled and pitiful, came from one of the sheds.

Ikmen said, 'You know this is illegal.'

Cuneyt grunted. As he opened the door, metal chains rattled.

The bear was old, its fur mangy, pus and blood wept from the hole in its nose where the chain that held it passed through the septum.

'God help us!'

It stank. Sitting in its own faeces, the poor creature's whimpering was punctuated only by the occasional impotent swipe of a massive paw.

Ikmen recalled Papatya *hanim*'s words.

'I tried to do what Pierre wanted, but I couldn't. I forbade my son. How could I make my only child a murderer? I asked Cuneyt to bring Erol ...'

The old man, once the witch's lover, had reached out to the bear that had finished what Papatya had started. Only Cuneyt had been able to stop the bear from eating what was his last kill.

'You know I'm going to have to arrange for this animal to be taken away,' Ikmen said.

Cuneyt bent down and rubbed the bear's head. 'All my other bears went a long time ago,' he said. 'Now you'll take Erol. I told mum you would, even if you said you wouldn't.'

Ikmen hadn't been able to promise the old witch that he'd keep the Cigarette Dandy's killer out of prison. Then they'd all heard Erol growl in response to a barking dog. Cetin Ikmen hadn't heard a bear for over twenty years, but as a child who had grown up around them—and their handlers—it was a sound he remembered well. Cuneyt was one of many dancing-bear men who hadn't been able to find a place in the world after their trade was made illegal. Cuneyt began to cry.

'This is all because mum made a promise she couldn't keep,' he said.

'To the Cigarette Dandy?' Suleyman said.

'To her prince,' Cuneyt said through tears. 'And my dad. She says he has to be buried with his hands because of his religion. You can do that, can't you?'

***

Papatya the witch knew her drugs. She had taken enough mandrake to kill herself yet leaving time to speak to Ikmen and Suleyman and tell them everything. The Cigarette Dandy had been the only man she had ever loved, and so it had been important that his story was told.

Pierre Yildiz had indeed been born to a woman called Nilufer. But she had changed her name when she entered the Imperial harem. She'd been French by birth. Whether the Dandy's father had been Mehmed Yildiz, even if such a person had ever existed, was open to question. What was said was that Nilufer was one of the last inhabitants of the imperial harem at Yildiz Palace. She had probably been one of the wives of the last sultan of Turkey, Mehmed V, and so possibly the Dandy had been his son. Papatya the witch had always chosen to believe that the Cigarette Dandy was of noble stock. But the Ottoman Empire was falling apart by that time, and it was quite possible that Nilufer had been married off to a court official by 1915. What happened after that was unknown. Somehow and somewhere, Nilufer brought her son up in the Catholic tradition until he appeared on the streets of Istanbul sometime in the 1940s. According to Gonca, a romance with a malevolent witch took place, and Cuneyt the bear man was born. But the Dandy, by this time firmly in his role as an artist of the cigarette, would not be pinned down by either women, convention, or even old age. And so he drifted around the city.

***

'Do you think that the Cigarette Dandy did actually tell Papatya the witch that story?' Suleyman said to Ikmen.

The Cigarette Dandy had finally been buried—with his hands— in Ferikoy Catholic Cemetery. Due to the affection of so many in the city, he had been given a fine funeral, which the two police officers were now walking away from.

'I don't know,' Ikmen said, as he fanned his face with his order-of-service card. 'It seems peculiar to me that a French woman should end up in the Imperial Harem in the 1900s.'

'Unless she was governess to the Imperial princesses,' Suleyman said. 'You know it's said that Sultan Abdulhamid II had a Belgian wife in his harem.'

'Well, we still have the Dandy's DNA if you ever want to compare it to your own.'

Suleyman frowned and rolled his eyes.

'What will stay with me from all this is the sight of Cuneyt standing by his father's grave, cuffed to that prison guard,' Ikmen said. 'I couldn't work out whether he was crying for his father or his bear.'

'Well, he wasn't crying for his mother. I know she said she didn't want to burden her son with murder, but she left him to deal with it all while she killed herself,' Suleyman said.

'She wanted to be with her prince.'

'How selfish.'

Ikmen smiled. 'Maybe.'

'I feel sorry for Cuneyt,' Suleyman said. 'He obviously has intellectual difficulties. How could his mother leave him? How could she have let him keep that poor bear, for that matter?'

'She loved her son, in her way. I think she even loved the bear,' Ikmen said. 'Do you know why your Gonca believes that Papatya was a witch of a dark persuasion? I really didn't get that.'

Suleyman sighed. 'After questioning me for hours about this so called "deal I do with myself" that Papatya told us about, Gonca admitted that she'd gone to the witch and asked her for some very powerful, and dark, love spells to keep me in line at the beginning of our relationship. Only evil people do that, apparently.'

'And do they work?' Ikmen, now at his car, stopped. 'And do you indeed do deals with yourself to—'

'No comment.' Suleyman held up a hand. 'And in answer to your next question, my reply is "no I don't feel bewitched".'

Ikmen smiled. Then he thought about Erol the bear, and his face dropped. A destruction order had been enacted that morning, and the creature was now out of its misery. In one way Ikmen was glad, but in another he felt only sadness. When the bear had been taken away from his master, both man and beast had cried. In spite of the poor conditions the animal had endured, there had been love between him and Cuneyt. And it was sad to see the last dancing bear of Istanbul go to his death, even though they had officially performed their last pirouettes back in the nineties. What a strain it must have been for Cuneyt and his mother to keep the bear a secret for so long.

When they arrived as Suleyman's car, Ikmen said, 'I miss the bear men. I know it was cruel, but it was also part of a lifestyle that has all but disappeared. I feel sorry for the gypsies. I feel only grief that eccentrics like the Cigarette Dandy are no longer with us. We are becoming homogenised.'

'We have more money these days,' Suleyman said. 'We have fine restaurants, shopping malls, and excellent pubic bathrooms.'

Ikmen knew he was being sarcastic. He shook his head. 'When I get home tonight, I will raise a glass to the Cigarette Dandy,' he said.

'I will too.'

'Whoever he was, that man was an original, and I will miss him,' Ikmen said. 'A man who died by mandrake root and bear. You couldn't make it up.'

When You Wish Upon a Star

Colin Cotterill

You had about four seconds, all told. You can't say a lot in four seconds, so it helps to have a plan. Some people prepared their wish, whittled it down to the bare minimum, and practiced it, just in case. But even then you'd waste a second as you looked up at the sky in wonder. Mr. Grabong had his wish standing by at one side of his mind, but the sky in Lang Suan was muggy with car exhaust and the lights of the town blurred the view. To see shooting stars, you'd usually have to drive to the coast and look out into the gulf and be patient.

But Mr. Grabong was putting out the garbage bin in front of his town house when he looked up at the roof and the meteoroid sliced across the sky above it. He didn't hesitate.

"I wish my wife would die in a car accident," he said.

Not every wish made upon a star bore fruit. It depended on the alignment of the night sky with certain supernatural elements he didn't really understand. Few people can claim success at this method of improving their lives, but on that warm southern Thai night in March, Mr. Grabong got lucky.

***

Only a week later, Auntie Sakorn sat on the balcony of her plywood hut waiting for a breeze that wouldn't come. The burning heat of the day had been trapped under a blanket of cloud that rolled in late in the afternoon. The languid river current couldn't shift it. The banana-leaf fan in Auntie's hand barely stirred the air in front of her face.

The toads grumbled. The insects shrilled off key. There were no lights along the riverbank, no human sounds. Not until Auntie heard the murmur of a car engine. Few people drove there at night. There was nowhere to go to or come from. But the sound got louder and the car accelerated and, within seconds, its full beam cast the shadow-puppet image of trees onto the far bank.

A speeding car was out of place in the drowsy community, and it was clearly heading for the river with no hint of slowing down. The motor roared, the tyres squealed, and the river was briefly illuminated in a glary yellow light. The car sailed majestically into the air like a bat, then paused long enough for Auntie Sakorn to gasp a warm breath. The bonnet dipped and the big black beast plummeted into the muddy water. It sank until the glow from the front and rear lights merged. It reminded Auntie of a pink phosphorous jellyfish deep in the water. Then, with a muffled click, it was gone. For a few seconds the wash sloshed against the riverbanks, but there followed an absolute silence when even nature held its breath. Then a dung beetle chirped, and all the animals and insects of the riverbank came out of their trance and yelled about what they'd just seen. And Auntie Sakorn crawled into her plywood hut and pulled shut the bamboo door.

***

I was working for the *Chumphon Gazette* at the time. It was a comedown from the crime desk at the *Chiang Mai Mail*, but sometimes family commitments took priority over happiness and common sense and a girl's career. I'd followed my mother, whose dementia had convinced her to sell our shop in the north and buy a rundown resort in a place nobody ever came to. That's how I ended up writing about school sports days and hair-styling competitions. It's not as if there was no crime in

Chumphon, but ours was a weekly magazine-style rag and, by the time it hit the streets, the police had already solved the cases or been paid off. My editor, Puk, steered clear of crime because he was a young startup novice using dad's money to make a name for himself in the media.

But there was something about the flying car episode that was mysterious, and, in an odd way, suitable for families. The victim and her husband were respected public officials. My editor saw it as a human-interest story. The police had already decided it was an accident. Of his three part-time reporters, I was chosen to write the story, not because Puk considered me his best writer, but because I lived very close to the scene of the accident. Any big newspaper ego I'd brought south had long since eroded.

Puk gave me two days to write a piece that could be stretched over two editions. He wanted emotion and good-quality, cell phone photographs so he didn't have to fork out for a professional photographer. The car was still languishing at the bottom of the Lang Suan River but was due to be fished out the next day. That would be his iconic, front-page photograph. He showed me how to hold the phone so it didn't shake when I was taking the picture, and which button to press. There were many times I was tempted to show him other tricks you could do with a cell phone.

***

"My name's Jimm Juree," I told the pudgy policeman sitting on a folding chair in the shade of a spreading duck-foot tree. His tunic was unbuttoned, and his white undershirt was soaking wet. He had a towel around his neck. It was March, and the temperature had hit forty-three Centigrade. There was still a month to go before Thai New Year brought its nourishing rains. Nobody in their right mind went out in the afternoon unless they were under orders.

"So?" he said.

"I've come to watch them lift out the car."

"You from Nissan?" he asked.

"No."

"Cause someone's coming from Nissan."

"Right."

"They have to check the brakes and steering and stuff."

"I see."

"But that's not you?"

"No. Can I go take a look?"

"I don't care."

I walked to the riverbank, where a small group of onlookers was gathered in the shade. In the middle of the river was a pontoon with a backhoe sitting precariously on top of it. On a concrete jetty about thirty meters away there was a crane truck, its rusty arm reaching out across the water. I joined the onlookers. I knew most of them.

"Don't you people have any work to do?" I asked.

I parried and sidestepped a number of jokes about my weight increase and my brother cohabiting with a woman old enough to be his mother.

"So, what's the plan here?" I asked.

"They'll use the backhoe to pull the car out of the mud, then connect it to the crane truck and winch it up the bank," said Meng, the plastic-awning salesman.

"No body in there?" I asked.

"They took her out the night the car went in," said fishwife Moo.

"She was alone?"

"Yes."

"Where did the car go in?"

"Over there," said Es, the cockfighter, pointing to another jetty on the far bank at the end of a small road.

"She must have built up a hell of a head of speed to get from there to the middle of the river," I said.

"Sounded like she accelerated before she left the road," said the policeman, who'd come to join us.

"Think it was suicide?" I asked.

"Drowning's a horrible way to go," said Nut, the squid-trapper. "I almost drowned when I fell off my boat drunk one night. It's like your lungs fill up with wet cement."

I wondered what other reasons there'd be for a woman to drive at speed into a river.

The crane operator took over from the backhoe and dragged the car slowly up the bank. It was a black Nissan Murano, one of the many cars I'd imagined buying when I got lucky on the lottery. I took several unshaken iconic photos as it emerged. The first thing I noticed was that the driver's window was closed, but the front passenger window was wide open and water poured from it.

"Who brought the body out?" I asked.

"Him there," said Moo.

The chocolate-coloured diver who'd connected the cable trudged up the bank wearing only a pair of briefs. He was like Ghandi in Y-fronts, but not as good-looking.

"He witnessed the sinking?" I asked.

"No," said Nut, "he's with one of them rescue foundations. They got here about an hour after it happened. Some man phoned them."

"No eye witnesses?"

"Look around," he said.

I did. The only livable structure in either direction was a deserted-looking hut about a hundred metres away. Everything else was vegetation, which begged the question, why would anyone build two concrete jetties in the middle of nowhere?

***

The diver was far more proud of his skanky body than he deserved to be. He sat on a rock under a blazing sun, and I had no choice but to hoist my Farmer's Bank umbrella and go talk to him.

"Hello sweetheart," he said.

"They tell me you pulled out the body."

"That's right."

"Did you bring her out through the window?"

"What?"

"The window's open."

"It was like that when I got down there. I just opened the driver's door, cut the seatbelt with me gutting knife, and floated her up."

"So her door wasn't locked?"

"No."

"Wasn't it too dark to see?"

"We've got a spotlight on the back of the truck. We should go for a ride in it sometime."

I could see he was starting to enjoy talking to me in the worst possible way, so it was time to go.

"Why did you cut the seatbelt?" I asked.

"Couldn't get it open."

"Thanks."

"You got someone?" he asked as I walked away.

***

Nuth Grabong lived in a two-story townhouse in Lang Suan, not far from the train station. It wasn't prime real estate. The rail-line slum was just along the street. There was no front yard, and I wondered where they'd parked the Nissan before it took its dip. It wasn't the kind of street you'd want to leave a new car on. The house had no bell, so I knocked.

"Come in," came a distant voice.

"It's me," I said. "Jimm Juree. I phoned."

"I'm at the back."

I walked through to the kitchen, where a man in white pajamas was slouched at the table. His eyes were bloodshot and he hadn't shaved for a few days. With a shaking hand he gestured for me to sit opposite him.

"I'm very sorry for your loss," I said. It was the best cliché I could come up with.

"She was such a warm and caring woman," he said. He looked like he might burst into tears at any moment. "Such a tragic, unnecessary thing."

"I was surprised you'd be willing to speak with the press."

"It's vital that we get the word out," he said.

"What word is that?"

"You were there, weren't you? You saw the road she was on."

"Yes."

That was a lie. It was a bloody hot day. I'd done all my investigative journalism from the far bank. The end of the road was visible, but I didn't get around to seeing where it went.

"Then you'll know there's no sign," he said. "The road just stops at the river. There's no warning. I went there the next day and I knew right away what had happened. My darling Malee was driving home. She took a road she'd never used before. It was a good, surfaced road. How could she have possibly known it ended where it did?"

He lowered his head and dry sobbed. There was no fan in the kitchen, and I was dripping with sweat and wearing an orange cotton top that changed colour when it got wet.

"What was she doing out there late at night?" I asked.

"She liked to drive at night."

"So she didn't go to Pak Nam to meet anyone or pick up anything?"

"No."

"According to the police report," I said, "you and your wife are both public officials.

"Yes. I'm at the provincial electrical authority. My wife was at the land office."

"So, a 2015 Murano ..."

"What? Oh, we were paying it off in installments. But look, I really think we need to focus on the lack of signage, don't you? It's a disaster area, no barrier, no 'Stop' sign, no 'No Through Road' sign. Anyone who drives along that road will meet the same fate."

"You're absolutely right," I said.

"I want everyone to know," he said. "I've alerted the police, who were very keen to dismiss this whole thing as an accident. I've made a formal complaint. I've delayed my wife's cremation so we can conduct an autopsy. I don't want anyone saying she was drunk or on drugs. No, it was the municipality that killed her."

That was a dramatic transformation from husband in mourning to vigilante. It wasn't the story I'd expected to come away with. I thought there'd be some reminiscences of a childhood romance and family life and … well, you get it. I wasn't sure how my editor would react. But I was on the case now, so I could hardly back out, especially as there were so many aspects of the death that worried me. I had a lot of research to do. I climbed on my Honda Dream and putted past the slum, where two-dozen pairs of eyes followed me.

***

The car had been taken to the Pak Nam Quality Garage after its rescue from the river. I knew Bob, the owner. The vehicular post-mortem had been conducted by Nissan's head motor technician, observed by a police mechanic, and by Bob, as an independent. Bob had been sworn to secrecy about the findings until the official report was released. But Bob's brain and Bob's mouth were often at odds with one another, especially when he'd had a few drinks. I turned up there at sunset with a half bottle of rum and a six-pack of Coke. Everyone had a fridge full of ice.

"This is off the record," he said, having no idea what that meant.

"I won't tell a soul," I said.

"There was nothing wrong with the car."

"Then why would you want to be off the record, Bob?"

"Not with the car ..."

"But?"

"But the seatbelt had jammed. The driver's door was unlocked, so if she could swim she'd have had a fifty-fifty chance of getting out of there before it sank. But she couldn't get the seatbelt off."

"Is it still here?"

"The belt? No. They took that with 'em. They'll be doing lab tests on it."

"Why was the passenger window open?"

"Hot night. Perhaps she wanted some air."

"The car had a/c."

"Right."

"Any idea why she accelerated before she left the road?"

"Could be panic," said Bob. "It was a manual transmission. A lot of people push down on the accelerator instead of the brake when they panic, especially women. No offence."

I took offence.

"Was there anything in the car?" I asked.

"No, just a few maps."

"Maps to where?"

"Couldn't tell. They were waterlogged. You could barely see they were maps."

"So it wasn't a street atlas?"

"No, just, you know, A4 size, loose sheets."

"Anything in the glove box?"

"No."

"No registration? No owner manual?"

"Not a thing. It was like the car was brand new. Nothing personal in there either. You'd think a woman would have a handbag. But no."

***

That wasn't such a mystery to me. A lot of wallets and handbags disappeared at the scenes of accidents. I went for a slow ride along the road to the river, the route Mrs. Grabong had taken that night. I went at exactly the same time. The husband was right. There were no signs. The surface was paved and had a few potholes, but that was to be expected on a road that went nowhere. There were about twenty houses spaced along the roadside but, as I neared the river, the houses grew fewer and the jungle thicker. The Lang Suan River was known to rise five metres in the rainy season, so nobody with any sense built near the banks. There were squid traps and rope coils, and even a fiberglass canoe marking the end of the road. I wondered whether the residents had put them there for fear of history repeating itself. I climbed from my motorcycle and went to stand on the spot from which the woman had launched her car. My headlamp beam caught the concrete jetty on the far bank, the place where I'd stood watching the car being raised.

There are times I think there are little creatures living in my mind, and they're employed to collect the obvious and flush it down the brain toilet. Yet there, at the end of a paved road, standing on one jetty looking at another, not even the toilet creatures could divert me from what was staring me in the face. At some point, the concrete jetties had been built as the first stages of a bridge. I didn't know whether it had been cancelled, like many other local projects, or whether it was still on the drawing board, but the fact was, the road should have continued all the way to Lang Suan. I didn't know how or why that was relevant to this case, but as sure as a squid can't dance, I knew I was on to something.

***

A handful of shanties had sprung up along railway land. The householders spent their time recycling garbage and producing bare-bottomed offspring. The heat on the corrugated iron roofs made it impossible to go inside during the day, so all the inhabitants were on the street under makeshift umbrellas. An aluminium specialist in a Metallica T-shirt and one boot was sitting on a stool, crushing empty beer cans.

"How are you?" I asked.

He stopped crushing and smiled. He looked like an unkempt monk.

"I could say, 'I can't complain'," he said, "but, of course, I can."

"My family makes more scavenging on the beach than they do from their day jobs," I replied, getting the empathy out of the way as soon as possible.

"You were down there yesterday visiting him."

"You've got good eyesight."

"He's had all kinds of people showing up there," he said.

"You know what happened?"

"They say his wife died in a car crash. Too bad. She was nice."

"What about him?"

"Miserable sod. Never said nothing to any of us. Works as a clerk in an office, and there he is with his big, posh car. Snob."

"I hear the wife liked to drive the car a lot," I said.

"Did she?"

"You didn't see her?"

"Didn't see that car go nowhere. They took a motorcycle to work. Seems he had pleasure just parking the car in front of his house for all to see."

"But it'd be gone in the evenings or at night," I said.

"Would it?"

"The woman liked to drive after dark."

He shook his head.

"You see that scruffy kid over there?" he asked. He pointed to a boy of about eleven smoking a roll-up.

"Yes," I said.

"The clerk gives him a few baht a week to keep an eye on his precious car. The kid can tell you when it was or wasn't there."

***

It was round about then that I came up with a hypothesis. The only problem was that it would only hold water—if you'll forgive the poor taste in idioms—if there was a motive. And I could see none. In fact, even if my suspicions were correct, it would have been an incredibly convoluted crime leading to no benefit whatsoever to the perpetrator.

My hypothesis was that Mr. Grabong had killed his wife. It all began as a result of the scruffy kid's assertion that both Mr. and Mrs. Grabong had gone out in the car the night she'd died. Of course it was possible she'd dropped her husband off somewhere and gone for her drive alone. But what if she hadn't dropped him off? What if he was in the car with her when she hit the river? What if he'd directed her to that unsigned road and leaned over and slammed his foot on the accelerator just as they reached the end? I wasn't sure if you could open the door to an electrified car under water. But what if he'd already arranged for her seatbelt to be jammed, and he'd lowered the window so he could swim away and leave her there to drown? What if he'd had a cell phone and a change of clothes and a bicycle on the far bank? What if it was Mr. Grabong who'd phoned in the "accident"? That was a lot of what-ifs.

I had no proof, of course. I'd exhausted all the usual "husband kills wife" motives. One of our neighbours worked at the land office and had been friendly with Mrs. Grabong. The woman had no life insurance, no savings, and, unlike most of the officials at the land office, didn't collect "tips" to expedite a client's paperwork. The neighbour said she was a very caring and tolerant woman who was committed to a rather obstreperous husband. It seemed she was an angel even before she died.

That unproductive line of enquiries led me away from domestic strife and in the direction of the journey and the car itself. At a stretch, Mr. Grabong might have been able to extort some silence money from Nissan. If there was a rumour about the reliability of the seatbelts, it would be a costly operation to recall all the vehicles that used that brand. He might also be able to claim compensation from the government for inadequate signage, but the paperwork alone would take an age.

No, I didn't see either of those as being the grand payola. If he'd gone to so much trouble to set all this up, he must have had a bigger fish at the end of the hook. I went back over the whole story to see if I'd missed anything, and that was when I arrived at the waterlogged maps in the car. They were the only personal items left in there. Why? It was as if she or he wanted them to be found. As we didn't have a landline at home, I joined the high-school kids in the queue at the Pak Nam Internet Café so I could get online. And it was there, over a sugary glass of green Fanta and a donut, that I found my motive.

***

"Mr. Grabong," I shouted from his doorway.

"Out back," came the reply.

"Did you know your front door's wide open?" I said.

He rushed through from the kitchen and looked around. He was still wearing the same pajamas and had a patchy beard.

"Bastard kids," he said, running to the front door. He stood in the sunlight looking up and down the road. "Did you see anyone?"

"No," I said. "You think someone was in here?"

"The little shits from the slum," he said. "Should have cleared that place out long ago."

"You think they got something?"

"Shit. My cell phone. It was right there on the coffee table."

By the time he returned to the living room, he was back in character. Tears welled in his eyes.

"How can they do things like this when they know I'm in mourning?"

He gestured for me to sit on the couch. It was vinyl and still covered in the plastic it had been delivered in. With a heat wave squeezing the juice out of everyone, the last thing I wanted to do was sit on plastic.

"I thought you'd be back sooner," he said.

"Yes, I've been busy following up on your wife's accident," I said. "You were right about that road."

"I told the local radio people this morning. It's a crime. That's what it is."

"If I were you I'd sue them," I said.

"Oh, I wouldn't want to cause any trouble."

"Really? I thought your lawyer had already been in touch with the district office."

That threw him.

"How did ..."

"Research, and a box of shortbread biscuits."

"Well, I don't know. My lawyer might have written to them. For my wife's sake."

"The letter also mentioned a sum of money to pour cold water on the media frenzy."

"That's ... that's just what lawyers do to show they're serious."

"He was serious with Nissan, too."

"You talked to them?"

"I'm very thorough," I said.

My thighs were as slimy as hocks of pork in oil. I was sliding around on the couch. Embarrassing when you're doing your best to act cool.

"I've been deeply affected by my wife's death," he said. "I want to hurt the people responsible."

"With all that grief, I'm surprised you could even summon up the strength to type. The letters arrived three days after your wife died. That means you sent them the day you were told about the accident."

"I didn't send them. The lawyer did."

"Well, that's another thing, you see. I've looked high and low for that lawyer of yours. I couldn't even find an office. Looks like he works out of a post office box."

His demeanor changed like an angry wind before a monsoon.

"Who do you write for again?" he said.

"The Chumphon Gazette."

"Well, I'm going to have to ask you to leave. I'm expecting a real journalist to come for an interview."

He stood up. I didn't, although I really wanted to.

"Those were domestic, of course," I said. "The international express letter only arrived yesterday. But I imagine Google prefer to get their mail online. They'd already received your ... sorry, I mean, your lawyer's email sent on the day after the accident. Personally, I would have left it a week or so just to make it look credible."

He walked to the door, closed it, and turned the key in the lock.

"I didn't make a note of your name," he said.

"Jimm Juree," I said.

"You seem to think you know something," he said.

He walked to a cupboard against the far wall and rummaged around through a pile of junk until he emerged with a tyre iron. I confess my panic set in around then. I took a deep breath.

"There's what I know, and there's what I suspect," I said. "What I know is that you were with your wife in the car that night, and you left her to drown."

He stood behind me. I could hear him slapping the bar against his palm, but I was certain he'd want to hear me out before smashing my head in.

"What I suspect," I said, "is that one day you were browsing through Google Maps and you came across the one for Pak Nam. And it showed a road that you knew to be incomplete. But on the map it was a through road with a bridge. I have no idea why put a bridge there, especially seeing as the maps originate from satellite photos. But there it was. A major screw up. And you saw it as a mega-dollar opportunity to sue an international organization that wouldn't miss a million or two. You just needed a car and a dead wife to put pressure on them. And the sad thing is you might have got away with it. There was no warning that the maps might be inaccurate. They might have settled, sooner than get involved in a long, drawn-out media battle and a court case."

"It's just as well I left the plastic on this seat," he said.

"You're not going to hit me with that," I said, hopefully.

"Why not? One more murdered woman isn't going to worry me."

"You won't until you know what evidence I've got against you."

"You have nothing."

"I've got this," I said.

I pulled his cell phone from my bag.

"You really shouldn't leave your belongings lying about," I said. "I bet I can find the log of your call to the Rescue Foundation the night you killed your wife."

He laughed.

"You stupid cow. You think I'd use my own phone? I rang them from a public call box."

"Well then, I've got this," I said, pulling Captain Chompu's smart phone from my bag. "Look. It's on 'Record'. And you just confessed. The police have heard everything you've said here. There'll be a knock at the door any second."

There was no knock.

"I said, there'll be a knock any second, but if that doesn't work, I've got this."

On my budget I couldn't afford pepper spray but I found mosquito spray was just as effective. I reached over my shoulder and let him have it full in the face. He was still screaming when they carted him off to the Lang Suan jail. Captain Chompu apologized for leaving me dangling in the void of impending death while he made sure Grabong's confession was strong enough to convict him. I forgave him.

***

I submitted my articles to Puk at the *Gazette*, and he rejected them.

"Too grim," he said. "Not suitable for a family audience. Offensive to the police and the local council. Treads on too many toes."

He was worried about my style, too. He said I should go in at weekends and he'd teach me how to write properly.

That night from my balcony I saw a star slide across the night sky. I had my wish for Puk all planned out.

Contributors

Leye Adenle is a Nigerian writer who has also appeared on stage in plays including Ola Rotimi's *Our Husband Has Gone Mad Again*. Leye is named after his grandfather who was also a writer, Oba Adeleye Adenle I, a former king of Oshogbo in South West Nigeria. *Easy Motion Tourist*, his first novel, is published by Cassava Republic Press (2016). Leye lives in London.

Website: www.leyeadenle.com
Facebook: https://www.facebook.com/leyeadenle
Twitter: @LeyeAdenle

Annamaria Alfieri's latest historical mystery *Strange Gods* is set in East Africa in 1911. *The Richmond (VA) Times-Dispatch* said "With the flair of Isak Dinesen and Beryl Markham, the cunning of Agatha Christie and Elspeth Huxley and the moral sensibility of our times, Alfieri permeates this tragic novel with a condemnation of imperialism, a palpable love of Africa." *The Christian Science Monitor* chose her *Blood Tango* one of ten must-read thrillers. The *Washington Post* said of her debut, "As both history and mystery, *City of Silver* glitters." Her next African mystery, *The Idol of Mombasa,* launches in October 2016.

Website: www.annamariaalfieri.com
Blog: www.murderiseverywhere.blogspot.com
Facebook: https://www.facebook.com/annamaria.alfieri
Twitter: @AnnamariaAlfier

Colin Cotterill was born in London in 1952. He trained as a teacher and worked in Israel, Australia, the US, and Japan before training teachers in Thailand and on the Burmese border. Since October 2001, he has written sixteen books, the most popular of these being the Dr. Siri crime series set in Laos. Colin lives in Chumphon in the south of Thailand with his wife, Kyoko. He rides his bicycle along the coast, eats a lot of squid, plays with his dogs, and occasionally sits down to write.

Website: www.colincotterill.com

_____

Susan Froetschel is the author of five suspense novels. *Fear of Beauty* and *Allure of Deceit,* both published by Seventh Street Books, are set in Afghanistan. She is also managing editor of *YaleGlobal Online,* which covers all facets of globalization and the interconnectedness of our world.

Website: www.froetschel.com
Facebook: https://www.facebook.com/susan.froetschel

Twitter: @Froetschel

_____

Jason Goodwin is a historian whose bestselling Yashim detective series is set in 19th century Istanbul. *The Janissary Tree* won the Edgar Award for Best Novel and the series has been translated into over 40 languages. He is the author of *Lords of the Horizons: A History of the Ottoman Empire*, among other award-winning nonfiction.

Website: https://jasongoodwin.info
Facebook: https://www.facebook.com/jsn.goodwin

Twitter: @jsn_goodwin

_____

Timothy Hallinan is the award-winning author of two current series: the Poke Rafferty series, set in Bangkok, and the Junior Bender mysteries, which take place in Los Angeles. His twentieth novel—the sixth Junior Bender, *Fields Where They Lay*—is set for publication this winter.

Website: www.timothyhallinan.com
Facebook: https://www.facebook.com/tim.hallinan.1

Paul E. Hardisty has spent much of his life in dry, hot, dangerous places, working as an engineer and scientist. His first novel, *The Abrupt Physics of Dying*, a thriller set in the deserts of Yemen, was short-listed for the CWA Creasy Dagger, and was one of the *London Telegraph*'s 2015 crime books of the year. The sequel, *The Evolution of Fear*, is set in Istanbul and Cyprus. He lives in Western Australia and works full time trying to solve some of our major environmental challenges.

Facebook: https://www.facebook.com/paul.hardisty
Twitter: @Hardisty_Paul.

Greg Herren is the award-winning author of over thirty novels and has edited twenty anthologies. His young adult novels *Sleeping Angel* and *Lake Thirteen* won medals for Outstanding Young Adult Horror/Mystery from the Independent Press Foundation. He has won two Lambda Literary Awards (and was nominated twelve more times). He lives in New Orleans with his partner of twenty-one years and works as a public health counselor.

Website: www.gregherren.com
Facebook: facebook.com/gregherren
Twitter: @scottynola

273

Tamar Myers is no stranger to sizzling temperatures. She was born and raised in the Belgian Congo (now the Democratic Republic of Congo) within a few degrees latitude of the equator. She went to college in the Middle East. Today Tamar lives in the Sonoran Desert of Arizona with her American-born husband. She is the author of 41 novels, as well as a number of published short stories, and hundreds of articles on gardening. Yesterday in Tamar's garden the thermometer read 120 F in the shade.

Website: www.tamarmyers.com

Barbara Nadel currently writes two crime fiction series, the Ikmen books set in Istanbul, Turkey and the Hakim and Arnold novels set in London. A psychology graduate, she worked in psychiatric institutions and in the community until she became a full-time writer. In 2005 she won the CWA Silver Dagger for her Ikmen book *Deadly Web*.

Facebook: https://www.facebook.com/pages/Barbara-Nadel
Twitter: @BarbaraNadel

Richie Narvaez was born and raised in Williamsburg, Brooklyn. His work has been published by *Murdaland, Out of the Gutter, Pilgrimage,* and *Thrilling Detective.* His book *Roachkiller and Other Stories* received the 2013 Spinetingler Award for Best Short Story Collection.

Website: www.richienarvaez.com
Facebook: www.facebook.com/rnarvaez
Twitter: @rnarvaez13

Kwei Quartey is a crime writer and physician living in Pasadena, California. He has practiced medicine for more than 20 years while simultaneously publishing his fiction. His first novel, *Wife Of The Gods*, made the Los Angeles Times Bestseller List in 2009. His Inspector Darko Dawson series also includes *Children of the Street* in 2011 and *Murder At Cape Three Points* in 2014. The fourth in the series, *Gold Of Our Fathers*, was published April 2016. The fifth, *By The Grace Of God*, will be published April 2017.

Website: www.kweiquartey.com
Facebook: www.facebook.com/kquartey
Twitter: @Kwei_Quartey

Peter Rozovsky writes the Detectives Beyond Borders crime fiction blog. He has contributed essays, introductions, and reviews to Maxim Jakubowski's *Following the Detectives: Real Locations in Crime Fiction*, Christopher G. Moore's *The Cultural Detective*, the *Philadelphia Inquirer*, *Mystery Readers Journal*, and *Words Without Borders*. He is a newspaper copy editor and a freelance proofreader/copy editor specializing in crime fiction.

Blog: detectivesbeyondborders.blogspot.com.

Jeffrey Siger is an American living on the Aegean Greek island of Mykonos. A former Wall Street lawyer, he gave up his career as a name partner in his own Manhattan law firm to write mystery-thrillers telling more than fast-paced stories. His Left Coast Crime and Barry Award nominated novels aim at exploring serious societal issues confronting modern day Greece in a tell-it-like-it-is style while touching upon the country's ancient roots. Jeffrey serves as Chair of the National Board of Bouchercon, America's largest mystery convention, and as Adjunct Professor of English at Washington & Jefferson College, teaching mystery writing.

Website: www.jeffreysiger.com
Blog: www.murderiseverywhere.blogspot.com
Facebook: www.facebook.com/jeffsiger
Twitter: @jeffreysiger

Michael Stanley is the writing team of Michael Sears and Stanley Trollip, both South Africans by birth. Both have been professors and have worked in business, Sears in South Africa and Trollip in the USA. Their mystery novels, featuring Detective Kubu, are set in Botswana. The third mystery – *Death of the Mantis*, involving the Bushmen of the Kalahari – won a 2012 Barry Award and was an Edgar finalist. Their fourth mystery, *Deadly Harvest*, was a finalist for an International Thriller Writers award. *A Death in the Family* was released in 2015. *Dying to Live* will come out in 2017.

Website: www.detectivekubu.com
Blog: murderiseverywhere.blogspot.com
Facebook: www.facebook.com/MichaelStanleyBooks
Twitter: @detectivekubu

Nick Sweet currently lives between Almeria and Malaga, in Spain with his wife and family. Works he has had published recently include a piece of short fiction in *The Mammoth Book of Jack the Ripper Stories* (edited by Maxim Jakubowski and published by Little Brown in November 2015), and his crime novel, featuring Inspector Jefe Velázquez, *The Long Siesta* (Holland House, September 2015.)

Website: http://www.nicksweet.co.uk
Facebook: https://www.facebook.com/nick.sweet
Twitter: @nickissweeter

———————

Timothy Williams is from London. He has lived and worked in Italy and the French West Indies. His first novel *Converging Parallels* was published in 1982 and was followed by four other police procedurals set in Northern Italy. The fourth novel won a CWA prize for the best novel set wholly or partly in Europe. The entire series has now been republished by Soho Press, along with the sixth novel, *The Second Day of the Renaissance*, set in Tuscany and Rome. He has written two Caribbean procedurals, featuring investigative judge, Anne Marie Laveaud. Now retired from teaching, Timothy spends his time in France, Italy, the USA, and Kenya.

Website: http://timothywilliamsbooks.com

———————

Robert Wilson has written thirteen novels: four West African noir, two WW2 Lisbon, four psychological crime novels set in Seville, and three international thrillers featuring kidnap consultant, Charles Boxer. *A Small Death in Lisbon* won the 1999 CWA Gold Dagger. The first two Seville books were filmed by Sky Atlantic in 2012. The first Boxer book, *Capital Punishment,* was nominated for the 2013 Ian Fleming Steel Dagger. *Stealing People* is out in paperback now.

Website: http://robert-wilson.eu
Blog: http://robert-wilson.eu/blog/
Facebook: www.facebook.com/robert.wilson.9634
Twitter: @robwilsonwriter

———————

Ovidia Yu lives and writes in Singapore most of the year and is exploring America one mystery convention at a time. After dropping out of medical school, she wrote over thirty plays before deciding to try to write murder mysteries. *Aunty Lee's Delights* (2013), *Aunty Lee's Deadly Specials (*2014) and *Aunty Lee's Chilled Revenge* (2016) will be followed in 2017 with *The Frangipani Tree Mystery.*

Website: harpercollins.com/cr-107711/ovidia-yu
Facebook: www.facebook.com/OvidiaYuDoggedAuthor
Twitter: @OvidiaVanda